Nine Years In The Hide

From the files of the Time-Share detective

Angelo Bartiromo

Printed in the United Kingdom

First Printing, 2020

Reissue, 2023

ISBN: 9798670298506
Imprint: Independently published
www.thetimesharedetective.com

"I was watching myself become who I was and who I am now, and it was exhilarating."

Contents

Chapter 1
The Catching Train

'Sixteen thousand pounds, that's all! What a bargain!'

He'd bought the place a couple of days ago and had started moving in earlier today. Five bedrooms, two bathrooms, an office, three very large downstairs living spaces, each with their own built-in viewers and a fully mod-conned kitchen that would have made a small restaurant jealous. To say the house wasn't bad for the price would have been the understatement of the century. It was perfect, and in Christopher Lowe's opinion, the crowning feature of the property was the garden. He made his way over to reception room number three's window and breathed in deeply as he took in the full extent of his new back garden, all the way to the fence that backed his house to the southwest corner of Hampstead Heath then allowed his thoughts to drift to his boyhood to recall his family visits to his granddad's fruit farm. For as far back as he could remember, he'd had that niggling dream about owning an orchard, and as he stared out of that window, he mentally planned what trees he would plant to rekindle the essence of his childhood visits to Gramp's.

"Ok, mate, that's the first lot of furniture, suitcases and the kitchen boxes in, we're gonna go back to the flat and load for another run, back in about an hour."

Christopher shook his head and turned around as the deep-voiced removal man snapped him from his daydreaming, just in time to catch a glimpse of him as he walked out the front door. "Ok guys, I'll be here." He sighed as he spotted the suitcases in the hallway and gave himself a nod of acceptance for resisting the urge to look back out the window. Slowly he moved away, *ok, come on, Christopher, plenty of time for that later, better get them unpacked before she gets back,* he thought.

The stacked suitcases, four in total, contained just the essentials and personals – the rest of the wife's and his belongings would arrive slowly throughout the day. Christopher walked through to the middle living room and headed towards the suitcases. "At least the living room furniture's here," he muttered, spotting the newly delivered sofa. Barely two steps past it, he stopped, looked back around, then back to the suitcases, *oh they can wait another five minutes.* He smiled as he felt that familiar wave of procrastination calling. Diverting over to the kitchen boxes, he opened a box labelled "*glassware and bottles*", lifted out a wine glass, a bottle of his favourite red, poured himself a glass of Malbec then made his way back to the middle living room. He simultaneously hooked his foot round a small coffee table as he passed, dragging it closer to the sofa and used the base of the half-filled wine glass to push a virtual newspaper along the table to make space before placing it down. Expertly, he flicked off his shoes, then with a soft *thump*, collapsed onto the mint-green, threadbare couch and closed his watery blue eyes. "It is gonna be a long, long, old day, I deserve a quick break," he told himself convincingly. *It's Thursday, it's September 25th, 2059, and it's the day my lovely wife and I finally get our dream home.* He was pleased with how his life was going. Opening his eyes, he looked around to take in the vast increase in living space his new house offered compared to his old flat. A smile fashioned on his face as he started to reminisce. *Everybody thought we'd be overpopulated by now. Apocalypse, without an apocalyptic event, they used to say.* He sank deeper into the sofa cushions as the pace of his reflections increased. *World population at twelve billion, limited living space, food shortages, air pollution at its highest ever, not a day had gone by that the media hadn't tried to be the scaremonger of world news*. He took a deep breath of fresh, clean air, then unsuccessfully tried to sink deeper into the cushions. *It's amazing to think that was barely twenty years ago. Then again, twenty years ago, I wouldn't have dared aspire to buy a house like this for a measly £16000. I doubt I would have got much change out of two or three million quid, not that two to three million pounds was anywhere near my budget then, or now*. Christopher chuckled to himself. *Now, everyone can afford a decent home. Living space is no longer a worry. In the last twenty years, I've seen the end of homelessness, end of poverty, the end of food shortages, just a better life and a better standard of living all around. This Time-Share system is amazing. I mean, housing people in the same location at different points in time! Crazy, when you think about it. What was it that salesperson said? This place is set in the year 2020s or something*. He shivered at the thought of the huge impact Time-Share had made on society, *come to think of it, I never could get my head around it, I'm probably sharing this house with a couple of hundred other people.* "I'm living in the same house as other people, at the same time, but at a different point in time," he said out loud. "AT THE SAME TIME BUT AT DIFFERENT POINT IN TIME!" he said even louder. *Wow, this is so confusing.*

The call of nature pushed the pause button to his daydreaming, and he heaved himself up from the sofa. Grabbing the virtual newspaper and the glass of wine from the small table as he went, he made a beeline for the stairs. Clumsily, he climbed the wooden staircase, his socks sliding on the highly polished steps. The thought of slipping and spilling more wine prompted the realisation that his new house offered another bathroom on the ground floor. He carefully turned around, descended the stairs, slipped again and made a mental note to wipe up the spilt wine and buy some slippers. Walking back through to the kitchen, he placed the now nearly empty glass of wine on the worktop and headed through to the downstairs bathroom, locking the door behind him as he entered. *It's going to be a long day,* he thought as he opened the virtual paper and his cobalt eyes started scanning the articles – They barely settled on the small news article positioned just to the left of a much larger advert stating, "*Killing*

Crime Is Legal", the new slogan for the Metropolitan Police, when he heard the front doorbell sound. The bathroom viewer automatically switched on to show a familiar face at the front gate, holding flowers and a bottle. Christopher pressed the intercom to greet the visitor. "Hi, I'll let you in." He pressed the touchscreen to automatically provide access to the Time-Share bubble of his house then returned to finish his business.

"Won't be long, just in the loo," shouted Christopher to his guest as he heard footsteps enter the house. His eyes returned to reading the article that had previously caught his attention. "*Are Time-Share Spaces Unsafe?*" He guffawed, *I've lived in a Time-Share flat for the past nineteen years, now we've got a massive new Time-Share house. I've been perfectly fine and happy, and guess what? I'm still fine and happy!* He gave out a series of small chuckles as he read the article's ridiculous questions about the very thing that had been a world-saver. "What a stupid article, Time-Share unsafe! Time-Share houses are perfectly safe. Why's there always got to be some do-gooder with too much time on their hands, who feels they need to moan about—" He stopped mid-sentence as his ears caught something, his senses picking up a faint *chug,*

chug-chug, chug-chug sound. His whole body became alert as the sound progressively became louder and faster – *Chug, Chug-Chug, CHUG–CHUG, CHUG-CHUG, CHUG, CHUG-CHUG*. He felt his body start to vibrate as the bathroom started to shake.

"Time-Share houses are perfectly safe! Aren't they?" The last words muttered by Christopher Lowe, as a National Rail bullet train appeared obliterating him and everything in its path.

Chapter 2
The Accidental Discovery

"Suddenly, we, humanity, would be tossed a giant lifebuoy, towed back to shore at high speed and greeted with cocktails, sunshine, and sweet apple pie".
- Dr Lukvinder Joshi

Something incredible happened in March of the year 2037. Something that would steer our once-inevitable future onto a different path and resuscitate humanity. You see, metaphorically, we, the population of the earth, had been haplessly drifting out to sea, holding desperately onto any floating bit of scrap we could find as we strayed further and further away from land. With society at a breaking point, civilisation had been close to drowning as we moved deeper into the ocean of despair with only the bleakest of futures on the horizon. With an unprecedented and rapidly increasing population, it had meant every estimate for natural resource consumption had been wrong, and we had been imminently running out of resources. With cold-fusion technology in the early stages of development – solar and wind farms not having been able to occupy enough land area to keep up with consumption – nuclear was the only realistic and feasible option left to keep up with demand. This was an option that would ultimately prove to be bittersweet to the ever-increasing section of society convinced that power stations were far from the taintless corporations they claimed to be and were, in fact, responsible for irreversible environmental damage to a once-beautiful planet.

Many a debate would take place, politicians selling conglomerate-influenced "nuclear power is good for you" ideology, versus various "keep the world green" organisations, fervently trying to conserve and save the environment.

Dialogues became heated, as keep-the-world-green vented annoyance over seemingly futile efforts to influence any palpable changes, inevitably pushing the groups' more draconian supporters to carry out unsanctioned terrorist attacks on power stations as their attempts to be heard and prove their point became increasingly desperate. Attempts that on many occasions would result in more damage to the environment than any power stations would have caused in the first place. Society was flawed and struggling, all that was left to do was to wait by the pier and pay Charon to take it across the river.

But then, like an answer to a prayer, everything changed.

*

Thursday 5th March 2037 – the day of the discovery

Knock-knock! The glass panel shook as the rap produced its unnerving rattle.

It was the entrance to Head Of Projects, Professor Lukvinder Joshi's office, and for the next twenty-four hours, at least, his name would remain there. Imminently due for reassignment, the office was about to be given to the next government-sanctioned, waste-of-public-money research project – given funding under the pretence that its results would benefit society when ulteriorly sanctioned in the hope that any outcome would deliver a military improvement so that this country would have an ever-so-slightly better toy to play with than that country in the international playground of world politics.

The professor, ignoring the knock, sauntered to the sink in the corner of the office and let out a deep sigh. Cupping as much cold water as his hands would allow, he tilted his head forward, then, with the majority seeping through his finger gaps, he raised his arms and threw the remaining water into his brown, care-worn face. As his head lifted back up, the water cascaded off the black ringlets of hair and into his almond eyes.

Professor Joshi, in his fifties, was a perspicacious man, chosen as project leader for his unchallenged theories on magnetic wormhole technology and award-winning work on the world's first true hoverboard. For at least one more day, he was to remain as lead scientist for the ill-fated Anglo/Indian/Chinese team of Project Gauntlet. A project that, at first, had been the envy of projects at the Cranfield Institute of Technology but had since reduced the once-stentorian Professor Joshi to toneless shadows of his former brilliance.

Knock, knock-knock! The glass repeated its rattle.

"Professor, it's me, we're all set up, we're ready and just waiting for you," said the voice from the other side.

"Yes, yes, Bartel, I'm coming," replied the professor.

"I've already let them know you're on your way," said the presumptuous assistant, Maddison Bartel. "I'll head back. Oh, I almost forgot, you have the GCPF waiting on line one," said the retreating voice.

The acronym GCPF stood for the Global Committee for Project Funding, a twenty-nation, inter-government organisation set up in 2025 with the primary objective to collect and distribute funding to projects that would be of benefit to mankind and the environment. Solutions to potential world food shortages and the discovery of an alternative fuel source were remitted as top priority. However, truth be told, since its formation twelve years ago, most of all fund-approved projects had leaned in favour of military advancement. It hadn't gone unnoticed but was rarely challenged successfully.

Professor Joshi leaned across his cluttered but highly organised desk to press the touchscreen on his tablet and accept the waiting callers then turned to his left to stare at a framed viewer. The screensaver on the viewer depicted a stunning and delicate watercolour painting of the Lake Palace on the island of Jag Niwas, as viewed from across the water, it was entitled *The Floating Palace.*

The picture blurred then disappeared and was replaced by a pyramid of three boxes, each one containing a progressively less pleasant view than that of the screensaver.

"Morning, Professor," said an adenoidal voice from the top box.

"Morning," reiterated the professor.

"Morning, Professor," said the left box.

"Morning," the professor batted back.

"Morning, Professor," came the croaky-voiced box three.

"Morning," repeated the professor.

"Progress?" asked the abrupt, rotund, middle-aged woman from the top box. She spoke robotically, with no human warmth behind her voice and her large, framed glasses moved slowly down her nose, giving the unnerving appearance of looking down on the professor, and this was exaggerated further by her box being at the top and the viewer being higher on the wall than professor's eye level.

Professor Joshi resisted the urge to let out another sigh and initiated his report. "Today, we are going to attempt a change in frequency to the quantum…"

"Stop!… We said PROGRESS," said an impetuous voice from the left box.

"Mm, I'm afraid, mm, I've nothing to add from, from, from yesterday's report," the professor stuttered nervously.

"We've received your request for an extension," said the condescending voice from box three to what was now a very awkward-looking professor. "You've had twelve unsuccessful months with Project Gauntlet, you have twenty-four hours left of your original funding. I suggest your team use them to pack. Goodbye."

Box three switches off.

"Goodbye," echoed box two, also switching off.

"Please, please, we are so close," beseeched the professor to the remaining box as its image took over the whole of the viewer screen.

"I'm sorry, Professor, we have a new project coming on Tuesday, the decision has been made, goodbye." The box followed the previous two and disappeared. The viewer crackled and reverted to the now less calming watercolour picture of the *Floating Palace* screensaver.

The defrocked professor exited his office for what he knew would be the last time in his official capacity. *This is it; I'll be the ridicule of the scientific world*, he thought. "The chances someone will want me helping on another project are slim, the chance of anybody giving me funding for another of my other ideas is completely nonexistent," he mumbled under his breath as he walked slowly along the corridor towards the project room. His deleterious thoughts made it impossible to see a clear future and made the walk seem longer than any of the previous three hundred and sixty-four days he'd walked it. His thoughts paused as the metal shutter opened slowly to the warehouse-sized laboratory. Two scaffolded structures encompassing large particle accelerator rings dominated either end, a cleared path of about forty feet lay between them, viewer screens and various electronic equipment occupying much of the remaining lab space.

The shrunken professor distractedly greeted his team as he contemplated whether it was worth going on – and not just with today's experiment. Strategically avoiding eye contact, he made his way over to the main control panel. "Ok, let's try this one more time, Bartel, catch." Picking up the first item reachable from a side desk, the professor hurled it to his assistant standing near one of the rings. He nodded, signaling the start of the experiment. Instantly, a bridge of energy and light connected the two rings as they whirred into life.

"Ready, put it through now!" shouted the professor.

Lab Assistant Maddison Bartel fed the golden statuette into the magnetic field and watched it disappear. "Ok, Professor, it's going through now."

Past tests had seen various objects either refuse to go into the energy field or enter and disintegrate as their broken parts scattered through it.

The dejected team waited for the all-too-familiar anticlimactic scenario to occur, but this time it didn't. Instead, something different happened, something that would slingshot the professor and his team not only to the pinnacle of the scientific world but to being the founders of the single most important discovery in the history of humankind.

The discovery of Time-Share was an accident, a pure fluke; no one had ever considered it, let alone thought to allocate funding for it.

Professor Joshi's team had been attempting large-matter transportation using a combination of quantum entanglement and magnetic wormhole technology, and it had been funded by the GCPF, which, as everybody knew, leaned favourably towards military advancement.

Unfortunately, or should we say, fortunately, due to the imminent demise of the project, and that Professor Joshi and his team's careers were hanging in the balance, a lacklustre approach to the final test had resulted in the frequency settings of the photon portal receivers not been calibrated to an exact match. They were out by a margin of 0.001678%. Whereas past discrepancies had resulted in equipment shorts, objects destroyed and a failed test, this time, the object – a small golden statuette resembling a raccoon – entered the magnetic field, disappeared, and the wormhole stayed active. More items were sent through; none reemerged, and the wormhole remained active. Eventually, a viewer camera was sent through and live-streamed back. The footage showed the top end of the laboratory, yet the camera wasn't visible on the other side of the portal. Several more tests, investigations, and excited scientists later, it was hypothesised that the objects had materialized in the same room but at a different point in time. The realisation that not only did the camera transmission stream back, but they were also able to pull objects back through the stream added to the excitement, it was a two-way portal.

After ascertaining the live stream and items were in the same room but seven days earlier, they reasoned that nobody had seen the objects the week before because any object in the new time period would only be occupying a moment and, therefore, a "bubble" of time. They called this "static time frame theory" The bubble encompassed an immediate area near the second portal as if freezing the moment like a snapshot of time. As luck would have it, no one had entered that distinct area of floor space during that particular time frame.

Without hesitation, money was thrown at the project, its potential immediately realised as a world-saver. Progress on the technology was unbelievably quick, further experiments uncovered the ability to manipulate the time frame to any point in time, expand and decreased to a given space, and the elimination of the receiving portal, which prompted the first of its world-saving uses. Modifications were made to contain and cover only a pre-determined area, meaning you could encompass a room then walk in and out of the portal the same as walking through a door. From the moment of entry, you could interact with whatever you found in that time frame, then any subsequent time would continue via a new Time-line, meaning it wouldn't manipulate or change the original timeline or any other Time-lines created from it. It wasn't meant to be time travel; the past wouldn't be affected, and there would be little or no chance of a butterfly effect when used sensibly. Obviously, the further back you went, the less information one had available as to what had been in that area in the past. For example, going back a thousand years and trying to share space with a lake that has since dried up, you could end up in very deep water, or imagine trying to share where a different building had once stood. And just as significant, if not the most important reason, you really wouldn't want to run into any people from the past. Those early Time-Share experiments could have been responsible for how some ghost stories got started throughout history. To be safe, you needed to choose a location in time you could be one hundred per cent certain about – places that had plenty of public records, for example, maps, building dates, blueprints, schematics, inhabitancies, CCTV footage, when and where buildings had been empty. It would be pointless to Time-Share a house that was already being used. Firstly, the occupants' belongings would be in situ, and even worse, you might run into them. A law was passed stating the furthest Time-Share space could go back to was 1995, the year when the internet had become commercialised and public records were easier to get hold of.

The first major modified use of the technology was on farmland, manufacturing plants and power-plants. The same fields and factories were used simultaneously at different points in time, each timeframe supplying power or exporting goods back through the portals to real-time. New workers in each time frame led to extra jobs, in turn, leading to a colossal drop in unemployment. Within one year of mainstream use, the technology had brought into effect a worldwide unemployment reduction of eighty per cent. Clean, sustainable power was no longer an issue, solar farms, wind farms and eventually, cold fusion reactors were built on the same land areas at different points in time, which generated many times power for the space they occupied. The technology was cheap to make, cheap to use and, most importantly, created an abundance of resources.

With the newly found plentifulness, production costs dropped, ushering in the new era of the "Counter-Industrial Revolution" as manufacturing reverted to using traditional methods and labour. Nearly forgotten tradesman's skills were retaught, giving birth to a more professional workforce. Traditional methods led to a reduction in automated machinery as the old ways made a comeback.

Technological advancements in lifestyle continued but with more vigour... society had developed a retro/techno lifestyle. Next, Time-Share was applied to housing. Pick a house, furnished or unfurnished, set dates for Time-Share and move someone in. As long as you ensured that within the selected dates and times the property was either empty or if already furnished, not in current use, you could endlessly keep selling or renting the same space to different people who would occupy it at different points in time, even if the property was already in real-time use. Pick a time, pay your money, receive your entry code and move yourself and your stuff in, it was that simple. A single house could hold any number of owners, inhabiting individual time bubbles, and if the timeframe chosen was empty, they could even fill it with their furnishings, fixtures and fittings. Freeholders would lease the same house to as many occupants as per demand, there was no limit, leading to a staggering drop in house prices and a massive increase in living space.

Venue capacities were also increased, bands and sports stars playing to record capacity. Wembley Stadium filled ten times over with every ticket holder watching the same performer on a real-time stage or pitch from a different point in time.

To sum it up, The Accidental Discovery was just simply incredible, and as long as its use was regulated and everybody adhered to the same set of rules, nothing the human race had previously accomplished could compare to how universally world-changing the new technology was to be.

Unfortunately, and inevitably, as the history books have taught us, with every great discovery there quickly emerges an element of society ready to exploit it for personal and illegal gains, thus prompting the necessary creation of the Time-Share Misuse Police Department, more commonly known as the TSM-PD, whose job it was to monitor and enforce against Time-Share crime.

Chapter 3
The Short Apology

Friday 26th September 2059 – the next day

Mirror awkwardly lifts his head from the sofa and agitatedly glares around his beige-walled living room. It is quiet, too quiet, and he needs something, anything that will stop the various "what I should have said and what I should have done instead" scenarios that have been so dominant in his thoughts the last few days. Looking back down at the sofa, he mutters, "How can the same sofa be comfortable one day and so uncomfortable on another? Does it get swapped when I'm not looking?"

The quietness would have been tranquil to most people, but today, that missing element of distraction is just another entry on the "*Things That Annoy Mirror*" list.

He composes a mental note of the "*the uncomfortable sofa*", listing it below the other newly entered irritation, "*the annoying quiet*".

The sofa and the quiet are both at least five items below the present list-topper, "*Detective Sergeant Jana Bailey*", the primary cause of his present mood.

Closing his eyes, he recalls his boyhood, growing up in the semi-detached house on the crowded outskirts of Bedford, and his dad's constant arguing with the neighbours as he would tell them where he would shove their sound system if they didn't turn the music down and keep it down. *Ah! That* thud, thud-thud, and thud *as the music emanated from the neighbours' house, all day and night. We could hardly think or hold a thought in our heads because of that* thud, thud-thud, thud. *What I wouldn't give for a bit of* thud, thud-thud, thud *right now.* Mirror ruminates on this rather distressing time for his parents as a good memory in the context of his present mood.

Time-Share has eliminated the noisy-neighbour syndrome, so even though you could be Time-Sharing the same house an infinite number of times, living next to an infinite number of neighbours, you are in your personal bubble of time, therefore, there isn't any possible way that sound from another bubble can travel through their wall and into yours.

An unwelcome flash reddens the inside of Mirror's eyelids to grab his attention and cut the distorted happy memory short. He opens his eyes and directs them to the screen of his mobile viewer. "Number twenty-three," he remarks and leans over and casually slides his finger across "*reject*" to send the caller to his viewer's growing list of "leave a message and I'll listen to you later if I feel like it", voicemail system.

It is "the department", calling "again", and he is sick of listening to any more of their ranting on about how he's missed yet another compulsory appointment with the police therapist for his session on the "how to get along better with your colleagues" issue. An issue which he doesn't feel is much of an issue. Basically, he prefers to work alone, or if he has to, I mean *really* has to work with someone, he prefers to work with people who will do things the way he likes them done – everyone else just gets in his way. He knows he prefers to work alone, and if that isn't an option, he also knows he doesn't want to work with most people, so where is the problem? To be blunt, Mirror blames the department's insistence that he be partnered with a straight-laced, by-the-book, always-correcting, fresh-out-of-college know-it-all called DS Jana Bailey for his being put on suspension. By and large, the most annoying police officer he's ever met, she's irritated him from the get-go, after he held the captain's door open for her and she didn't thank him. When he'd first heard her talk, it had got worse; she has a monotonous voice, and as she talks, her lips barely move, and the sound that emanates between her barely parted teeth gives her voice a vibrating tone that makes Mirror shiver whenever she speaks, which is too often. In his opinion, she'd have made a much better ventriloquist than a detective.

Mirror and DS Bailey have very different personalities, Mirror may seem a bit of a maverick type of copper, but he has the utmost respect for the law and enough common sense and awareness to loosen up or cut a corner if he thinks it could work better to get that lead. He is very in touch with his surroundings and works hard to get results, which, in turn, has led him to become the best detective in the department by a long shot. He is empathetic to people's moods and will go above and beyond to help anyone if he can. He's even been known to give money to total strangers for taxi fares or buy them something to eat if they look in need. Unfortunately, he is just as reactive to anyone that annoys him. It is this clash of intolerance that has led to the current predicament of being suspended.

DS Bailey has been with the Time-Share Misuse Police Department for three months, fresh out of Glasgow

University where she'd studied Time-Share Criminology, achieving the highest grades ever seen. Over-impressed by her grades, an overzealous Home Office MP had fast-tracked Jana to the rank of Detective Sergeant, straight from basic training, and subsequently enrolled her as the official poster person to help promote recruitment to the police force, and to encourage study in Time-Share Degree courses. It was also suggested, in a weighty way to the head of the TSM-PD, Captain Marshall Mason, that not only did he take the newly promoted DS Jana Bailey into his department but that he also partners her with the department's best detective, who, as everybody will tell you, is DI Gabriel Alex Mirror.

Barely a couple of weeks had passed since DS Bailey had teamed up with the reluctant-to-be-partnered-with-anyone DI Mirror, and a fair number of her "procedure dictates" conversations had already ensued. Mirror had surprised himself that he'd lasted as long as he had without previously sharing a few choice words. It was a week ago today that he had been told by the captain – who, in turn, had been specifically told by the Home Office – that their fast-tracked future superstar of law enforcement, "DS Bailey", and her partner were to attend a benefit gala on

Saturday 20th September 2059 to represent the TSM-PD. The event in question, to be held at the Barbican Conservatory, was a fundraiser for the New Homes for Wildlife charity and would be hosted by the police commissioner.

*

Saturday September 20th, 2059 – six days earlier, the day of the benefit gala

Mirror's personal feelings were that it was a pure waste of time, and he could think of a multitude of things to make better use of it. *The two dead bodies case at St Thomas' Hospital, I should be working on that*, he thought. The captain had ordered him to close the case, but he'd had that familiar gut instinct which had served him so well over the years. It was telling him something didn't quite add up, so he'd purposely delayed closing it. He looked over to a smug DS Bailey, sitting as far from him as the back seat of the limo would allow, then returned to staring out the window and drifted back to his thoughts, *Or, I could be seeing my girlfriend, Frances, or brushing my teeth, come to think of it, anything would be a better use of my time! Instead, I'm being driven in a driverless limo to be a sidekick to a poster person at an NHW charity gala, while wearing the most uncomfortable tuxedo ever.*

The New Homes for Wildlife charity, abbreviated to NHW, rehoused animals to a more individual, natural and environmentally safe Time-Share bubble, where they'd be free from exploitation of themselves or their habitats.

Mirror completely understood why the police commissioner and Home Office had invited DS Bailey but couldn't fathom the need for him to be there. *The only reason we've been invited is so that they can, once again, thrust their so-called poster-person and the future of Time-Share law enforcement into the limelight.* Mirror was less than enthusiastic as he stared out of the window and looked for any distraction or reason that could delay the impending farce of an evening that the limo was steadily making its way to. His attention perked up as he spotted an incident. A car parked, slightly skewed, on a red zone, a man in his fifties, seemingly arguing with two traffic officers while pointing to an area about fifty meters in front of them where a small crowd had gathered and were staring up the road at the furthering of blue flashing of lights. Mirror, deciding it was the perfect "delay me getting to the snobby event I don't want to go to" opportunity, ordered the limo to stop, in doing so, eliciting a questioning glare from his co-passenger.

"Why are we stopping, sir?" Mirror shivered as her words vibrated through him. "There's no need for us to interfere here, sir, there's an appropriate and official response to the situation, and stopping will only make me unnecessarily late for my speech at the gala, so why are we stopping? Sir!" said the unimpressed DS Bailey. Mirror turned to look at her, opened his mouth to reply, then held back, managing to stop his already lined up and inappropriately sarcastic response to her question. He exited the limo, placed his shield on his belt and walked at pace towards the traffic officers and the arguing man.

"What's the issue officers?"

"Please, sir, step back," barked one of the traffic officers, turning to face Mirror, his demeanor quickly changing from in charge to subordinate as he spotted Mirror's shield. "Sorry, sir," he said, purposely louder than necessary to alert his partner to DI Mirror's presence.

"Err, we have everything under control, sir," said the second traffic officer. "This gentleman has parked illegally, we have temporarily laser-clamped his car and are awaiting an override controller to reroute his car's navigation to the impound yard, it's all routine. Unfortunately, the gentleman has just started to get a bit abusive."

"Is this what I get for trying to help?" shouted the visibly distressed man towards Mirror.

DS Bailey joined the group; she gave the man a once over. "Sir, if you continue with this confrontational behaviour, these officers will have no other choice but to arrest you." Feeling like she had just controlled the situation, she turned to Mirror, "Nothing more we can do here, sir, it's all under control. Can we get back to the limo, please?" Mirror gave her a nod. The traffic officers misinterpreted this as confirmation to continue and grabbed the agitated man, laser-cuffed him and read him his rights. Mirror reluctantly started to follow DS Bailey back to the limo but could sense a small murmur from in his gut. Was it just a churn because he was about to climb back aboard the limo and head to the dreaded gala? Or was it telling him there was more to the incident than he could see? He watched her climb back aboard then turned back to follow his instincts towards the small gathering, fifty metres up the road. "Where are you going now, sir?" said the despairing voice from inside the limo. The thought of being even a minute late for the event was unbearable, she was always on time, more to the point, she was always early, for everything. Evidently, Mirror wasn't taking this event or her seriously and that just wasn't on.

Mirror called out to the group, "Hi, guys, what's just happened?" He heard how the man currently being arrested had seen a woman pushing a buggy get knocked over by a bunch of kids who had stolen bottles of spirits from a local supermarket and were being chased by the shopkeeper. As they had barged past the woman, knocking her over, they had also dropped some of the bottles. As she had fallen, she had landed onto a long shard of glass from the neck of one of the now-broken bottles and impaled her stomach. The man had witnessed the incident as his car had driven past, but his reactions had been slow to make sense of what he'd just seen, and his car had travelled some way up the road by the time he had asked it to stop. He had quickly run back to see if the woman and baby were ok. Realising the extent of her injuries, he had helped her, making her comfortable, applying pressure to the wound and stemming the blood flow until the ambulance had arrived. His quick actions had more than likely saved her life. When the paramedics had taken over, the man had returned to his car to find the traffic officers clamping it. A combination of shellshock from his recent experience and the obnoxious traffic officers completely misreading the situation had resulted in the scene that was leading to his imminent arrest.

Mirror jogged back over to the traffic officers just as the police department's driverless car tech crew were arriving. He explained the situation, then, much to the annoyance of DS Bailey watching from the limo, the traffic officers released the man and waved the tech officer away. She then watched in further disbelief as DI Mirror shook the man's hand, told him that he was free to go and how there should be more people like him in the world, none of which sat well with "abide by the rules" DS Bailey, who, at the first opportunity, reported DI Mirror for the triple misconduct charge of letting a traffic violator away without charge, misuse of rank in interfering with the traffic officers arrest and the worst offence of all, making her late for the charity event.

The triple allegation in its entirety wasn't the full reason Mirror had been suspended, but it had been the trigger. Called into the captain's office, the Monday after the gala, and asked to comment on the newly filed complaints involving two traffic officers and misuse of rank, Mirror knew that once he explained the 'why' of letting the man go, being cut from the same old-school police cloth, the captain would decide Mirror had acted appropriately and in the best interest of both the public and the police force. Unfortunately, Mirror quickly surmised that it hadn't been the traffic officers that had raised the complaints, it had, in fact, been DS Bailey complaining on their behalf, believing she was sticking up for them against a bullying senior officer. This had been the straw that broke the camel's back, pushing Mirror over his tolerating-DS-Bailey tipping point, and he decided that it would be the perfect moment to storm out of the captain's office and share some colourful words with her, colourful words that he had, up that moment, done well to hold in. But in sharing those colourful words, Captain Mason had been left no other option but to suspend him, after deciding it was best for Mirror to take some time off and have a break from DS Bailey.

*

Friday 26th September 2059 – present day

As far back as he could remember, Gabriel Alex Mirror had wanted to be a detective. His dad loved all those twentieth-century detective shows, and Mirror had loved sitting next to him watching them. The difference had been that while his dad would always be left wondering who the bad guys were right up to the show's final curtain call, Mirror had already guessed the who and why halfway into the show. Therefore, his chosen career path had been no mystery and he'd joined the Bedfordshire police force at eighteen. He accelerated through the ranks on merit, becoming one of the youngest detectives in the Met, and at twenty-eight, Mirror had been first on the transfer list when asked by his long-time friend, Captain Marshall Mason, at the tail end of 2039, if he would like to join him at his new command and help lead the newly commissioned TSM-PD task force in London, Time-Sharing the same building as New Scotland Yard.

Now forty-eight, and with thirty years' field experience under his belt, the one thing he knows he doesn't need, nor want, is a partner half his age with a degree in Time-Share Criminology dictating procedure to him.

Looking at the mobile viewer in his hand, Mirror again decides not to call back. He lifts his arm, flicks his hand and propels the mobile-viewer, spinning it towards the sofa just as it starts ringing again. "Call twenty-four," he murmurs. But something is different, the spinning viewer screen catches his attention, it lands on the sofa with the screen facing up and draws him in closer. It *is* the department. It *is* call number twenty-four, but there is a difference. Unlike the previous twenty-three calls, all of which had displayed the department's main-line number, this time, the screen is displaying Captain Marshall Mason's private extension. Without thinking, Mirror moves towards his mobile viewer and hovers his finger above the flashing screen, moving it side to side over the green accept and the red reject symbols. His hovering outlasts the ringing, and the call forwards to the video mail system.

A slight panic strikes Mirror: he'd always answered a direct call from the captain. In his haste to pick up the mobile viewer, he sends both his hands at the same time and they get in each other's way. With his right hand eventually winning, he picks the viewer back up, "Play video mail twenty-four," he says.

"Message received at ten twenty-four a.m. on Friday 26th September 2059," says the mobile viewer's smooth but slightly automated female voice.

"Mirror, we need you at the department, so stop sulking, or whatever the hell you're doing, and get here now!"

It is the captain, his voice, but his tone confuses Mirror. There was no mention of a missed appointment with the therapist, instead, he'd used the words "we need you". Staring around the beige room he focuses on a small 1950's jukebox-shaped clock sitting on the mantel. 10:31 a.m. – it has already been five minutes since the call. A stubborn streak screams at him not to go, but he is struggling to work out why the captain has called him personally. It has thrown spanner in the works of his mulish attitude, and now, his every instinct is to get to the department as soon as possible.

*

Mirror fidgets impatiently as he sits in his car, agonised by its steady speed as it makes its way through the slow-flow, train-like streams of the other driverless vehicles in the London traffic. The positive thing about driverless cars has been that they have almost eliminated traffic jams in cities and on major routes; satellites guide computers in the vehicles, on-board viewers process the multitude of information streamed to the vehicle's sensors from street

CCTV, traffic reports and other vehicles as they adjust speed and course accordingly to keep the traffic flowing. Without the human element making mistakes or bad driving decisions, it has greatly reduced the number of accidents and breakdowns. The roads are almost always moving. The driverless system has worked so well that it is now illegal to self-drive within congestion zones or major motorways unless they offer a self-drive lane option. The main issue, in Mirror's opinion, is that getting to your destination is comparable to getting your teeth pulled without an anesthetic. He often recalls his dad, who would never allow anyone else to drive, and how much he would have hated being a passenger. The car pulls up to the barrier at the police headquarters secure car park and Mirror wonders if he is missing out by not driving himself. *At least when you drove yourself to a destination, back in the old days, you would have been preoccupied with concentrating on the road,* he thinks as he gives a nod and a frowned smile to the barrier guard. She responds with a "Good afternoon, sir" and sets the Time-Share to the Time-Share Misuse Police Department's time bubble. Mirror's car enters the car park and stops by the lifts. He gets out, walks over to the lift and presses the call button, and the car drives off to self-park.

The lift doors open to the foyer of the TSM-PD hive, the ever-bubbly Elaine Wallberry at her usual place at the helm. Behind her, partitioned by glass panels, is the buzzing personnel-filled main office of the department. “Good afternoon, Detective Inspector Mirror,” says the Glaswegian-accented Elaine from behind her shiny mirror-fronted counter, she gives Mirror a big ear-to-ear smile as he walks towards her.

“The captain has asked to see you as soon as you’re in. I’ll let him know you’re here.”

“Don’t worry, Elaine, I’ll tell him myself,” says Mirror, dropping his head and uncharacteristically walking straight past her. He feels awkward not stopping to chat, but he wasn’t there to stop or chat with anyone, he has come in for one purpose and that is to have his say with the captain. He ignores all calls and salutations thrown at him as he walks quickly through the department and straight to the captain’s office at the far end of the large main room.

“Knock or don’t knock,” self-questions Mirror as he approaches the captain’s office. “What the hell, I’m already on suspension.” He increases his pace and bursts in, pausing at the entrance as he notices the office is busier than he had expected it to be. The captain has visitors. Making an on-the-spot decision – considering he's already committed to bursting in, in a make-a-statement way, he feels he has no choice but to carry on. "Well, I'm here," he says. "I guess you really wanted me here." He takes a step further into the office and knocks a picture frame over from the low-standing table with his replica 1970's raincoat tail. "So, what is it? Am I getting a further suspension? Has Bailey reported me for not being on my suspension in accordance to article 'blah' of the *Detectives On Suspension* manual?" he asks sarcastically.

Captain Mason breathes in deeply and lets out a long, contained, if not slightly louder than required, breath. He turns to his guests, sitting on the couch opposite him. "Sorry, gentlemen, can we pick this up in a few minutes? If you would like to make your way back to the waiting area." He stands, looks at the two men as warmly as a stone-faced poker player, lets out another long audible breath, then gestures them to leave. The two men, one wearing a black suit, the other a grey, stand and start walking towards the door. The black-suited man backtracks and attempts to pick up a small statuette sitting on the captain's desk. "I'll take the golden raccoon statue with me, shall I?"

"No, I think I will take the golden-red panda with *me*," says the grey-suited man.

The captain quickly moves from behind his desk, intercepts them both and puts his hand on the statuette first. "I think we will leave this here for now, shall we?" He gestures toward the door again, the two men bow, thank him, then leave, walking out sideways through the gap left, due to half the exit being blocked by DI Mirror.

The moment has only lasted a few seconds, but being surreal, it feels a lot longer.

Captain Mason looks at Mirror. "See what I have to deal with? Both claiming ownership of the first item sent through a Time-Share vortex. One calls it a raccoon, the other a red panda. Same bloody thing if you ask me."

Choosing to ignore the captain's small talk, so as not to distract him from his goal, Mirror continues his rant, but with the sarcasm toned down from when he first burst in. "Guess what? I didn't want to come, believe me, I nearly didn't. Twenty-three missed calls from the department, I looked at my viewer each time, I couldn't have cared less about answering any of them." Mirror struts deeper into the captain's office, judges his position to be roughly the centre and stops. "Happy to ignore all of them and more than happy to let them all go to mail so they wouldn't disturb me from my very busy day of doing absolutely nothing." Full sarcasm is back and turned up to ten. "'Nothing?' I hear you ask. That's correct, nothing, because I'm *suspended*."

Captain Mason adjusts his view and looks past Mirror, the door is still open, and the rest of the department can hear Mirror's rant. He walks past him, lets out another of the most obvious blows of breath and shuts it as Mirror continues his moan. "Then, call number twenty-four!" Mirror rocks his head left and right then pauses as if making the last sentence the point of his rant. "That was the one! That's the one that made me stop and stare longer! Because it was you who called on twenty-four! Well, now that intrigued me, what could it possibly be? I don't even have words to find as to what it could possibly be. I mean, what could possi—"

"Will you shut the hell up?" Mirror's jaw drops mid-sentence, and he stares in disbelief at his superior's uncharacteristically raised tone.

“Shut the hell up? You know what? You can…” Mirror pauses, his good sense returning just in time to stop him saying something he knows he’ll later regret. “I knew I shouldn’t have come!” He turns to walk out, and even though he is still a good three meters away, lifts his hand, holds it in front of him to the same level as the doorknob and starts walking.

“Mirror stop, STOP! Please, just stop.” The captain’s voice disconcertingly increases in volume, then calms as he turns to look towards the office wall viewer. The screensaver on the viewer displays a view from the top of Primrose Hill, NW1, in the summer of 2009. He tilts his head then walks towards it with an uneven step, his imagination trying to make the BT tower look more like the pre-fallen tower of Pisa. “You were right.” The usual reassuring and calm temperament has returned to his tone, “I’m sorry.”

Mirror stops mid-step, turns and slowly walks back towards the desk, his facial expression filled with confusion, “What?”

“Don’t make me repeat it,” says Captain Mason, staring harder at the viewer, as if trying to spot something new in the picture.

"No! Repeat it!" Puzzled that he is getting a rare apology from the captain, Mirror feels this is something he needs to savour. But to do that, he first needs to know why he is being apologised to.

Captain Mason looks away from the viewer, walks back behind his desk, picks up a virtual newspaper, slams it on the coffee table in front of Mirror then points towards it. The newspaper gives off a series of crackles and frame changes, reboots and as it recovers from the slam, displays its headlines.

Mirror, slightly off-balance, stares at the virtual paper and reads out the main headline, "*Olympic Athletes Banned for Illegal Use Of Nanorobot Limb Enhancement*".

Captain Mason shakes his head in disapproval and adjusts his finger, pointing to a smaller article below the main headline. "*Thirty-One-Year-Old Man Dies on Toilet*". Mirror slowly looks up from the paper, giving himself as much time as possible to search through his mind's filing system for any reference as to when he might have mentioned a man dying on the toilet and whether he deserves an apology for it. Nothing comes to mind and his head has lifted to its destination. His eyes refocus on the slightly taller and weathered-face of Captain Mason.

"That's the third one. The third Time-Share-related accident this week. I've checked, and all three names are on your juror list," explains the captain.

"Juror list," echoes Mirror, looking back to the article. The words are all he needs to eclipse the entire recent debacle between him and DS Bailey and re-infect him with the detective bug his recent suspension had taken away. The base of the article reads, "*continue on page 21*". Mirror passes his hand over the virtual paper as if grabbing at real pages. On the bottom corner of page twenty-one, his eyes briefly glance over an advert for self-drive cars – *Be the driver, not the driven, and feel the road again!* – then refocus on the small section continued from the front-page article.

"*Christopher Lowe – aged 31 – from Finchley, was killed on his toilet by a freak accident involving a train. Mr Lowe was a barber and the owner of family-run retro hairdressers, Lowe Priced Cuts, which was originally opened by his granddad in 2019. Friends describe him as a charming man who loved his job and will be sorely missed by his wife, friends, family and customers.*"

Captain Mason opens the top drawer of his desk and pulls out Mirror's warrant shield and laser cuffs. "As of now, you're off suspension. There's a team waiting for you in Time-Share incident room one. Get it solved and keep a low profile." Captain Mason sits, pulls himself closer to the desk and closes his top drawer. "One more thing, Mirror, work with the team – that includes DS Bailey. Give her a chance, she might just surprise you."

Regardless of how much Mirror chooses to deny it, he is fazed by the captain's perceptive speech, suggesting he understands Mirror better than he does himself, knowing him well enough to be confident that he will come in after receiving a direct call, pick up his warrant shield and get straight back to work. So confident that he's also arranged a team, all ready and waiting for him in the incident room.

The intuitive captain has been, of course, one hundred per cent correct.

Mirror bites through his pride reluctantly to pick up his warrant shield and laser cuffs, nods towards the captain and walks out the office.

Chapter 4
The Case Opens

Friday 19th September 2059 – the week before Mirror's suspension

Taking longer than normal to work out which direction the loud ringing noise was coming from, a drowsy Mirror struggled to lift his head from the pillow. Normally, he'd have instantly woken and been on full alert to any unnatural noise, but today, he was a lot less enthusiastic. His eyes slowly calibrated as they followed his ears to source the ringing, then slowly focused on the profile picture of his girlfriend flashing up on his mobile viewer screen.

"Morning," said the ever-cheery Frances. "You weren't still sleeping, were you?"

"What time is it?" asked Mirror sluggishly.

"Twenty past eight, I thought you would have been up, dressed and ready for work by now, Gabriel, Guess I gave you a glass of wine too many last night then?" A full-on Frances-smile hit both sides of his mobile viewer screen.

"It's been such a slow week at headquarters, Frances. Believe me, if you had to work with Bailey, you wouldn't be too enthusiastic about getting up and going in either."

"Oh, Gabriel, I'm sure she's not that bad. Maybe if you gave her a bit of a chance, she might surprise you. I tell you what, get washed, get dressed, I'll pop the kettle on. Come over and have a cuppa with me before you go to work."

"Sounds like a plan, Frances, I'll be there in ten," replied Mirror, climbing out of bed and heading for the bathroom.

The washed, dressed and more alert Mirror headed out of his house, picking his key cards up from the entrance table as he passed them. He closed the door behind him, walked out of his front gate, turned back around to face the same house, flicked through his key cards, selected the key to Frances's house and held it against the gate post keypad to reset the Time-Share to Frances's time bubble then walked back through the same gate and into the same building.

Mirror and Frances had met ten years previously at an open-house event. Viewing the same property, they'd clicked immediately, much to each other's surprise, as neither were the other's usual type. They inevitably bought the same house at different Time-Share locations. The friendship upgraded into a relationship, and even though they'd kept to their separate Time-Share houses, they'd been an item for the past nine and a half years, a situation that suited them both and had been the main contributing factor to how they'd stayed together as long as they had, given that Frances had more than a few obsessive-compulsive quirks.

Mirror let himself into Frances's house, took off his shoes and placed them neatly to the sidewall in the hallway.

"Hi, tea's on the side, be down in a min," shouted Frances from upstairs.

The shoeless Mirror made his way through to the living room, grabbed his slippers from their usually neat and parallel place against the side of the sofa then ritualistically walked through to the kitchen and over to the sink to wash his hands. Frances was extremely OCD, and over the years, Mirror had become empathetic to her ways, so whenever he came over to her house, he would follow a certain set of rules and make the necessary adjustments that he wouldn't normally do in his home or anywhere else.

Mirror picked up his tea just as Frances walked into the kitchen, she gave him her usual smile and asked the inevitable question, "Did you wash your hands?" A question he had taken offence at when they'd first met but had become so commonplace over the years that even though he automatically washed his hands the moment he entered her house, he knew it would still be asked.

"Yes, of course, my dear," he said, cheekily raising his eyebrows and tilting his head in reply.

Frances picked up the hand towel Mirror had just used to dry his hands, threw it on the laundry pile near the washer then washed her hands, grabbed a clean towel, dried her hands, threw it on the washing pile then replaced it with another clean one. "What you got planned today, anything nice?"

"Well, hopefully, something a little bit more exciting than what I've been doing so far this week," replied Mirror, purposely keeping his answer uninformative and short, knowing full well there was no point expanding or adding any more information. Frances liked to talk, I mean, she *really* liked to talk, so even when she asked him a question, at some point during his answer, she would stealthily start telling him something else, something very longwinded, the kind of conversation that would take you circle every possible pathway just to get to the point.

Just as anticipated, she cut in, "Well, I'm off to see my mum today, we might pop over to Camden. Oh, that's what I meant to tell you, I was driving along the High Street yesterday, just going past the turning for Greens Lane, you know Greens Lane, it's the one that if you go down past the post office, turn left into Dors Close, which is the turning just after the old church where that little park is, you know, where I used to take my old dog, Charlie. Well, as I said, I was going past Green Lane..."

Mirror faded out as she continued to talk. He'd already guessed or had a good idea where the story was going and was convinced it would take a while to get there, a perfect time to zone out slightly and work out his plan for the day. He patted his pockets, and realising he'd left his mobile viewer at his house, he looked up at the kitchen wall clock and adjusted the time by the ten minutes – Frances had set the clock fast to fool herself into never being late. "Sorry, Frances, I need to get going." He rinsed his cup under the tap and placed it on the side, knowing full well that even if he had thoroughly washed it, she would do it again anyway.

"Ok love, I can finish telling you about it later," said Frances. He hugged her, placed his slippers in the usual place, walked back through to the entranceway to put his shoes on, waited as Frances readjusted his slippers so that they were even more parallel to the sofa, gave her a wave goodbye then left to go back into his Time-Share bubble to collect his mobile viewer.

Mirror picked up his mobile viewer, huffed then rolled his eyes as he noticed the screen was showing a missed a call from DS Bailey. He exited his house, headed for his driverless car and mentally re-edited his day accordingly to include returning a call to DS Bailey. Leaning back in his seat, he commanded the driverless viewer system, "Drive to headquarters and, err… call Detective Sergeant Bailey."

Instantly, DS Bailey appeared on his viewer screen. "Sir, I've been trying to reach you," she snapped, giving Mirror a look of annoyance.

Mirror ignored her gaze and wondered if her mobile viewer had even rung since she'd answered so quickly. "What is it, Bailey?"

“We had a call-out, sir, but I couldn’t get hold of you, *again*. There has been a Time-Share incident at St Thomas’ Hospital, I’m here now; it’s all in hand and seems to be a justified accident, but as you know, I need a senior officer to sign it off,” she said grudgingly.

“What’s the incident, Bailey?” asked Mirror.

“It’s in hand, sir, I just need it signed off,” replied DS Bailey.

“What’s the incident, Bailey?” Mirror asked again with an edgier tone.

“Two accidental deaths, sir,” replied DS Bailey, sheepishly trying to make the incident less dramatic.

“Bailey, stay there, I’m on my way.” He hung up without waiting for a reply and instructed the car to reroute to St Thomas’ Hospital.

Much to the annoyance of DS Bailey, the drawback to her fast-tracked promotion was her lack of field experience. Captain Mason’s condition to DS Bailey joining the TSM-PD was that the department should have due diligence, so, for a probationary period of six months, Detective Inspector Mirror was to be her assigned guarantor and assessor for all her reports.

A frustrated DS Bailey was paced by a squad car as Mirror arrived at the hospital. “Bailey, what have we got?”

“As I was trying to tell you on the viewer, sir, it is in hand, I have checked both areas personally, both accidents are…”

“Bailey, stop!” Mirror gritted his teeth, refraining himself from adding further, would-be unfiltered words to his sentence. “I’m not signing anything until I’ve had a look for myself. Now, once more, what have we got?”

DS Bailey quickly adjusted her tone, sensing the change in Mirror’s temperament. “Yes, sir, sorry, sir. There have been two deaths. Both happened within minutes of each other and in two different locations. I’ve looked at both scenes, and I agree with the hospital security report that concludes both the doctor and the nurse’s deaths are unfortunate but accidental Time-Share mishaps.”

Mirror instantly deduced that with her limited field experience, DS Bailey had concluded the deaths were accidents because the hospital report had said so. She had accepted without question that two people could die within minutes of each other in different parts of the same hospital, and after reading the report, it would be a waste of her talents to search for any evidence to the contrary. She didn't seem the slightest bit inquisitive, and that worried him. He needed to view the scenes for himself and would never dream of signing off any report handed in by a third party until he had seen all the facts first-hand. He was a bit of a control freak in his personal life, but it went into overdrive when it came to his police work. He had to ask his questions, not the standard ones – he would leave those to DS Bailey. "Show me." He walked straight past DS Bailey and headed towards the nearest of the two accident scenes.

Mirror looked around slowly as he vividly imagined various permutations of events that might have led to the untimely death.

"Show me the second scene, Bailey."

As he took his time to look around the second scene, DS Bailey's body language and irritation made it apparent that she perceived disrespect by his presence. He blocked her out as he listened as his gut; it was shouting to him that something didn't quite fit. Over the years, he'd learned to trust his gut instinct, even if his gut had no answers but was merely saying, "Mmm, not sure," it was enough for him to look again or think twice about a situation.

"Ok, Bailey, I'd like to go back over to the first scene, let me see the hospital report."

DS Bailey exhaled with volume and abruptly handed over her tablet viewer. "Here you go, sir." She purposely showed her frustration at his interference of her first solo incident.

"This doesn't feel right, Bailey," said Mirror, ignoring her obvious discontent. "Ok, if you collect copies of CCTV then collect statements from this floor, please."

"Yes, sir," DS Bailey replied abruptly but also felt the slight relief of not having to follow Mirror, even if it was just to ask pointless questions, questions she deemed would be a waste of her precious time.

Mirror hid his annoyance and felt proud of himself for not reacting in a what Captain Mason would have called an "unprofessional manner". He walked along the corridor, away from Bailey, looking for someone to question and found the operating theatre staff nurse's room. Knocking his usual *ta-da ta-ta*, he entered without waiting for a reply. Six nurses looked up to stare at him as their paired conversations paused mid-flow. "Morning all, sorry for disturbing your break. I'm DI Mirror, I'd like to ask you a few questions on this morning's events," he said as informally as the subject matter would allow. "Well, not so much questions, guys, it's more to find out a little bit of gossip." He calmed his body language and looked around the room.

The gossip revealed the deceased had been valuable members of the team, liked by all, and what's more, they were an item. After a chance meeting a few years previously, they had kept in touch and had "hooked up and got seriously loved up", as one of their colleagues adequately put it, when the nurse had joined the hospital a few months ago. DI Mirror wondered if that might be the reason his gut had been nagging him. *Maybe*, he thought as he headed back to find DS Bailey.

"Ok, Bailey, let's get back to headquarters. I want to look something up on the central system."

DS Bailey looked at him with a puzzled expression, convinced Mirror was purposely trying to belittle her. "Have you not read the hospital report? they are straightforward and justified accident."

"Yes, Bailey, I've read the report, but I've found out they weren't just colleagues. They were a couple, so unless I am one hundred per cent satisfied with two people who were in a relationship dying in a different part of the same building within minutes of each other, and I find proof it was nothing more than a random occurrence, it stays an open case. Oh, and just for future reference, it's 'have you not read the hospital report, *sir*' next time, ok, DS Bailey?"

DS Bailey struggled to hide her frustration; her mind was made-up on it being a coincidence. "Yes, *sir*, they may have known each other, but they were obviously still both accidents," she replied with voiced contempt.

Even with the sharpest of knives, it would have been difficult to cut the atmosphere as they were driven back to the department in Mirror's car. Mirror's gut was nagging, and as tempting as it would have been just to sign off on the case so he'd spend less time with DS Bailey, he just wasn't the type that would accept a neat solution if it didn't add up. It felt wrong, and it kept rotating around in his head. It bothered him that the doctor and nurse were a couple. *Their deaths do seem like accidents,* he thought, questioning himself. "There must be something else, something I'm not seeing yet," Mirror talked out loud, but found he was only speaking to himself as the doubt-filled DS Bailey heard but chose to ignore.

The security gate officer waved them straight through the barrier as they arrived at TSM-PD headquarters. As the car slowed to a crawl, DS Bailey hastily exited and headed straight into the already open elevator. She momentarily paused, but Mirror waved her to go on, content to let her use the lift by herself. Welcoming the thought of not having to share another confined space so soon after the car ride, he stayed in the car as it self-parked. He checked the rear-view viewer as DS Bailey looked over to the car, huffed and let the doors shut. Mirror climbed out of the car, walked over to the second lift and got in. *What was it that that nurse had said?* he mused, revisiting his earlier conversation with the nurses as he rode the lift. *The victims had met each other a few years ago and had hooked up when the nurse transferred to St Thomas' Hospital.*

The lift opened to the very familiar view of the shiny TSM-PD front desk. The ever-bubbly Elaine Wallberry, sitting at its helm, was on a viewer call. She acknowledged and halted Mirror with the gesture of holding her index finger straight up, instructing him to wait, then pointed the same finger at her viewer screen to state the obvious then back upright to reiterate her wanting DI Mirror to stay. "No problem at all, madam, I will make sure that she gets the message directly," she said, enunciating her every word to the caller while continuing to keep her finger upright until she had ended the call. "Thank you, and I hope you have a very nice weekend as well, madam."

"Detective Inspector Mirror – 'n' how's mah fave boaby doin' t'day?" said Elaine, her posh telephone accent instantly changed as she reverted to a less forced Glaswegian dialect.

"Afternoon, Elaine, how's it been around here today?" replied Mirror.

"It's been stowed, bit ye know me, ah love mah jab." Elaine gestured Mirror to come closer, "How's it goin wi' ye fresh birdie? Is she still driving ye dooially?" Mirror understood every other word when Elaine unleashed her full accent but could still piece just enough of what she had said to translate the question and concluded she had asked if DS Bailey had been driving him crazy today.

"She's hard work, Elaine, but the captain insists I show her the ropes. I'd certainly like to show her a rope," he joked, giving Elaine a raised-eyebrow look. "Any idea where she is?"

"Och, DI Mirror, yer terrible! She's in with the captain – he cried her in as soon as she got here."

"Thanks, Elaine, let's hope the captain has a very, very, very important media role for her to promote and glamorise the department that would also, quite sadly, take her away from us for a day or two, or three," said a straight-faced Mirror. Unless you knew his true feelings, you would never have guessed he was being sarcastic.

"Och, DI Mirror," said Elaine as her viewer started to ring. Instantly, her elocution lessons kicked back in, and with her poshest pose and viewer-voice, she answered the caller. "Good afternoon, Time-Share Misuse Police Department, Elaine Wallberry speaking, how may I help?"

The sudden change in Elaine's accent always brought a smile to Mirror's face. He continued to his office, sat at his desk and called his viewer. The viewer lowered from the ceiling and stopped just short of the desktop. *Ok. What am I missing*? "Viewer, show me linked files on this morning's fatalities at St Thomas' Hospital." He gestured at the screen with his fingers and slid each of the files into a separate part of the screen then dragged the two victims' names together to the left-hand top corner of the viewer. "Viewer, search the database for any associated links, and show files only where the names are paired together." The viewer brought up a list of seven main results, five from a public server, covering a period between August and September 2059 and two from a government server: media articles dating from 20th October 2050 to 18th December 2050.

Date	*Short Details*
1. 19th September 2059	*TSM-PD report*
2. 19th September 2059	*St Thomas' Hospital accident log*
3. 12th August 2059	*Union mobile and utilities*
4. 8th August 2059	*Mortgage acceptance*
5. 1st August 2059	*Credit application*
6. 18th October 2050	*Court services juror release*
7. 24th July 2050	*Court services summons*

Mirror scanned both lists, *they were looking at mortgages; they were living or planning to live together.* His eyes widened as he stopped on the sixth and seventh items from the government server list. *They were on jury service together.* Mirror's gut pounded its drum. The link had expanded. *They worked at the same hospital, they were romantically involved and had met years earlier when they were called up for jury service.* The findings gave him a familiar buzz as they fed his gut. “Viewer, expand item six from government server results.” The viewer displayed details of a court case.

“Viewer, expand top result on the public server.”

The viewer expanded a newspaper headline dated 20th October 2050.

“*CASE OF THE CENTURY JURORS REVEALED*”. Mirror’s jaw dropped slightly as he absorbed the main headline then slowly tightened back up as he read the main article, his deducing mind moving through its gears as the familiar process of organising and processing information started to gain its momentum, only to be ground to a halt as the viewer screen flashed. It was an incoming call from the captain. “Oh, for… ok, viewer, save contents to Detective Inspector Mirror file number forty-two and accept the call.”

The captain’s image engulfed the viewer screen, sweeping away its previous content. “Yes, sir.”

“Mirror, can you come over to my office, please,” ordered the captain.

“Sir, I’m just in the middle of…”

“Now, please, Mirror.”

“Yes, sir.”

Mirror knocked his usual *ta-da ta ta* and waited, but instead of the usual “come in”, the door opened, and a self-righteous-looking DS Bailey walked out of the captain’s office. “Sir,” said the smug DS Bailey manoeuvring past him.

“Mirror, come in, take a seat.” The call snapped Mirror out of his moment of confusion. He entered the office and sat facing the captain. *The chair was quite warm. I wonder how long they’ve been talking for, and what was it about?* He guessed it was more likely to be Bailey complaining about how he’d interfered with her case by not signing it off.

“Gabriel, now, I’ve known you a long time, and I’m grateful that you’ve tolerated DS Bailey this long, but knowing you as I do, I have to ask if you’re purposely hindering this St Thomas’ incident just to wind her up?”

“No, sir, I’m double-checking all the details,” replied Mirror, staring into a blank space to avoid eye contact with the captain.

“I’ve checked DS Bailey’s report and the hospital’s report, and I agree with them both. I want you to close the case and file it, please.”

Mirror's usual reaction would have been to jump up out of his chair and shout, "You *what*, sir?" then continue to argue his point until he either got his way or the captain kicked him out of the office. But as this involved Bailey, he decided it might be best to hold back, opting that a smoother approach might be the better way to proceed.

"Sir, I was going to investigate it further, there's something that doesn't make sense, there seem to be a couple of unanswered questions. I've found a link between the two victims dating back nine years. They were on the same jurors' list." With his new, calmer approach and professionalism in his presentation, Mirror was convinced his point was being put across well. Unfortunately, judging by the captain's reply, his new style hadn't been as effective as he had hoped.

"Mirror, stop and calm yourself. What jurors' list? Nine years ago? What the hell are you talking about? Stop trying to find a reason for every little incident. They were accidents, sometimes they just happen. I want you to close the case and that's the end of it. Now, get out of my office, get your speech written up, go home and get ready for the benefit gala."

"But sir, there *is* a link! My gut's telling me it can't be that simple, it's not just a coincidence—" He froze mid-sentence, "What bloody benefit dinner and what bloody speech?"

Chapter 5

The Tale Of Two Lists

Friday 26th September 2059 – present day

Mirror puts his badge in his pocket, attaches the laser cuffs to his belt and carefully shuts the captain's office door behind him, feeling somewhat disconcerted about how the captain presumed to know him so well and annoyed with himself that had he pushed that little bit more in keeping the hospital case open last week, three people might still be alive today.

He sighs, walks three rooms up, presses *Incident Room Number One* on the Time-Share keypad and watches the door slide open.

Mirror glances around the glass-walled conference room. Six Time-Share officers are sitting around a large oval conference table which is positioned in the centre. Three large and two smaller viewer screens dominated the top end. The two larger of the viewers display profiles and photos of the recently deceased trio of Christopher Lowe, Ravi Binning and Carmela Rosa.

“Afternoon, sir. Would you like a cup of tea?” asks PC Polly Killy, her greeting closely followed by nearly all the other officers.

“Good afternoon, Guv.”

“Guv.”

“Afternoon, sir.”

“Good to have you back, sir.”

Salutations are offered in turn as Mirror makes his way past PC Gordon Reeves, DS Yik Chang, PC Sangeet Gill and PC Pedrag Dragan, all of whom are sitting with their backs to the room’s River Thames-facing windows. He makes his way to the viewers and draws his attention to the opposite side of the unbalanced table as he hears a sheepish, yet still managing to vibrate through her teeth, “Good afternoon, sir,” from DS Bailey, who is sitting by herself. A sudden realisation hits Mirror as he nods back to her greeting, his animosity towards her has subsided, the case has taken priority. He still finds her slightly annoying, but more in a fly-in-the-room-like way.

“Afternoon all, and yes, please, Polly,” says Mirror, turning to look at the images of the three victims. *Could I have saved any of them had that stupidness with Bailey not distracted me from my work? I don’t know,* he wonders.

Being away from work the last few days has given Mirror a sense of urgency, and he is eager to catch up. Not that his life solely revolves around work – yes, work has been the predominate part, but in the last few years, he has developed a nice balance of work, home and social life. He loves going out to live events, walks, visiting new places and so on. He has a tried-and-tested method of pushing individual thoughts or problems from each different corner of his life into a separate file in his mind and can continue processing them in the background without affecting another file. Whether it is working on a case or what he is doing later, which bills he must pay or which messages he has to reply to, he has become an expert at keeping each part of his life to itself. He is very systematic, he is adaptable and very good at improvising within a given situation, whether that means being a lifesaver, solving the clues, finding something to do on a night out or making something for dinner from whatever he's found in the cupboards. Nothing seems to stress him as long as the main elements of his life are kept apart and balanced. Which, of course, they haven't been this week. His suspension has destabilised him, his mind files have merged and become jumbled. But being given his warrant shield back has rebooted him, a balance has returned, and the files have quickly reordered.

Mirror swipes at his mobile viewer and loads the St Thomas' Hospital deaths files to the two smaller viewers. "Ok, this is Doctor Anthony Chand, forty-three years of age."

PC Polly Killy walks over and places a brown-and-gold TSM-PD shielded mug next to him. "Here you go, sir," she says.

"Thank you, Polly," replies Mirror appreciatively. "Dr Chand died last Friday; he was, by all accounts, a brilliant surgeon. At nine sixteen a.m., as he was entering the third-floor Time-Share elevator, the doors suddenly closed, trapping the doctor. Half of him was in real-time, half in Time-Share. The elevator continued to move upwards, severing the doctor in two. The hospital reports a malfunction in the elevator's Time-Share system had caused the safety overrides to fail and forced it to shut."

The officers look at each other like a class of college students wondering if they have turned up to the wrong lecture. Mirror continues, ignoring the puzzled looks, "And this is Ophelia Schmidt, who also died last Friday. She worked at the same hospital, thirty-seven years of age, ex-army nurse, recently transferred to St Thomas' and for reasons yet unknown was on the hospital's roof helipad. At 9:15 a.m, the emergency helicopter came through a Time Share window and landed on top of her. The helicopter was originally scheduled to land in a Time-Share bubble, but once again, due to a *glitch*, it landed in real 'time." There is a noticeable scepticism in his voice. DS Bailey clears her throat, "Sir, hasn't the hospital incident been closed? It was concluded that a Time-Share glitch between 9:15 a.m. and 9:16 a.m. had been directly responsible for both accidents. The captain has already signed off on the report."

"Thank you, DS Bailey," Mirror answers sharply but with satisfaction that his response has remained professional as he blocks out Bailey's voice vibration from distracting his train of thought.

DS Yik Chang's left eyebrow, as if in slow motion, rises an inch above his other as he turns to face Mirror. "Sir, are we not here to discuss the three recent deaths?" He turns to scan round his colleagues, ending his sweep to face PC Reeves, who instantly nods back in support then double takes as he registers DS Chang's expression.

DS Chang is an intense-looking man, which is the complete opposite to his personality, so, he tries to make light of any given situation in the hope that humour might help compensate for his consuming looks, humour which often backfires, leaving his colleagues confused.

"Yes, Yik, we are," says Mirror, looking up at DS Chang then back down to his mobile viewer and sends a list to one of the larger viewers and to everyone's viewer tablets.

The list shows the five recently deceased victims and is entitled "*List Number One*".

List Number One:

Anthony Chand – 43 – surgeon – deceased Friday 19th September 2059

Ophelia Schmidt – 37 – nurse – deceased Friday 19th September 2059

Ravi Binning – 72 – retired – deceased Monday 22nd September 2059

Carmela Rosa – 48 – shop owner – deceased Tuesday 23rd September 2059

Christopher Lowe – 31 – hairstylist – deceased Thursday 25th September 2059

Mirror surveys his officers to gauge reaction, and the expected blank expressions stare back. Before anyone could make comment, he sends a second list to the tablets, and the viewer splits the screen to show the two lists side by side. “And this is list two,” he says with a raised tone, expecting this one to cause more of a stir.

List Number Two:

Juror list – the State vs Maddison Bartel, October 9th to October 15th, 2050

Juror 1	*Carmela Rosa – age 39*
Juror 2	*Lindsey Clark-Carter – age 24*
Juror 3	*Lucy Victoria – age 19*
Juror 4	*Ravi Binning – age 63*
Juror 5	*Michael Craven – age 30*
Juror 6	*Christopher Lowe – age 22*
Juror 7	*Calvin Wireless – age 18*
Juror 8	*Jade Andrews – age 31*
Juror 9	*Betsy Thorn – age 44*
Juror 10	*Michele Esteves – age 55*
Juror 11	*Anthony Chand – age 34*
Juror 12	*Ophelia Schmidt – age 28*

One by one, puzzlement and anticipation replaces the blank expressions as the realisation that this is no longer a meeting to look at three deaths, confirm their accidental status and sign them off spreads through the room.

"Is that the 'Slate Killer' trial, sir?" asks DS Chang, vocalising the media name given to the convicted serial killer, Maddison Bartel.

No matter how accidental each death had initially seemed, it is clearly much too much of a coincidence for the names of five people who'd met for a brief period back in October 2050 to now show up on a different list.

"This can't be a coincidence. They sat next to each other in the courtroom," mutters DS Bailey, noticing jurors eleven and twelve were the same doctor and nurse recently killed. She places her hand between her forehead and hairline and looks back to her tablet, she can't understand why, when all the signs pointed at accidents, something had niggled DI Mirror enough to stop him signing off on the case. A rookie feeling hits her as she reassesses her position, realising that her now very apparent over-confidence has revealed her inexperience and the professional gulf between her and DI Mirror.

Mirror gestures PC Killy to join him. "PC Killy, please bring me up to date on the three incidents I've missed."

"Yes, sir," says PC Killy. She swipes on her tablet, changing the picture on the first of the larger screens.

"This is Christopher Lowe – thirty-one years old," she reports. "Found yesterday by his wife on her return to the house they had just bought. Mrs Lowe had been at work, and Mr Lowe had taken the day off to oversee the house move."

"Who did they buy the house from?" asks Mirror.

DS Bailey looks at Mirror, wondering why the question was important and why it hadn't occurred to her to ask when she had attended the scene.

"Erm…" says PC Dragan, furiously tapping away on his tablet. "It was Diamonds Time-Share Estates, sir."

"Thank you, Pedrag. Carry on, please, Polly."

"Yes, sir. DS Bailey and I attended the scene. There wasn't much left of Mr Lowe, but his remains were found in his ground-floor bathroom. The room was approximately fifteen by twenty feet." PC Killy changes the image on the viewer to show areas of the scene. "As you can see, sir, the rear of an old train carriage covers the back of the room and Mr Lowe's severed legs are still standing by the basin portion of the toilet." She cringes as the images force her to recollect the scene she had witnessed. “As you can see, sir, the identification number of the train is visible.”

“What were your findings as to how this so-called Time-Share accident happened?” Mirror diverts his gaze over to DS Bailey, “Can you fill us in, please, DS Bailey?”

“Yes, yes, of course, sir,” DS Bailey quickly reacts and sends her findings to the first viewer. “The plot of land used for building the house was in the south-west corner of Hampstead Heath Park, right next to the old train line that used to link Gospel Oak and Hampstead Heath train stations, sir,” says Bailey as she sends a second image of an old newspaper clipping. The headline reads “*TRAGIC MONDAY – Sports Centre Destroyed by Runaway Train*”. Below is a picture showing a building on fire, the newspaper dated Tuesday, May 30th, 2023.

“The train originated from 2023, there was a track running close to the plot of land where the house was eventually built in 2025. After a bit more digging I…,” she pauses, “I mean, PC Killy and I managed to trace the train’s serial number. It was retired from service on May 29th, 2023. Further digging revealed National Rail had been testing a driverless bullet train the same day along the Northern Line. National Rail had been conducting secret driverless train tests in the prelude to their 'increase reliability' campaign. For reasons yet unknown, the train derailed, ending up in Parliament Hill Athletics Track and Sports Centre."

"Luckily, nobody had been using the centre at that time as it was a bank holiday and closed, so no injuries," adds PC Killy.

She looks over towards DS Bailey who nods and continues, "After a media hoo-ha and a long investigation National Rail were eventually fined. The centre never reopened and the land was instead sold as building plots for luxury and highly sought-after housing, though, looking at the original price list, not very affordable housing, sir."

Mirror was reluctantly impressed with her report. As if finally seeing a bit of blue emanating from her, his feelings towards her calmed slightly, which made his mood more forgiving. "Thank you, Bailey, good work."

DS Bailey was used to receiving compliments, due to her impressive academic achievements, she has been complimented or honoured all her life. Top of the class or a test had been so much the norm, she'd rarely taken praise as a sign of achievement anymore; to her, it is nothing more than a few words strung together. But a "thank you" and a "good work" from DI Mirror ignited something in her, something that had been missing for a long time.

"Ok, next, please, Polly."

"Yes, sir." PC Killy taps on her tablet viewer. "This is Carmela Rosa – she's on your juror list as juror number one, forty-nine years of age and was killed in her coffee shop three days ago. Witnesses say Mrs Rosa had been at the counter, and there was a loud bang. A picture of a ballerina, covered in holes, appeared on the wall, and Mrs Rosa fell to the floor with shotgun wounds to her head. CCTV was thoroughly checked inside and outside the premises but no signs of any gunman in proximity. The shot seemed to come out of nowhere. DS Chang and PC Reeves attended the scene."

DS Chang stands and, in a single motion, gestures PC Reeves to join him. He picks up his tablet viewer and swipes to send his coffee shop incident to the second of the larger viewers. "Sir, I had already signed this incident off as an accident, but I now realise I might have been slightly premature," he admits with sprit-level straight eyebrows, an expressionless face and his brow unfurrowed. "Mrs Rosa had recently set up the coffee shop, 'Rosa's Pantry'.

Friends say it had been a lifelong dream after working production lines since leaving school. The shop was a Time-Share unit and shared space as one of five other shops, a launderette, pic'n'mix sweet shop, pawnbroker all of which had individual coded access systems, and the real-time luggage accessories boutique."

PC Reeves joins the conversation. "Mrs Rosa was hit in the head by a wide burst of shotgun pellets, which would indicate the shooter had to be nearby. We have checked CCTV footage of both the coffee shop and the street and can't see anyone that it could have been."

DS Chang's left eyebrow breaks its levelness. "We looked back at the shop unit's history and discovered that during most of 2017, the building had been empty, so the year was chosen for Time-Share space. Before being vacant, it had been a post office with cash machines on the outside of the building. The post office was closed in December 2016, but the cash machines stayed in use for a few years after. On June 23rd, 2017, an armed robbery of the security van emptying the machines took place. One of the thieves used a shotgun blast through the then empty shop unit's window as a scare tactic to convince the van's security staff, they were serious and to cooperate with their demands. The lead pellets from the shotgun blasted through the window, through the empty unit and into the left-hand wall where a picture of a ballerina hung. The picture had been left behind when the post office closed. Rosa's coffee shop counter had since been built along the same wall."

"Thank you, DS Chang and PC Reeves, you said that she had only recently set the coffee shop up?" asks Mirror.

PC Dragan anticipates the question, "Diamonds Estates, sir."

"Diamonds Estates sold the property. Yet another coincidence," says Mirror, making a note on his mobile viewer. "Next, please, Killy."

"Next we have Ravi Binning, aged 72, killed in an MRI mishap four days ago at…" PC Killy pauses realising what she is about to say, "St Thomas' Hospital, sir." She looks around at the others, wondering why no one apart from DI Mirror had even considered any of the deaths could have been linked before today. "Mr Binning was attending an MRI appointment at St Thomas' for a lung check-up. A lifetime smoker, he suffered from emphysema. Mr Binning carried with him a portable oxygen tank. The MRI department uses Time-Share bubbles so they can increase the number of patients seen at the same time with each machine. He was asked to go into MRI Time-Share five, and for whatever reason, on entering the MRI suite, he arrived in Time-Share four, where the MRI machine was already active and scanning another patient. The magnetic field from the MRI pulled the metal oxygen tank towards it with the seventy-two-year-old Mr Binning in tow. The shock was too much for Mr Binning, who died of a heart attack brought on by shock and breathing difficulties."

"Poor sod," says PC Gill. "I took statements at the time, sir, from staff, patients and members of the public around the area. It seems that all had been doing their jobs correctly, and logs show that Mr Binning did enter Time-Share five. It did seem to be just another Time-Share glitch," he reports. "I must admit, sir, since the incident took place at the same hospital that yourself and DS Bailey attended last week, I was happy to conclude, as I think we all were up until today, that the hospital was having issues with their Time-Share equipment. The hospital itself is conducting thorough checks on their systems, and that was good enough for me to sign it off as another accident or bubble mishap."

The week's suspension fades to his distant memory as Mirror assumes full control of the case. "Ok, until someone gives me proof that these deaths are not related, we are going to work on the assumption that they are somehow linked. So, for now, the juror connection is the lead we follow."

Mirror turns to look at DS Chang. "I want you and Reeves to work on Diamond Estates. Find out everything about them and why their company is linked to at least two of the victims and are they linked to any others." He turns to look at PC Killy. "PCs Killy, Dragan, Gill and…" Mirror pauses – he was going to add DS Bailey's name to the group but stops short. "We need more information about the court case. I want you to track the remaining names on that juror list and put together a matrix of anyone else involved in the original court case." He looks down at his viewer tablet and swipes. "I want everything, every finding, no matter how small, added to my file number forty-two, I've given you all access."

A complement of, "Yes, sir," follows. Then, much to her and everyone else's surprise, Mirror turns towards DS Bailey and adds, "Detective Sergeant Bailey, you're with me."

Chapter 6

The Court Case

Monday 4th July 2050 – nine years earlier

Newsflash — 7:02 a.m. — *Newsflash*

An eye-catching headline went viral as it hit media and viewer platforms worldwide, alerting the public to the story of the decade.

A newsreader dramatically directed a concerned look toward the camera and greeted his viewers, "Good morning, Britain. The Slate Killer has been caught." Pausing to add intensity, he semi-pouted his lips and stared harder into the camera. "A police raid on a house last night in the sleepy village of Cranfield near Bedford has led to the apprehension of a man our sources believe to be the serial killer who's been terrorising Britain for the last two years and is linked to at least eighteen murders."

*

Wednesday 6th July 2050

"A police spokesperson has confirmed that a thirty-six-year-old Bedfordshire man has been charged with multiple counts of murder."

"With incriminating evidence found at his home, police believe they have caught the Slate Killer."

"According to our sources, we are led to believe the man's name is Maddison Bartel."

*

Tuesday 12th July 2050

"Maddison Bartel appeared before magistrates today for a plea hearing. The trial has been set for 10th October 2050."

"Join us at ten thirty tomorrow evening when we will have an extended program to take a closer look at this suspected evil serial killer and try to answer why and what drove him to kill so many people."

*

Wednesday 13th July 2050

"Good evening, tonight we are going to find out a bit more about Maddison Bartel. Who is he? Why are the police convinced that he is the killer, and if he is, what drove him to brutally murder eighteen poor souls?"

"We have to stress, Mr Bartel has not yet been found guilty of anything, we are simply having a hypothetical discussion based on reports from our sources and recent statements from the police."

"Joining us this evening is Captain Raj Solomon from the Herts–Beds–Bucks three counties' police force, and psychologist and profiler for the International Behavioural Science Unit, Barbara King. Welcome and good evening to both of you," said the newsreader.

"Good evening," said Barbara King.

"Good evening," replied Captain Solomon.

"Captain Solomon, if I can start with you, why the nickname, 'Slate Killer' for this particular murderer?"

Captain Solomon looked at the newsreader then faced the camera.

"Thank you and good evening. Whilst working on the case, it was quite fair to say we were very puzzled. There didn't seem to be any set pattern to the murders, each one being very different. The victims were of different age and gender, found in different Time-Share locations, and they were all killed by different methods. The only thing we had to go on was that the murders were happening consecutively on weekdays, Monday to Friday, and seemed to stop at the weekends then restart on a Monday. We originally nicknamed him The Weekday Killer. The murders didn't seem to have anything else in common. Eventually, as we worked the case and dug that little bit deeper, we had a breakthrough and started linking some of them together via lists. The seemingly unconnected deaths did have at least one factor in common but only once we knew where to look. The various victims had been listed together at some point in their past. The first five names were all people who had volunteered to help at a disabled rally, the next seven were national amateur writers and competition finalists, and they were followed by the first six names from an online petition against smoking in public. It was that last list that finally gave us the lead we needed. The name in common and the name that kept popping up was 'Bartel'. He was one of the main organisers for the disabled rally, a non-finalist entry in the writers' competition, and he'd signed the petition. We nicknamed him The Slate Killer as a play on the word 'list'. You know the old saying 'on the slate'," explained Captain Solomon, looking at the newsreader then back towards the camera to continue. "I'd like to also state that even though we have charged Mr Bartel and evidence seems to strongly suggest that we have our man, it will be up to the courts to decide on his guilt. We have done our job to the best of our given knowledge in the given time."

The newsreader nodded in agreement, showing understanding towards the captain, then smirked. "Captain Solomon, I understand why you have to say that, but I think we all know the trial is heading for a foregone conclusion and is merely a technicality – you have your man," he stated as he turned to his second guest of the evening. "Barbara, you are a psychological profiler and have often aided police in the past with many other cases. Can you tell us a bit more about Mr Bartel and whether he fits the profile of a serial killer?"

Barbara King pushed her glasses back up her nose, placed her fingers in an overlocked position and hovered her hands slightly above the table. "Yes, yes, of course. Well, Mr Bartel. He is a very, very clever man, university educated, degrees in physics, mechanical engineering, computer science, and of course, as we all already know, he was part of the original Time-Share discovery team. He was a member of several community groups where other members presumed to know him and held him in regard as a very nice man, but he never, it seems, gave much of his actual life or lifestyle away. When we questioned the neighbours and groups, no one seemed to know him as well as they first thought. All struggled to say much more than, 'He is a nice man.' This is typical behaviour for a psychopath trying to blend into society without giving too much away," said the intuitive Barbara, lifting and lowering her hovering interlocked fingers, using them to emphasise the last part of each of her sentences. "His personality, his lifestyle show traits highly regarded within professional circles as 'red flags' for a possible psychopath. We know he had recently returned to work at Cranfield University in the water science division. He had been relocated to four different jobs in the last year. When arrested, he bragged that he had inside information about the murders but would not admit to doing them. These are also typical psychopathic traits, not holding down a job, being a power junkie, bragging about what they know but manipulating the sharing of that information to maintain control and keep everyone on the back foot, Psychos love that – they love manipulating people and watching the chaos that ensues."

"Thank you, Barbara," said newsreader. "Of course, we are not allowed, currently, to divulge any information about the murders or the case until after the hearing. One thing I will say, this is going to be one of the most high-profile court cases in history, and we will bring you any, and all developments as they happen, so stay tuned."

*

Monday 25th July 2050

Out of an estimated four hundred and fifty thousand jury summons sent out in Britain every year by the Ministry Of Justice, fifteen randomly selected postboxes received a notification informing the addressees that they had been selected for jury duty and were to attend the Central Criminal Court for England and Wales on Friday 7th October 2050.

*

Friday 7th October 2050 – 8:49 a.m.

The heavy droplets of rain bounced back up as they hit the ground, a soaking wet Anthony Chand arrived at the Old Bailey and momentarily stood in the doorway. Thankful to be out of the torrential downpour, he shook his head, swept his hands across his eyes to brush the excess water off his face and lifted his head to realise he was blocking the access behind him. "Oh, I'm sorry," he said. He backed into the rain, moved to the side, and opened the door for the smartly dressed woman.

The woman hurried into the building and was immediately followed by Anthony, both happy to be out of the rain. “Thank you,” she said, attempting to figure out what to do with her dripping wet umbrella. “Have you been summoned too?” she asked in a jokey voice, widening her eyes and lightly shaking her head from side to side. “I’m Ophelia Schmidt.”

“I’m Anthony, and I’m afraid so.” He smiled back and noticed she was only slightly drier than him.

“Guess we join the queue,” said Ophelia, pointing towards the busy check-in desk.

They stood side by side in a line of twenty people, and their attention was instantly drawn to the front where a sunglasses-wearing man was speaking very loudly to the check-in clerk.

“Mr Wireless, unfortunately, there is nothing I can do. You have been summoned, and you are law bound to stay if you are needed unless the judge releases you.” The clerk seemed to be doing well just to keep her cool, remaining calm as she repeatedly explained the situation to the insufferable man.

“For fuck's sake! You are not taking me seriously! You’re acting like you can’t see me. I’ve got a tour – a chance of a lifetime, I'm supporting—" the obnoxious Calvin Wireless stopped short of finishing his sentence as he noticed the clerk wave over a very large security man. "Sir, please move into the next room," said the deep-toned heavy-set guard, whose shadowing presence instantly quietened Calvin to contain his moaning to just under his breath as he was quickly moved into a room labelled "*JURORS ONLY*".

The woman in front of Anthony and Ophelia turned around to look at them.

"Did you hear that? Making out we can't see him, dressed in tight green trousers and a bright orange top. I'm pretty sure everyone can see him very well indeed," she laughed. "Hi, I'm Camela Rosa. Don't know what he's moaning about anyway. I've been looking forward to this – beats work. I'm treating it like a holiday." Both Anthony and Ophelia nodded in agreement, introduced themselves then turned to look at each other in an almost mutually telepathic pretence of already being in conversation so they didn't have to continue chatting with the talkative Carmela.

The line quickly moved forward. When they reached the front, Anthony invited Ophelia to check in first and felt a buzz when she waited for him to check in so that they could enter the second waiting room together. Inside the room were about eighty people, some sitting some standing, or in Calvin Wireless's case, pacing furiously backwards and forwards while muttering obscenities under his breath. Anthony attracted Ophelia's attention, and at first, she just smiled back but then failed to hold in her laugh as they watched a streak of lime-green trousers and bright orange shirt pacing in front of them.

"Well, I guess we wait in here then," said Ophelia, chuckling. She looked at Anthony, content that even though she'd only just met him, he seemed nice and approachable, alleviating the nervousness she had felt about the day.

"Guess we do," he replied. "It's a bit strange that we got asked to attend on a Friday. I thought it would make more sense to start on a Monday."

They found a table with vacant seats and sat, chatting away, enjoying each other's company. About an hour and a half later, a court officer called their attention. "Good morning, everyone. Those of you continuing your cases, please follow your appointed court officer now. Anyone here for the first time, please wait here. We will be with you soon," he said in a loud high-pitched voice.

A few "London underground station at rush hour" minutes followed, and the majority of the people made their way to their relevant destinations; one by one they left until only fifteen remained. "Maybe, if we're not needed, we can go for a coffee instead?" suggested a hopeful Anthony. Ophelia's eyes widened, and she nodded back in agreement.

A couple of minutes after the exodus, the court officer came back in. "The rest of you here should be new and here for the first time today, thank you for coming in. You will not be needed until Monday."

"YES!" shouted a relieved Calvin Wireless from the far side of the room and momentarily stopped wearing out the carpet.

The court officer turned towards him and gave him a stern look, "But, as you will be part of a special hearing, you will be sworn in today, and arrangements have been made for all of you to remain in the Crown's care and under observation from now until the end of the court case. If you can all follow me, please."

“WHAT?” The re-aggravated Wireless frantically lifted and lowered his opened hands as his sotto voce obscenities directed towards the clerk and the court system rose to full volume.

Looks of confusion and annoyance spread as each of the new jurors allowed the court officer’s words to sink in.

“Does that mean we’re getting put up in a hotel?” said the excited Carmela, giving a thumbs-up to the woman across from her and receiving a frowned look back.

“Please follow me,” ordered the clerk.

A mixture of emotions flowed through the group as they followed the clerk towards a “*JUROR’S ONLY*” hallway that led them into the main courtroom.

The clerk stopped by the Time-Share control panel to the left of a door.

The court had six Time-Share bubbles, one to five were showing occupied; the clerk pressed button six. They entered and were ushered immediately to the right to sit along the juror’s bench.

“Wow, look at this courtroom, it’s amazing! So much polished wood, it gives such an olde worlde look, doesn’t it?” commented Ophelia.

Before Anthony could answer, the court clerk shouted from the front of the courtroom to bring everyone's attention to a wooden panel that was opening behind the judge's chair. "All rise for the Honorable Judge Edward C Crowley the Second."

The silence in the court only broke for the sixty-eight-year-old judge's movements as he slowly sat on his highly polished and extensively carved wooden throne then unconcernedly took his time looking through his paperwork, periodically placing random sheets to his side as the rest of the courtroom remained standing and waiting in silence.

"Morning, you may sit," said the judge without looking up. He picked up the top sheet from his pile which listed the jurors' names. "Can John Mullins, Joanne Smith, Calvin Wireless and Lonnie Logan-Smythe stand," he ordered.

"Oh, for," an audible Calvin let out a huff to bring attention to his frustration of being told to stand so quickly after being told to sit and of what he deemed a waste of his time and talents.

The judge looked at each of the four standing jurors in turn.

"I have received, today, requests from each of you, asking to be excused from your duty. Mr Mullins and Miss Logan-Smythe, please identify yourselves." Two of the jurors cagily put their hands up. The judge looked at them in turn then back down to his paperwork. "I am satisfied with your request; you are both excused. Looking at the other two requests, I don't find the excuses offer sufficient reasons as to why Mr Wireless or Mrs Smith shouldn't be able to continue, but one of you is surplus to our requirements so…"

Calvin Wireless crossed his fingers and held his hands in the air as he hoped that the first and only judgement he would witness would be the judge's verdict on whether he would be allowed to leave.

"Mrs Smith, as you have children, I will accept your request. Mr Wireless, please sit," ordered the judge, whose verdict was met with, "Oh, my *God*!" as Calvin threw himself back onto the bench.

"Mrs Smith, Miss Logan-Smythe and Mr Mullins, you are excused and released from duty. Please exit the court." The judge placed the sheet of paper back in its place and waited for the three released jurors to leave. Then, with a change of persona, he glared over to the remaining inhabitants of the jury benches. “You twelve have been selected for a very, very disturbing case indeed. Unfortunately, due to the expected heightened media attention this case will attract and because this will be a live viewer-streamed trial, it is best to choose the jury early and keep you under the Crown’s protection for the duration of the hearing.”

Various looks of amazement, panic and fear of the unknown cycled through the jurors’ benches as the judge continued, “You will hand in any mobile or tablet viewers you may have on your persons. We request that you do not communicate with anyone outside of this courtroom and only talk with either each other or the officers assigned to you. You are not permitted to discuss the case with each other until the hearing is at a point that you are asked to deliberate on your verdict, do you understand?”

The twelve jurors looked at each other, but before any of them responded, the judge continued, “Good, you will, of course, be allowed to communicate with your families, and the court officers will be at your disposal to assist you with your families should it be required. Again, I stress you cannot and must not divulge any of what you hear inside this courtroom, and your calls will be monitored. If you have any questions, please see the court officer afterwards."

Before anybody could comment on their pending situation, the court officer snapped their attention away from the judge. "Please stand. You will now be sworn in. In front of each of you, you will see a viewer. On the screen, there is a declaration. Please raise your right hand, and in the presence of Judge Edward C Crowley the Second, we will read the declaration together."

The judge took an unhurried sip of water, looked towards the court officer and nodded. "Repeat after me," the clerk continued. "I swear by the laws of England and Wales, that I will faithfully try the defendant and give a verdict according to the evidence presented to me."

The slightly out-of-sync jurors repeated the declaration as the surreal situation started to sink in.

"Please follow me," ordered the court officer, and the sheep-like jury followed.

*

Monday 10th October 2050

An animated Christopher Lowe entered the hotel's breakfast room then stopped to look around. Most of the chairs and tables were empty, but his attention was drawn to the far side as he spotted Carmela Rosa waving him over to join her and the rest of the jurors sitting around a single table.

The mixture of emotions was evident, reluctantly eating, some sitting staring and some, like Christopher and Carmela, trying to make the most of a bad situation.

"Un-be-lieve-able! I feel like royalty! I mean, this is like the Ritz, people, and it's all for us," said a child-like Christopher.

It wasn't the Ritz, but it was a very nice two-hundred-room hotel in a secret location on the outskirts of London, booked in its entirety by the Crown, all for them. The Crown was taking every step necessary to make sure nothing could go wrong and that nobody involved in the case could or would tamper with anything: security was tight.

A guard entered the breakfast room. "Ok, everyone, it's time, the coach has arrived, please follow me."

The twelve jurors and as many security guards took turns to climb aboard the window-blackened coach.

"Well, at least it's not driverless," said the all-approving Michael Craven, spotting the driver in his seat. Being a true gear head, Michael was a connoisseur of self-driving and was always daydreaming about engines and vehicles. His thoughts today were of his vintage Ducati scrambler 1100 motorbike. He'd only ridden it a couple of days ago, but that now seemed a lifetime away. *It must be so lonely, it's just sitting there in the garage, not being ridden,* he sighed.

The coach ride ensued mainly in silence as the twelve nervous passengers wondered what the day would bring and for how long they would be locked away from the rest of the world.

The pending trial turned out to be a media whirlwind with press and viewer news reporters from all around the globe, ready to pounce and be first to beam any new bit of information they could.

A multitude of journalists, media drones and the public were gathered outside the New Old Bailey, the coach driver sailed straight past, stopping further along the road at the side entrance. The gates opened, and the coach pulled into the security of the building's inner courtyard.

The trial took place between Monday 10th October and Tuesday 18th October 2050. There were no reporters or members of the public allowed in the courtroom, but there was a series of remote camera viewers to stream live as they followed the trial with vigorous detail.

During the trial, the judge and jury listened to vividly recalled accounts and testimonies from victims' families and police officer reports from all eighteen murder scenes. Maddison Bartel smiled and listened as every piece of evidence was recounted and even laughed as the jury flinched when shown the brutally horrific images of the murder scenes. Maddison never once admitted his guilt, but his aura, his actions, his body language throughout the trial were proof enough of his evil.

Maddison's solicitor was Harrison Mann, a scrupulous being, whose primary goal was to ride the wave of the high-profile case and make a name for himself. He pulled every trick he could in the *How To Be A Weasel Lawyer* book as he attempted to lead the jury, badgered every witness and scrutinised every decision by the police force in an attempt to find the loophole that would dismiss the case and free his client. But the jury was far from being swayed from the obvious decision they would make.

*

Monday 17th October 2050

The court hearing ended at 11:50 a.m., and the judge sent the jury out to deliberate. They returned barely ten minutes later, having made a unanimous decision.

The judge turned to look at the jury then to the clerk and gave him a nod to start. The clerk immediately addressed the court, “Will the jury please stand.”

The jury rose in perfect unison, having had plenty of practice over the past week.

“Will the defendant also rise and face the jury,” ordered the clerk. “Madam Foreperson has your jury agreed upon a verdict?” he said, addressing the timorous-looking Jade Andrews.

“We have, Your Honour,” replied the shaky-voiced Jade.

The expressionless clerk turned to the judge to receive a second nod then back to Jade. “What say you, Madam Foreperson, as to complaint number 266199-266199 wherein the defendant is charged with multiple murder? Is he guilty or not guilty?”

“Guilty,” said the visibly shaking Jade.

Judge Edward C Crowley the Second looked over at the jury. His expression seemed different and warmer than it had been the past week. “Thank you, jury, for your service in this most horrendous of trials. You are discharged from duty. The court is adjourned and will reconvene tomorrow at eleven a.m. for sentencing. Can the Jury, please follow the clerk to fill in your release forms. Bailiff, please take the prisoner down."

*

Tuesday 18th October 2050

Newsflash — 10:59 a.m. — *Newsflash*

"Welcome back to the Slate Killer trial special, guest psychologist Barbara King joins me, and we are moments away from going live to the courtroom, where Judge Edward C Crowley the Second will pass sentence on the convicted serial killer Maddison Bartel," said the newsreader.

"Over the last eight days, we have witnessed details on the most heinous series of crimes ever seen in this reporter's lifetime."

"I said it before, and I'll say it again, bring back the death penalty. Hold on, we've just got word that the judge is ready, let's go live to the New Old Bailey."

"This is the moment we have been waiting for. Judge Edward C Crowley the Second is addressing the smirking Maddison Bartel," commentated Barbara.

"The court has considered the nature and circumstance of the offences and I have considered the decision found by the jury. After considering all factors, the court finds as the jury found that the crimes were especially cruel. The offences were committed with different weapons and other instruments that were used as weapons. The crimes involved substantial planning and organisation. The defendant has shown no remorse for his victims, destroyed evidence at the crime scenes and gone to great lengths to conceal his involvement in the crimes. I have also considered the emotional and financial harm these crimes have caused the victims' families. I acknowledge that the defendant's counsel has asked for leniency towards the defendant but has shown no valid reason as to why it should be granted. It is, therefore, the court's ruling that the defendant is given a life sentence and is to be imprisoned for the rest of his natural life without parole. Bailiff, please take the prisoner down," ordered the judge.

"There you have it, *life*, no parole," said the newsreader.

"Life in prison is too good for him," said Barbara.

“Join us later when we will discuss the case, and whether the death sentence should be reinstated,” said the newsreader.

*

Tuesday 18th October 2050 – evening, the same day as sentencing

Newsflash — 6:37 p.m. — *Newsflash*

“Good evening. Maddison, ‘The Slate Killer’, Bartel is dead,” said the first newsreader.

“Found guilty by a jury of his peers and sentenced earlier today to life in prison without parole, The Slate killer was then escorted to the secure car park under the courthouse. Reports indicate that as they headed to the transport, prison escort driver Mr Brian Smale used a fire extinguisher to prop open the heavy car park door. Accidentally knocked over by the bailiff escorting Maddison Bartel, the fire extinguisher fell, the hose snapped, and the water pressure forced the extinguisher airborne, hitting The Slate Killer in the head, knocking him out cold and causing severe haemorrhaging to his head” reported the second newsreader.

“An ambulance was called, but Maddison Bartel was pronounced dead on arrival at the hospital,” said the first newsreader.

“Needless to say, this reporter is more than happy with that result – a fitting end to the hearing, I’d say,” said the second newsreader.

“Yes, I wholeheartedly agree, and I must add that even though he may not accept it quite yet, Mr Brian Smale, I’m sure a lot of people, me included, consider you a hero today. I’d also like to add, the killer was extinguished!” joked the first newsreader.

“Ha, ha, ha, very good! Oh, and let’s not forget to mention it’s going to be a huge saving to the taxpayer, not having to keep that cold-hearted killer in prison,” said the second newsreader.

“*Justice was served*,” the first and second newsreaders said together.

Chapter 7
The Rockstar and the Elephant

Friday 26th September 2059 – 3:55 p.m.

"Ok let's get to it!" Mirror bangs his hands flat on the table emphasising the urgency, his thoughts predicting more puzzles will need solving before this case will be over.

The oval desk empties bar DS Bailey and DI Mirror.

"Sir, can I have a quick word?" asks a cagey DS Bailey.

Mirror, anticipating what she is about to say, tries hard not to give any kind of negative look. "Bailey, what happened last week is in the past. Let's just leave it there, shall we?" The captain's words of "give her a chance" echo through his head louder than DS Bailey's vibrating voice, "Fresh start?"

Much to her surprise, DS Bailey was relieved. She'd been feeling the frost from her colleagues this past week and had become fully aware they blamed her for Mirror's suspension. For the first time in her twenty-four years, she had felt completely out of her depth. "Yes, sir, a fresh start, sir, thank you, sir," she replies. "Sir, I remember the Slate killings from when I was still at school. I remember being terrified, sleepless nights for two years, I drove my mother crazy. We only had a good night's sleep once he was caught. It was seeing justice done to him that made my mind up to join the police force."

A week ago, Mirror wouldn't have thought a proper conversation with DS Bailey would have been possible, let alone a personal conversation, but he has found that they do have one thing in common. "You weren't the only one that had sleepless nights, DS Bailey. I was already with the TSM-PD and remember how much tension there was in the department. For two years, he had the whole country terrified and us chasing our tails," he says. "These five incidents are giving me the same sense of dread I had back then." He gestures her to start moving towards the door.

"But it can't be Bartel! There's no way it can be him!" exclaims DS Bailey as she starts to walk towards the exit then stops suddenly to face Mirror as a horrible thought strikes her. "A copycat, sir?"

Mirror overtakes her and turns the handle. "I hope not, Bailey, I really hope not."

They leave the room, turn around and re-face the same door. Mirror presses the second button on the keypad, and they walk back in, but at a different Time-Share bubble.

The room buzzed as a multitude of officers on tablets or viewer screens searching for information on the latest murders.

"Sir!" calls PC Gill, waving to attract Mirror's attention, "We've found another one."

Mirror and DS Bailey divert to the centre where PC Gill and Dragan are looking at PC Killy's viewer. "We were working on the list of court case personnel, sir and—"

Before he can continue, DS Chang jumps from his seat and runs over to PC Killy's viewer, waving his hand to interrupt PC Gill. "Sir," he shouts and then goes on to talk at speed without taking a breath, hoping to reach the end of his find before PC Gill reacts to being cut off. "Diamonds Time-Share Estates was opened eight years ago by a forty-four-year-old man called Albert Diamonds. I phoned to speak to Mr Diamonds, who wasn't in, but his secretary, Toni, spoke highly of him and said he's been away in Manchester for a business meeting and is due to return to work later today. Also, apparently, he's been having dizzy spells since having a blood test last week and she was a bit worried about him. She said he's been working too hard, and supposedly, sir, he paid a visit to a hospital's walk-in centre on Monday to get checked…" He breathes in, deeply refilling his lungs with the oxygen lost from talking so quickly.

"Which hospital?" asks DS Bailey, anticipating Mirror's next question.

"St Thomas'," DS Chang replies then grins as if the case had been solved simply by him uttering those words.

"Looks like we have our first person of interest, Bailey," says Mirror. "DS Chang, phone Diamonds Time-Share Estates, talk to the secretary, find out more about this Mr Diamonds and ask her to pass on a request that we would like to speak to him ASAP, and would very much like him to pop into the station tomorrow morning for a voluntary chat."

"Yes, sir," replies DS Chang, lowering his head pretending to make notes on his tablet as he returns to his desk, to avoid eye contact with PC Gill.

"What have you got, Constable?"

PC Gill turns to make sure DS Chang has completely walked away, half-expecting him to interrupt again as he repeats his earlier sentence. "We've been working on the rest of the juror list and the court personnel, sir. Out of the other seven jurors, four of them live here in London. These are the addresses, sir." PC Gill passes DI Mirror his viewer tablet. "Out of the others, one of them is Calvin Wireless who is '*the*' Calvin Wireless, lead singer of the supergroup, Wireless for Sound. The band arrived in from the states this morning and are due to perform at Wembley Stadium tonight as part of their *One Country One Night* world tour, after which they fly straight out to Germany," reports PC Gill.

PC Reeves' eyes light up, "I'm going to that tonight, sir, they are fantastic!" then spontaneously hums *Take It With Ice*, one of Wireless for Sound's biggest hits. He then instantly reality checks himself as the realisation that the more complex the case becomes the less chance of him doing anything other than working could be the more likely outcome for the evening.

Mirror ignores PC Reeves' singing and looks at the address list on the tablet. "What about Lucy Victoria?"

PC Gill points to PC Killy's viewer, showing details of the twenty-eight-year-old Lucy Victoria. "That's what I meant, sir. We've found another one.
She was found dead two days ago, allegedly drowned."

PC Killy takes over to speed up the pace, "Lucy Victoria settled in Manchester permanently six years ago after studying at the university. She was part of the university swimming team and a promising prospect for the national diving team. After graduating, she carried on her training for the coming Olympics, coached swimming and undertook lifeguard duties for the local swimming baths."

"A lifeguard and Olympic swimmer and she drowned?" says DS Bailey, voicing what everybody is thinking.

PC Killy continues, "Yes, ma'am, Manchester Time-Share Misuse PD is not treating it as a suspicious death. Apparently, as well as the swimming baths being an Olympic standard pool and diving facility, they're also public swimming baths. They utilise Time-Share technology to empty and clean the pool, periodically switching to the Time-Share bubble pool for a day while cleaning gets done, thus allowing swimming and diving to continue uninterrupted. An investigation showed a short circuit momentarily caused the Time-Shared pool to switch back over to the non-Time-Share pool, and since it was undergoing a routine clean, it had a low water depth. Unfortunately, the glitch happened just as Miss Victoria had dived with not enough water to break her drop, she hit the bottom and knocked herself out. The pool returned to real-time, and she drowned."

"I can count on one hand the number of glitches in Time-Share that have happened since commercialisation nearly twenty years ago, and now we have six in less than a week," mutters DS Chang under his breath.

"Exactly," says Mirror, surprising him with a reply. "So now, we have six murders."

Mirror's use of the word "murder" instead of "accident" instantly brings a new reality to the investigation.

"Lucy Victoria died on Wednesday the twenty-fourth. We now have parallels to The Slate Killer's murders. We have a list of names, there's been a death each weekday, starting last Friday, and as in keeping with the original pattern of murders, he, or she, so far, has excluded the weekend."

DS Bailey, trying again to anticipate Mirror's train of thought, brings up the list of the remaining six ex-jurors to the room's main viewer.

Lindsey Clark-Carter – 33 years old – senior investment banker

Michael Craven – 39 years old – motorcycle mechanic

Calvin Wireless – 27 years old – musician

Jade Andrews – 40 years old – medical robotics engineer

Betsy Thorn – 53 years old – optician

Michele Esteves – 64 years old – retired musician

Mirror thanks DS Bailey with a nod then continues in a much louder tone to draw everyone's attention. "Today is Friday, someone on that list is being hunted right now and will be the next victim unless we do everything we can to stop it."

"Do we have a copycat, sir?" asks PC Killy, reiterating DS Bailey's earlier comment and again saying out loud what everyone else is thinking.

In a less loud voice Mirror answers, "I don't know, Polly, but my guts telling these deaths aren't just a coincidence." His tone turns back up to "give me your attention" mode. "Right, I want officers and armed security on every name on that list, and I mean every name on that list. DS Chang, keep working on Diamonds Estates – I want to speak to Mr Albert Diamonds in person, and find me details of Maddison Bartel's defence solicitor, where is he now? See what else he can tell us about the original case that we don't already have in our files."

Mirror turns to look at DS Bailey, “My gut’s telling me Calvin Wireless is the next target. The band is in this country for one day, and that’s today. Bailey – fancy a bit of live music tonight?”

“Yes, sir,” nods DS Bailey, surprised that DI Mirror has chosen to keep her with him rather than sending her off to investigate another element of the case.

“PC Reeves, it looks like we’re all coming with you to the concert,” says Mirror, sensing a relief in PC Reeves that even though he will be working, he is still going to the concert that he’d been so excited about earlier.

*

Friday 26th September 2059 – 6:55 p.m.

Wembley is at its new full capacity. After recent upgrades to their and the surrounding infrastructure Time-Share technology, this is the first time all seats have been sold. In real-time, the capacity is ninety thousand, but with an extra nine Time-Share bubble timelines added to every turnstile, it now means each of the nine Time-Shared stadiums and the original timeline has its own sold-out crowd. With a negatively charged electromagnetic field around the stage, preventing each of the Time-Share bubbles closing around it and keeping an open portal to the real-time stage, all

Time-Share stadium crowds can and will, theoretically, be watching Wireless For Sound perform at the same time. With all tickets sold out, nine hundred thousand fans are going to be part of the biggest stadium concert in history, and Wembley is buzzing.

Mirror watches the gates as they open, letting the excited concert-goers into the stadium. He walks over to DS Bailey and PC Reeves. “Ok, we’ve got officers on every entrance and around each of the inner stadiums, but even with stadium security helping, this is going to be like searching for a needle in a haystack. Bailey, have all positions check in, then meet me in the security viewer booth. I’m off to have a chat with the star of the show, probably a wasted trip, but let’s hope I can either persuade Mr Wireless to cancel the concert or, at least, wear a bulletproof vest.” Mirror walks away from DS Bailey and PC Reeves, shows his badge to a curious security man and walks past him into the backstage area.

PC Reeves looks at DS Bailey with the realisation of the job in hand. “This is crazy, ma’am, how are we going to cover everywhere? There are nine hundred thousand people in here, and that’s not including staff.” He’d been looking forward to the evening and being part of the record-breaking concert as a concert-goer, and this wasn't the way he'd imagined it. He stumbles backwards towards a wall as he makes his way through the endless hordes of people, turns slightly to judge his distance from the portion of wall and subconsciously reads the out-of-date poster advertising the previous week's big Wembley event, *Walking With Elephants*, "*live on stage, an intimate look at the world's largest land mammal*", before backing up to lean against it.

As he makes his way to the backstage area Mirror notices each member of the band has their own room. He scans the signs on the doors and spots Calvin Wireless's name written in a large gold star. *Of course,* he thinks as he walks over and knocks loudly.

"What?" comes a husky voice from the other side.

"Mr Wireless, I'm DI Mirror. Can I have a quick word, please?"

"I'm busy," Calvin laughs and is closely followed by more laughter from a slightly higher voice.

"Come back after the concert – when I've gone," says a sarcastic Wireless.

His reply triggers Mirror's more "reactive than is good for him" persona. He enters to witness more of Calvin Wireless and a companion than he would want to.

"Who the hell are you? Who the hell do you think you are, you prick?" shouts a naked Calvin, picking up a make-up bag and throwing it at Mirror, as the partially-dressed make-up girl scurries away to the bathroom, picking her clothes up as she moves.

"Sir, I am DI Mirror," Mirror says as he skillfully dodges the make-up bag, avoiding its spilling contents. "As you know, we have reason to believe that your life is in danger."

"I'm immortal, you bell-end. Nothing touches me," says the egotistic Calvin, now standing but still naked.

Mirror ignores Calvin's narcissistic comment. "My advice would be to cancel and rearrange the concert and allow us time to defuse the threat."

"Go away, little man… Cancel the concert? I don't think so, you knob," Calvin responds with a God-like attitude, trying to belittle Mirror.

The heat rises to Mirror's head and his patience is past being tested but keeps his replies calm and professional. "I would advise that you do, sir, or at least wear a bulletproof vest…"

Calvin turns away from Mirror and sits, blatantly looking everywhere and anywhere but directly at the man standing in his dressing room, childishly acting as if Mirror is no longer there. Calvin's stardom has gone to his head, he thinks so little of other people that he unquestionably believes Mirror is not worth his time or acknowledgement anymore.

Calvin Wireless has given this mere mortal enough precious time, thinks Calvin.

Mirror knows it is best to leave, and if he doesn't, there might be another reason that the concert gets cancelled. He closes the dressing room door behind him to head up to the security viewer camera booth. *What an idiot*, he thinks as he walks away.

DS Bailey enters the security booth. It is full of state-of-the-art viewers showing various angles and covering multiple views across the nine Time-Share bubbles and the real-time stadiums, each viewer running face and voice recognition, continuously scanning faces and picking up any keyword chatter that stands out as a possible danger. Mirror tries to take in as many of the live streams on the multitude of viewers as can. "Bailey," he greets her without looking away.

"Have all positions checked in?"

"Yes, sir, we are covering as much of the stadium as possible, but we have no idea what we're looking for, sir, Is it a sniper, a bomb, someone from the crowd? We don't even know if Mr Wireless is a target, let alone next on the list." Mirror's concentration on the viewers momentarily shares itself with the thought that DS Bailey's voice no longer seems to bother him. Maybe his run-in with Mr Wireless had recalibrated the *Things That Annoy Mirror* list.

"No, we don't, Bailey, but my gut's telling me that Wireless has it coming to him one way or another tonight." Noticeably still reeling from Calvin's efforts to belittle him, DS Bailey looks at Mirror, slightly confused, then redirects her eyes to the viewers.

*

Three hours later

PC Reeves enters the security booth.

"Sir, ma'am, I've just checked with the teams covering the other jurors, nothing to report with any of them."

Mirror acknowledges him with a nod. "Ok, everyone, the band's coming back for the encore, everyone, stay focused."

Wireless for Sound returns to the stage to a fanatical roar from the crowd. The night has been amazing, and Calvin Wireless knows it; he is lapping it all up, and his already out-of-this-world sized ego inflates even more.

"*Take It With Ice*! *Take It With Ice*!" the crowd chants and shouts, anticipating the moment has arrived when Wireless for Sound will hit them with their biggest hit to date. Calvin moves to the front of the stage, all ten Wembley Stadiums buzz, looking to the man on the stage for more. Calvin turns to the drummer and nods. The famous heartbeat drum intro sends the crowd wild.

Calvin brings the microphone up to his mouth and sings…

"I see you waiting for him
When it should have been me
I hide my face in the shadows
So the tear I weep you won't see
For just one nite's full of lust
I gave up a life's worth of love
Woke up looked in the mirror

Realising wot I'd lost.

When she said..."

Calvin extends his arm out and holds the microphone to the nine hundred thousand-strong crowd as they all sing the chorus together.

"Take it with ice, take it or leave it

Take it with ice, yeah, you better believe it

Take it with ice, there's no second chance twice.

Take it with ice, babe, I don't need you in my life."

Calvin runs to the left-hand side of the stage and brings the microphone back to his mouth.

"I see his car pulling up

As you go to get in

I look down to the rain

The reflection I see is a

Man full of hurt and broken dreams

As memories flood in of how life used to be

I guess it's over now

'Cause she said..."

The crowd sings with Calvin,

"Take it with ice, babe, take it or leave it

Take it with ice, yeah, you better believe it

It's a spice for life, and you're the one that seasoned it

Take my advice, leave me alone

Stay outta my life

Yeah, take it with ice."

Calvin turns around, holds his hand up to the band and the music stops. He then turns back to the crowd and holds his hands up, summoning silence. The audience quietens to as silent as such a huge gathering can. Calvin brings the microphone towards his mouth, it is now time for the famous talking part of his classic song, the audience is awestruck.

"I've been walking around for days on end

I can't sleep at nite, I hold my hands tight and pray

Oh, show me, God, show me

If this tunnel has light

And tell me wot love's got that

Gives pain without a fight

Cause she said..."

The band start playing again, and instantaneously, the crowd joins him, singing,

"Take it with ice, take it or leave it

Take it with ice, yeah, you better believe it

Take it with ice, there's no second chance twice

Take it with ice babe, I don't need you in my life!!!

I see you for the last time

I'm so sorry for the fault is all mine

I'd try change your mind

But deep down I know

I'd be wasting my time

You seem to be doing all right without me

And to think I believed

It would always be you and me

I was wrong

So, I...

Take it with ice, there's nothing else I can do

It's no easy life, believe me, I've been all the way through

Doubt I'll live twice; hope the one I've got turns out all right

Babe, I guess it's time for goodbye

Take one more look into my reflection

Hold your glass up real high...

And...

Take it with ice."

Calvin stops singing and holds himself in his famous after-show pose: centre stage, holding the microphone to his mouth, legs apart, a slight sideways stance to the crowd and his left hand in the air. The crowd roars.

Calvin drops the microphone, throws himself to the floor and lies face up on his back, his head slightly to the side and his arms outstretched, the numerous viewer screens throughout the stadiums showing him in a Christ-on-the-cross pose at the centre of the stage.

The crowd cheers, screams and calls his out name. The noise from the massive crowd is truly unbelievable. Calvin stays motionless, lapping it all up. Then, in the blink of an eye, the same joyfully screaming crowd momentarily falls silent, then starts screaming again, a different kind of scream…

In that same blink of an eye, an elephant had appeared on the stage, crushed Calvin Wireless then disappeared.

"Oh, my God!" yells DS Bailey.

"What the…?" murmurs PC Reeves.

Everyone in the security room is stunned by what they've just seen.

Panic sets into the audience as they run for the exits.

DS Bailey looks over to DI Mirror then shouts over the police communicator, "Every officer and stadium security to the exits. Do not let anyone leave."

“What the hell just happened?” mouths Mirror, momentarily stunned. He snaps himself out of it and grabs the police communicator from DS Bailey.

“This is DI Mirror. Do not follow that last order. Open all exits and control the flow. The priority is to make sure the public leave safely.”

PC Bailey turns to DI Mirror, “Sir, protocol says we should not let anyone leave,” saying the words out loud, but as she watches the viewer screens, she realises the danger of her instruction. The crowd is in all-out panic, “I’m sorry, sir, you’re right, it’s too dangerous to hold them back.”

Relieved by the change in order, the stadium security opens all the exits and controls the mass exodus, avoiding any stampedes, as all Time-Share points leave at once.

Acknowledging Bailey’s quick change of mind and Mirror tries hard not to direct any anger and annoyance from the current situation to her.

“We should, Bailey, you were right, but locking the gates now, we’d end up with crushed concerts-goers and a lot of innocent bystanders injured. PC Reeves, get me copies of all CCTV footage and backups of all facial and verbal recognition files taken tonight and for the last three weeks."

PC Reeves looks at one of the security viewer team, "You heard him, show me the files."

Mirror calls the stadium's head of security over. "As soon as the last member of public leaves, lock this place up, *tight*, all staff to stay. Also, get that stadium roof fully closed, it won't be long before the media drones arrive." The head of security is happy to follow his orders as he gives Mirror a "this wasn't in the training manual" look.

Looking at his DS, he nods his head sideways in the direction of the main gate. "Let's go, Bailey."

Chapter 8
The Aftermath

Friday 26th September 2059

Newsflash — 23:35 — *Newsflash*

"Calvin Wireless is dead,"

"The world of rock is in shock tonight. Reports are flooding in of a terrible Time-Share accident. Moments after giving the performance of his life to more than nine hundred thousand fans, twenty-seven-year-old rock star, Calvin Wireless, of super-band, Wireless for Sound, has been cut down in his prime,"

"Goodbye, Calvin Wireless, you were a true legend, and you have earned your place in the 'Twenty-Seven Club', along with the other greats taken from this world far too soon," says the newsreader.

The stadium was empty of all concert-goers. DI Mirror and a full crime scene investigation team scrutinized all areas. Venue security and stadium staff have been ordered to sit in the disabled seating areas of their respective time-shares, told they won't be leaving until interviewed and officially released by one of the crime scene officers, which, frustratingly for them, doesn't seem likely to happen anytime soon, since every police officer is busy fine-tooth-combing across ten Time-Shares.

Usually, when a stadium or venue empties from the show-goers and the military-style operation of clean-up and make ready for the next event gets underway, there's a calm ambience called the "after silence", a very welcome silence that holds a rhapsodic buzz in the air.

That's not to say that the ecstatic cheering, the frenzied singing, the euphoric screaming of crowds and the deafening thunder from the band – sending their masterpieces to the multitude of speakers to radiate a sound that vibrates through your whole body – isn't welcomed at the time, but as a worker and part of the team that has made it happen, the after silence is always appreciated. The moment when you get to take in the evening and reflect on the masterclass of performance you have witnessed as it starts to sink in. That perfect after silence, meaning you only have to look at someone who was part of the same fantastic evening and with no words exchanged, you know what the other is thinking. As you clean and prepare the venue, you're mutually unique in that after-silence euphoria. But tonight's silence is different, it isn't a joyful silence or calming or fantastic in any way. The only similarity to the usual after silence is that you can still look at another person from the same event, and with no words exchanged, know what the other is thinking: neither one of you want to be there any longer.

"Oi! We do have homes to go to, mate," shouts one of the stadium workers towards DI Mirror as the rest of the staff noisily support him.

Staring at the group of agitated staff then back around to the crime scene forensic personnel, running around busily, trying to piece together the craziest of evenings, Mirror calls his DS's over "Bailey, Chang, how the hell did this happen?"

DS Chang stares down to read from his tablet as PC Reeves joins the group. "Apparently, sir, the stage was meant to stay in real-time, but for reasons yet unknown, an overload at the end of the concert caused the Time-Share equipment surrounding the stage to power up for a few seconds. I'm still trying to figure out where the elephant came from, sir."

"Last week," answers PC Reeves with a quiver to his voice.

Mirror and DS Bailey look past DS Chang to PC Reeves standing directly behind him. DS Chang turns around to face him, all three inquisitive as to why and how he knows about the elephant.

"It was on last week, sirs and ma'am. Earlier this evening, I saw a poster advertising it – *Walking with Elephants*, on last week," PC Reeves struggling to believe his own words.

Mirror looks back to DS Chang. "DS Chang, get a team, start taking statements from the staff. I think their evening's been long enough."

"Yes, sir," replies DS Chang, calling a couple of PCs to join him with taking statements.

"Eight days and seven murders, Bailey. How the hell did they do this one? And why does it feel like they're copying The Slate Killer?" DS Bailey isn't quite sure whether to say something or whether Mirror hasn't yet finished talking. She turns to him and slowly nods her head in a silent show of "I know, sir, and I agree, sir". "The one thing we'll have to hope for now, DS Bailey, is that, if they *are* copying The Slate Killer's pattern, we've only got until Monday to stop the next name on that jurors' list becoming victim number eight. Bailey, you finish up here.

As soon as Time-Share forensics have finished, make sure they upload everything, every finding, no matter how small, tonight. We need a head start on this one. I'm going back to the station, see you in the morning. Oh, and get Chang to send all his findings on the solicitor, estate agent and remaining jurors to my mobile viewer."

"Yes, sir. Do you want me to come back to the station after as well?"

"No, don't worry, Bailey, it's been a hell of a long day. Go home, get some rest, I'll see you in the morning," replies Mirror, turning to head for the main exit. As he approaches, he sees the squadrons of world media outside, reporters peering in, squashed up against the windows like zombies attacking the mall in *Dawn of the Dead.* Media drone viewers hover above them, ready to pick up anything journos might miss and waiting to pounce on any person coming out of the stadium and get their version of what had happened. Behind the reporters, an increasing mass of shocked public and fans, gathering to pay their respects to their hero. Turning back for the inner stadium, Mirror looks up to see the media drones buzzing over the top of the closed roof like wasps flying around an unattended fizzy drink.

DS Bailey walks over to Mirror. “Sir, you’re back? Everything ok?”

He looks around, making sure nobody is in earshot, then covers his mouth to avoid his lips being read by the hovering drones. “Bailey, the media is everywhere, and we’ve got to give them something. But we need this to look like an accident for now. If they get wind of our suspicions before we can confirm anything, they will run wild with the story, and cause a panic.”

“Ok, sir. What would you like me to do?” replies DS Bailey.

“Follow me out, Bailey. We’ll give the press a statement, or should I say, *you* will give the press a statement, and I’ll use the moment to get away and back to the station,” says Mirror cheekily.

DS Bailey is taken aback and stares at DI Mirror in surprise, “Er, ok, sir.”

“Just stick to the basics, Bailey. Suspected Time-Share accident and we are still processing the data.”

DS Bailey follows Mirror to the exit, breathes in deep and signs to the security to let them through. As soon as the gate opened, swarms of reporters home in and fire their questions.

“I’m Detective Inspector Mirror, and this is Detective Sergeant Bailey, who will now give you a brief statement regarding this evening’s events. Thank you. DS Bailey, if you would.” Mirror hands the spotlight to the slightly taller DS Bailey, who steps forward to absorb the full focus of the media, allowing DI Mirror to make his escape.

“Thank you, Detective Inspector Mirror,” says the nervous DS Bailey, who isn’t a stranger to being in the public’s eye, but this is completely different, and her usual confident self is far out of its comfort zone “We can confirm that during the last song of the evening, Mr Wireless was involved in a terrible accident. Medics were on the scene immediately, but unfortunately, could not save him. It is with regret I have to report that, due to the substantial injuries sustained, Mr Wireless has sadly passed away.”

As soon as she stops talking, a barrage of questions is fired at her. An unfamiliar sorry-for-her feeling hits Mirror as he looks back to the shrinking DS Bailey, standing in the stadium’s main entrance. He turns and paces towards his police transport.

Mirror walks through an eerily quiet TSM-PD, opens the door to his office then looks at his viewer phone to check the time. *1:45 a.m. and twenty-one messages* he thinks – the twenty-one messages all from Frances to see if he is ok. She's been watching the evening's events on the news and is worried. He sits at his desk. "Viewer, send a message to Frances." The viewer's screen changes to the messaging app. "Message to say the following, 'Hey you, sorry. It's been a bit of a night, still at work. I'm ok, so don't worry, will catch up with you tomorrow.' End message and send."

The viewer sends the message and instantly receives a reply from Frances: *Ok, hope you're ok, talk to you tomorrow, love Frances.*

Mirror swipes the message to the side. "Viewer, open file number forty-two alongside Maddison Bartel's court file and personal file." Mirror starts to read the shared file forty-two. A knock startles him, and DS Bailey walks in.

"Bailey!"

"Yes, sir."

"I thought I said go home?"

"Yes, I don't think going home would have done much good, sir. I think I'd be more useful here, helping to piece this together," replies the young detective sergeant.

"Thank you, Bailey, sit." His respect for her is growing, and he is almost starting to accept that he'd misjudged her on his first impressions. Unfortunately, those first impressions had been partially influenced by the multitude of social media profile posts and the bigging up she had received by the TSM-PD prior to her starting. *Maybe it was just Bailey trying to live up to the expectations of the mouthpiece figurehead role she'd been given, and now, I'm getting a glimpse of what the real DS Bailey can be like as a person?* he thinks. He pushes a button on the side of his desk, and the desk splits in two, long-ways, and a chair rises from the floor. Three more viewer screens move in from the sides, the set-up allowing DS Bailey and Mirror to sit side by side and be able to see all the viewers.

"Where shall we start, sir?"

"Well, Bailey, I may be wrong, and these indeed are random Time-Share accidents – which I doubt – or we're looking for a very, very clever person or persons, someone competent with complex computer systems and an expert at Time-Share programming. Now, from what I understand, once a bubble has been set, reprogramming of the Time-Share is impossible. So, if these incidents aren't accidents, then we're looking for some kind of computer genius."

"And someone with a knowledge of the original Maddison case, sir."

"Yes, Bailey, so, I guess the best place to start is at the beginning. This looks like a copycat killer, so let's find out more about the person he's been copying – Maddison Bartel."

"Viewer, bring up Maddison Bartel's file and read out loud," asks Mirror.

The viewer opens the file and in a soft female voice, reads the information.

"Professor Maddison Bartel – aka The Slate Killer. Born Maddison Constantine Bartel on April 12th, 2015. He died October 18th October 2050, aged thirty-five. Cause of death – massive brain trauma. Maddison Bartel was a professor of Time-Share technology at Cranfield University and on the $5^{th\ of}$ March 2037 was part of the original Time-Share bubble experiment as a member of Lukvinder Joshi's Time-Share discovery team. He has since received many acclaims for his Time-Share theory thesis and time-bubble coding in the post-discovery years."

"Viewer pause. I didn't know Maddison Bartel was a computer genius or that he was on the original Time-Share team," says a surprised Mirror. He turns to DS Bailey who lifts her hands, shakes her head and shrugs back to indicate she hadn't been aware of this either. "Viewer, continue."

"On the 18th of October 2050, Maddison Bartel was convicted of murdering eighteen people from 2048 to 2050. Post-death, it has been debated that he could have been responsible for a further three hundred and twenty deaths between 2041 and 2050, meaning, if correct, Maddison Bartel would become Britain's most prolific serial killer,"

"Oh, my God, that's horrific," says DS Bailey, shocked at the sheer volume of possible victims.

"Viewer, state common factors between the eighteen victims Maddison Bartel was convicted for and crosslink with common factors of the three hundred and twenty further victim possibilities," asks Mirror.

The viewer buffers while processing the information. DS Bailey looks at DI Mirror, whose eyes are glued to the viewer, waiting anxiously for the results to show.

"Patterns found for the victims and possible victims of Maddison Bartel. All victims died whilst in a Time-Share bubble. Victims were either killed as a result of a Time-Share mishap or taken to a dark-web Time-Share bubble and tortured then killed in Time-Share kill rooms. All victims were—"

"Viewer, stop." DS Bailey looks at Mirror, "Dark-web Time-Share bubble? What the hell is that?"

"Unfortunately, Bailey, dark-web Time-Shares are one of the things they don't teach you about at basic training, and it doesn't help that the police hierarchy refuses to acknowledge them. Ever since 'the technology' was created, we've seen our society improve. Time-Share has literally saved humanity, but inevitably, the bad apples soon found ways of skipping the Time-Share bubble registration process, and unmonitored Time-Share bubbles are sold to the highest bidders as safe rooms. As you can imagine, a bubble that can't be monitored, can't be overheard in, and you can store all your illegal goods in is a pretty sought-after commodity amongst the less desirable elements of society. The mob, prostitution, paedophiles, black-market traders and, by the looks of this, serial killers as well. You get the picture," he says, showing Bailey the unwelcome reality and serving her a wake-up call to real policing as he highlights the truth of the Time-Share Misuse police department's less-savoury responsibilities.

An unhinged DS Bailey hadn't realised how dark the world still actually was. Her whole life has been post-Time-Share discovery, and the deep-rooted world issues are now a thing of the past. Hunger, wars, overpopulation, disease all but vanished, either before she was born or in her childhood. The police force has always projected a "we keep crime off the streets" persona. In her lifetime, she has wanted for nothing and has been kept safe from any real harm. Her version of the world has been spoon-fed to her through the media, her family, and her friends, and they have all led her to believe it is a safe and a prosperous world for everyone.

"Are you ok, Bailey?" asks Mirror.

"Yes, sir, just taking it all in. Viewer, please restart pattern analysis from the beginning and continue reading out."

The viewer buffers and then continues.

"Patterns found for the victims and possible victims of Maddison Bartel. All victims died whilst in a Time-Share Bubble. Victims were either killed as a result of a suspected Time-Share mishap or taken to a dark-web

Time-Share bubble and tortured then killed in Time-Share kill rooms. All victims can be grouped into lists of different types and sub-categories. Each list was completed when a final victim was found clutching a paper list of names, showing all previous victims from that group in their right hand and a pen in their left hand, all the names on the list, apart from the victim, found clutching the list had a tick next to their names. Profilers believed that the pen was meant as a symbol for the final victim to tick their name after death."

"Anything else?" asks Mirror.

"One other pattern link has been blocked and classified and cannot be accessed without appropriate authorisation. Further information on Maddison Bartel has been blocked and classified and cannot be accessed without appropriate authorisations," says the viewer.

"Viewer, continue to read out final pattern link. Authorisation, Detective Inspector Gabriel Alex Mirror." Puzzled by the viewer's last report Mirror looks at DS Bailey.

"Authorisation not recognised," replies the viewer.

“What the hell does that mean? Viewer, explain authorisation and list authorised personnel,” requests Mirror.

“A sealed authorisation for a final pattern link and further information on Maddison Bartel’s death was put in place on the 18th of October 2050 after his death. The block classification was authorised by Judge Edward C Crowley the Second after the court case. Files can only be released by Judge Edward C Crowley the Second.”

“Isn’t that the same judge who sentenced Bartel?” asks DS Bailey.

“Yes, Bailey, but why would the judge block the files? Viewer, locate contact details for Judge Edward C Crowley the Second,” says Mirror.

“Judge Edward C Crowley the Second died Tuesday 11th July 2056, aged seventy-three, cause of death – heart failure.”

DS Bailey kicks back on her chair in frustration. “Well, that’s just bloody brilliant, sir. What are we meant to do now?”

“We’ll get DS Chang onto it in the morning, Bailey, if anyone can break into those files, it’ll be him,” replies Mirror, hiding his own frustration.

“Yes, sir.” She would have normally tutted and immediately filed a report at the slightest hint of someone wanting to hack into an official file, but she is becoming quickly aware that police work is not as straightforward as she has been led to believe and some rules should be slightly bent. The important thing is knowing when to stop bending so that you don’t cross over that thin blue line.

“Viewer, send sealed files to share drive file forty-two,” says Mirror.

Mirror’s tablet buzzes, indicating an incoming file, and he sends it straight to the viewer. “DS Chang has just sent the Wembley staff interviews and all his findings on the solicitor, estate agent and remaining juror names.” He looks over to the clock. “It’s three o’clock, Bailey. I think you should go get some sleep.”

“Are you leaving now sir? I’m ok, and I’m staying if you’re staying.”

Mirror gives a tired semi-smile and nods, “Ok, Bailey, let’s start with the name that has popped up on more than a few occasions, we already know he was at the hospital and his company has been directly involved with both Christopher Lowes’ house sale and Carmela Rosa’s shop unit sale.”

"And we also know he's been to Manchester this week. Albert Diamonds is starting to look a very likely candidate, sir."

Mirror's eyebrows rise, *could it be that easy?* he wonders. "Viewer, open and read Detective Sergeant Chang's files on Albert Diamonds."

The viewer opens the notes and starts to read out loud. "Albert Diamonds, aged forty-four, occupation salesman and owner of Diamonds Time-Share Estates. Records show he was abandoned as a baby and left on the doorstep of a children's home in East Ham. No further information could be found for the children's home after it was closed in 2050, due to a fire which destroyed all records. No information on Albert Diamonds attending university or higher education or from any examination board computer system, presumably meaning that he left school with no valid qualifications. Albert Diamonds' National Insurance number shows he's worked for several small independent shops, restaurants, and door-to-door sales, never staying too long in any one job, therefore not making much of an impression. In October 2050, whilst working at a distribution warehouse, Albert Diamonds was involved in a driverless forklift accident where he was hit on the head by a pallet of wooden panels, there were no witnesses, but as a result of the accident, he suffered a severe head injury, leading to some memory loss. After successfully suing the distribution company – which in turn sent them into bankruptcy – he used the money to set up Diamonds Time-Share Estates."

"Well, he doesn't sound like a computer genius so far, Bailey," says Mirror, interrupting the viewer. "Viewer, continue with Detective Sergeant Chang's report."

"Married three years ago to Carol Ann Diamonds, also known as Carol Ann Christie, her surname from a previous marriage, and her maiden name, Appleby. Albert and Carol live together in north London with Carol's two children from her previous marriage."

DS Bailey slowly shakes her head. "Not quite the profile we're looking for, sir."

"No, it's not, Bailey," agrees Mirror.

"Maybe our killer is using Albert somehow, sir?"

"Viewer, show details on Carol Ann Diamonds. Show previous marriage details," says Mirror, following a hunch.

"Do you think it might be connected to Carol's ex-husband, sir?" asks DS Bailey, impressed by how DI

Mirror would even think to search for links that hadn't occurred to her.

"We need to rule out all possibilities, Bailey," replies Mirror.

The viewer's result makes Mirror and DS Bailey look at each other in surprise as another link between Albert Diamonds and The Slate Killer is found. "Carol's ex-husband was one of Maddison Bartel's victims, sir," says DS Bailey in amazement.

"Neil Christie, died July 1st 2050, leaving behind wife, Carol Christie, and two children. Neil Christie was the last known victim of The Slate Killer, Maddison Bartel."

"Oh, my God, sir, I think Albert and his family could be potential victims. The profile I read on The Slate Killer stated that he would research and follow future list victims in preparation, even before completing his present lists. Maybe the copycat is doing the same with Albert because his wife has links to an original Slate Killer victim."

"I don't know, Bailey, but we'll get a better idea when we question him in the morning. He's scheduled to come in for a voluntary interview with DS Chang. I think maybe we will take that interview instead, Bailey. If he's in danger, we can either protect him or, better still, use him as bait to lure the copycat out."

"Yes, sir." DS Bailey unfamiliarly finds herself agreeing with DI Mirror. Just the thought of using someone as bait a short time ago would have seen her quote procedure after procedure straight out of the police code of conduct rule book, but after this last week's events, she now has no doubt in her mind that this is an option, and she's not going to rule it out just yet.

"Ok, Albert Diamonds is looking less like a potential killer and more like a possible victim. Let's try the solicitor." Mirror swipes at the viewer screen, saving progress and opening DS Chang's files on the lawyer who had represented Maddison Bartel. "Viewer, read out file."

"Harrison Mann aged thirty-nine years, former solicitor at Harrison Mann LLP. Held in high regard and ranked high on the legal five hundred top criminal defence lawyers list of 2044 to 2050. Harrison Mann was touted in 2049 to become one of the best lawyers of the modern age. He'd never lost a case before the Slate Killer conviction. Harrison Mann stopped practicing law and closed his firm shortly after the Maddison Bartel trial. Speculation indicated that a combination of losing his first case, it being so high profile and that he was defending such a heinous killer were all factors that ended a promising career. Harrison Mann has since moved to Lizard in Cornwall, where he set up and runs a gipsy caravan and glamping holiday site."

"You've got to be kidding me! He gave up being a solicitor and a promising career at thirty to run a holiday camp at the furthest edge of the country. That does not sound convincing, sir!" says DS Bailey.

"No, Bailey, it doesn't. We need to speak to ex-solicitor and holiday-camp-owner, Mr Harrison Mann."

"Yes, sir, I agree. I doubt he'll be willing to just pop into the station, so I'll contact him in the morning and arrange a viewer interview. Failing that, and if need be, arrange a little field trip to Cornwall," says DS Bailey.

Mirror looks at the clock. He isn't tired, but he knows that unless he leaves, Bailey won't leave either, and if they don't get a bit of rest now, it will catch up on them later that day. He types a message to Captain Mason, attaches access to his shared drive file forty-two and presses send.

"It's already morning, Bailey, quarter past four in the morning, to be exact, time to go. Get a couple of hours rest – back here at nine, ok?"

"Ok, sir."

Chapter 9

Nine Days in Albert's Life

Friday 19th September 2059

Albert Diamonds' eyelids snapped open. Waking, as was usual, in a bright, positive, and cheerful mood, he turned over to look at his alarm clock: *6:59, oh yes! Up before the alarm again* he thought as he leaned over, stretched out his hand and hit the alarm stop button on top of his retro clock, silencing it just as it was about to go off on the hour.

Albert prided himself on his positive phycology; he was a glass-half-full type of guy, and the last couple of years of business had been so good that his glass was almost brimming. With a can-do attitude, self-employed Time-Share salesman Albert had a 1980s double glazing salesman's charm and natural spiel that could sell magic to a magician. He'd opened Diamonds Time-Share Estates just over eight years ago after receiving a payout for a work-related injury.

"Morning, love." Albert leaned over to give his sleepy wife, Carol, a kiss on her cheek. "I'm gonna jump in the shower then get the kettle on," he said in his happy-go-lucky tone. He leapt out of bed and headed to the bathroom, singing his made-up version of Rogers and Hammerstein's *Oh What A Beautiful Morning* whilst Carol pulled a pillow over her head.

In one sharp movement, Albert bounced out of the shower, picked up his towel from the floor and looked in the mirror. He pointed his right index finger at his reflection, giving himself an I'm-a-success pose then went back into the bedroom to get suited, booted and ready for a day of selling Time-Share. Albert was addicted to his reflection and would often be found staring into anything shiny enough to reflect enough of him. He always talked to his reflection in the second person, as if he were admiring someone else, and he gave himself the type of attention a groupie gives their favourite pop star. Thoughts of, *You're looking good* or, *If looks could kill* often accompanied the appreciation for the person reflected back. His wife and her kids were the closest anyone else came to being loved more than his reflection.

A sleepy-eyed Carol finished tying her dressing gown and walked into the kitchen to join the somewhat annoyingly over-cheerful Albert making the tea.

"Here you go, love," said Albert placing two cups of tea on the kitchen table. "Have you woken the kids?"

“Yes, they’re up and getting themselves ready. Don’t forget you have blood tests this morning at St Thomas’. The department opens at eight-thirty,” said Carol as she joined Albert sitting at the table. “I tried to get the earliest they had. Oh, and I think they’ve moved the department since you were last there, so you might need to ask where it is when you get there.”

“Well, as long as I’m back at the office by ten-thirty. I’ve finally been given the green light on the Time-Share options for the old OXO tower, and I’m meeting with the group of investors from Manchester. They’re interested in buying the lot, and, my love, if all goes well today, it’ll be a quick trip up north next week for some signatures and hello, big bonus cheque and a luxury holiday for us this year” Albert spotted his reflection in the kitchen cabinet door glass and gave himself a nod. His self-admiration was instantly cut short by Carol jumping up and screaming, “Oooh! Squash it!”

Albert turned away from the cabinet to see a large house spider crawl across the kitchen worktop. “Oh, bless it,” he said. He cupped the spider in his hand and gently picked it up.

"Don't you bring that near me!" shrieked Carol, squeezing her eyes shut.

"Oh, love, he ain't gonna hurt anyone, he's harmless." Albert opened the back door and gently placed the spider on the ground outside.

"You're so sweet, you just haven't got it in you to hurt anything, have you? I guess that's why I love you." Carol's mouth curved into a smile as she looked up at the kitchen clock. "Oh, you'd better get going, or you'll be late."

"Yes, right, I'm off." He kissed Carol on the cheek, picked up his viewer tablet and headed out.

"Bye, love – have a nice day!" shouted Carol after him.

"Bye, love," replied the happy-with-life Albert.

Albert sat in his driverless car and stared at the rear-view viewer, which had purposefully been lowered to reflect him instead of the road behind.

"Call office," he said to the car's viewer.

"Good morning, Diamonds Time-Share Estates, Toni speaking," said the secretary.

"Morning, Toni."

"Oh, hello, Mr Diamonds, happy Friday to you, sir," said the cheerful Toni.

"Thank you, Toni, and to you too, darlin'. Just calling to let you know I'm on my way to the hospital, so I won't be in first thing. We have the Manchester group coming in at ten-thirty. I should be back in plenty of time, but just in case, make them as comfortable as I know only you can."

"Hospital? Oh, my God, Mr Diamonds! Everything ok?"

"Yes, Toni, I've got my annual private medical insurance health check coming up. Just need to get a blood test so they'll have the results ready for the appointment, nothing to worry about, love."

"That's a relief, Mr Diamonds, and don't worry, I'll make sure they're all comfortable. See you soon."

"See you soon, Toni."

Albert arrived at St Thomas' Hospital, climbed out the car and sent it off to self-park. "Right, let's get this done," he said convincingly as he caught his reflection in each window he passed. He looked up and studied the ample signage. Working out where to go, he headed off, continuing to look at his reflection at every opportunity. Arriving at the blood test area, Albert joined the queue, his eyes eagerly looking around the waiting room, his ears trying to catch any bits of conversation, *Who knows, pick the right person, I might even get a sale in before I get out of here* he thought. He took a couple of steps forward to catch up with the queue then looked up to the clock behind the front desk: *8:31 – plenty of time.* He restarted his people-watching around the waiting room and spotted a doctor and a nurse talking, *Closer quarters than they should be, I'm guessing they might be more than just colleagues,* thought Albert, spotting the doctor's hand touch the nurse's for a second then return to his side.

"Well if body language tells me anything, they are so obviously a couple," said a voice from the front of the queue. Albert followed the voice to a long-bearded, long-haired man looking towards same doctor and nurse. The man turned to look at Albert looking at him and smiled. Albert gave a familiar nod of agreement and smiled back.

Maybe they could be the next Time-Share sale for Diamonds Estates, thought Albert as he started to daydream about selling them a Time-Share property.

"Sir are you next?" said the voice from the front desk.

"Sir, can I help you?" called the voice again.

"Sir, you are holding up the queue!" said the voice, louder.

"SIR!" shouted the voice.

Albert felt a tap on his shoulder and snapped round to give a fierce look at an older lady behind him, “WHAT?” he snarled.

“They are waiting, you’re next,” said the frail old lady, now shaking fearfully from Albert’s aggressive response.

Albert shook his head, realising he had got carried away with his daydream and had snapped at the old lady quite uncharacteristically. “I’m so sorry. I didn’t mean to be rude. I was in a world of my own there, I’m so sorry.” He turned around and walked over to the frowning women at the check-in.

Ashamed, Albert continuously apologised to the older lady and the rest of the people behind him in the queue, offering them his place. He looked up to the board on the back wall, the number ticker was showing serving ticket number thirty-seven, and he was now ticket seventy-eight. He looked at the clock, *8:37, well, looks like I’m going to be here a while*. He looked over at the soft drinks machine and caught his reflection smiling back. “I don’t know what you’re smiling at,” he muttered as he shut his eyes and gathered his thoughts to settle in for a long wait.

Albert opened his eyes just wide enough to focus on the serving number screen as it changed to number seventy-seven. He moved his eyes over to the clock: *9:22, and I'm next. Well, at least I should still make it back to the office in time*, he thought.

Albert repeatedly pressed the "call driverless car" app on his tablet viewer, attempting to get his car to meet him at the pickup area as he quickly walked to the hospital exit. As his car pulled up, two police cars arrived, and he watched as three uniformed police officers and a plain-clothed female officer climbed out and ran inside the hospital. Albert reluctantly jumped into his car. Usually, he would have been nosey and stayed to see what was going on, but it was nearly 10:00, and he had to head back to the office to meet the Manchester committee.

"Morning, Toni," he said, out of breath after running into the Diamonds Time-Share estates office.

"Morning, Mr Diamonds. I've shown the Manchester committee to your office. They got here a little early. I've made them comfortable, so all's ok. They have drinks, and I ordered breakfast rolls from Rosa's Pantry. How did the blood test go, were you scared? Did they give you a sticker after for being brave?" Toni smiled as she teased Albert.

"That's fantastic, thank you, Toni, I hope you included me in that Rosa's Pantry order? I could kill someone over one of Rosa's breakfast rolls right now. I think they might have taken a bit too much blood. I've been feeling a little bit lightheaded since – bloomin' vampires," he said, smiling back at Toni.

She let out a girly giggle, "Of course I've ordered you something. Oh, Mr Diamonds, was everything ok at the hospital? I heard on the viewer that there had been some kind of incident?"

"I did see some police cars pull up just as I was leaving, but not overly sure why. Oh Toni, I nearly forgot. Mr and Mrs Lowe are waiting for a call this morning to let them know what time they can pick up the keys. We should be getting confirmation on the contract exchange anytime now, so if any news comes through, I'll let you know." Albert walked over to his office and held the handle, "Wish me luck."

"Will do, and good luck, Mr Diamonds. Oh, I told Rosa's Pantry that you'd pop in early next week and pay for today's order. Good luck again with the meeting, sir."

*

Forty-five minutes later

Albert tried hard to hide his joy as he stood up from his desk to see his guests out. "Thank you, gentlemen. I guess it's nearly done then. I'll message the paperwork to you later. Have a look at it over the weekend, then, shall we say midday, Wednesday the 24th of September at your Manchester office to digitally sign the virtual paperwork?" He walked the Manchester committee out of his office, watched them leave the building then turned to Toni, "That's the one, Toni! That's the deal that's going to put Diamonds Estates in the big time!"

Toni gave a jubilant clap, "That's fantastic, Mr Diamonds! Does that mean I can have my company car now?"

"Cheeky, Toni! But it just might, when they sign on that dotted line on Wednesday, it just might," he teased.

"Oh Toni, I nearly forgot. The contracts for Mr and Mrs Lowe have come through. I've just got to finalise and register the Time-Share dateline for their new house, which won't take two minutes. Give them a call – tell them to pop in any time after twelve-thirty to pick up the keys." He winked at Toni as he walked past her and headed back into his office.

Albert sat at his desk. "Viewer, finalise OXO contract from the most recent draft and print virtual master copy."

For the first time in as far back as he could remember, Albert had a headache. *Wonder if it was the blood test? Or maybe it was the stress of running around this morning and the importance of the meeting?* Albert closed his eyes to alleviate the pain then started to daydream about the deal that was going to make him significantly better off being only days away. *What's my impending spending spree going to involve?* He mused as his mouth lifted at its sides and turned into the biggest of smiles.

Knock, knock, knock!

Albert opened his eyes. Bright and alert and his head felt clearer. He stood, quickly grabbed the newly created virtual paperwork, packed it neatly together by patting it on the desk as if it were real paper and placed it into a folder named "*OXO Tower Contract*".

"Come in," said Albert.

"Hello, Mr Diamonds. We've just heard you've got some good news for us," said a smiling Christopher Lowe as he squeezed his wife's hand tight.

Albert smiled at the couple, opened his desk drawer, took out a set of Time-Share key cards and waved them in front of the couple. "Hello, Mr and Mrs Lowe, how are you both on this loveliest of days?"

“Excited!” said both Christopher and his wife in unison as their eyes followed Alberts’s hand as if being hypnotised. “It’s really happening, we are finally getting our own house!” Christopher turned to look at his wife who, in return, gave an incredulous look back.

“Ok, folks. All you have to do to wrench this lovely set of key cards from my hand is sign on this dotted line, then twenty-four Gospel Oak Avenue at Time-Share Bubble commencing 9:35 a.m. on June 20th, 2025, will be all yours,” said Albert cheerfully. He loved the excited looks on first-time buyers’ faces as they realised their dream home was only a digital signature away. Christopher and his wife took turns to sign the virtual forms. “Ok, here’s the keys. The Time-Share bubble will activate on Wednesday 24th September around midday. You will get a message sent to your mobile viewers when it’s ready. So, once you’ve received confirmation, start moving in as quickly or as slowly as you like,” instructed Albert.

“Thank you, thank you, thank you!” the happy couple repeated as they took turns holding the key cards and shook Albert’s hand.

Albert caught a glimpse of his reflection in the door glass, winking and smiling back at him as he escorted Mr and Mrs Lowe out of his office. “Goodbye, guys, good luck and congratulations on your new home. You’ve got a great location there that most people,” Albert turned to look straight into Christopher Lowe’s eyes, “would kill,” then he turned to Mrs Lowe and smiled, “for.”

Albert felt elated with how his day was going. “Toni let’s take the rest of the day off, I tell you what, why don’t you take rest of the weekend off, paid. I’m gonna take the wife and her kids for a surprise getaway for the next couple of days to celebrate.”

*

Sunday 21st September 2059 – 9:17 p.m.

Albert’s car pulled up to his house, he pressed the Time-Share keypad on the car’s viewer screen to open the front gates and allow access to his bubble. Carol turned to look at the back seats, “Ok kids, out you get, straight upstairs, get washed, brush teeth and bed. You have school tomorrow,” she looked tired. The kids sluggishly exited the car and trailed after Carol into the house. Albert grabbed the bags from the boot and followed them in.

“That was a wonderful weekend, love, and a fabulous surprise,” said Carol attempting to kiss and hug the suitcases-laden Albert.

"I'm so tired," said Albert. He dropped the bags and hugged Carol back.

"Are you, ok, love? You seemed a bit different over the weekend, not your usual cheerful self." She released from the hug, took hold of his hand, and led him into the kitchen. "Tea?"

"Yes please, love. I must admit I've not been a hundred per cent since I had that blood test – been feeling a bit weird and a lot more tired. My eyes just want to shut all the time. I think I'll pop back to St Thomas' walk-in centre in the morning."

Carol put teabags in two cups and held them under the instant hot water dispenser. "I don't think you need to do that, love, you're just a bit anxious. Maybe it's the Manchester contract preying on your mind. You'll see, after they sign on Wednesday, the worries will be off, and you'll be a lot better."

Albert nodded in agreement then gave himself a wink as he caught his reflection in the opening fridge. "Maybe, I know it's in the bag, but until I get that signature on that contract, I guess I'll worry."

Carol placed a cup of tea in front of Albert then jumped back as she spotted another house spider crawl out from behind the bread bin and scurry across the kitchen worktop, just past her retracting hand. With lightning reflexes, Albert cupped it, trapping it before it could escape down the side. Carol moved quickly to open the kitchen door for the anticipated releasing of the creature into the back garden, but instead, her jaw dropped, she shut the door and watched in horror as Albert un-cupped his hand, pulled the spider's legs off one by one then squashed the motionless trunk of the once eight-legged beast.

"Albert, I think you're right. Maybe you should see someone in the morning," she said.

*

Monday 22nd September 2059

Albert Diamonds woke up to the drilling sound of his alarm clock. *7:00, oh my word, I feel like I've only just put my head on the pillow.* He leaned over, stretched his hand out and slapped the stop button on the retro clock to silence the alarm, knocking it onto the floor at the same time.

Albert was not feeling positive. He was usually a glass-half-full type guy, but right now, the glass was well below that.

"Morning, love," Albert leaned over and gave his wife, Carol, a kiss on her cheek. "I'm gonna jump in the shower, then I'll get the kettle on."

He crawled out of bed as Carol pulled a pillow over her head. "You were up a lot overnight, love. Hope you're, ok?"

Albert stepped out of the shower, picked up his towel from the floor, looked directly into the mirror and pointed his right index finger at his reflection. "Come on, Albert, get that mojo flowing, you're in charge," he said repeatedly. He sluggishly left the bathroom, got dressed and headed to the kitchen.

A sleepy Carol finished tying her dressing gown as she walked into the kitchen. She looked worriedly at Albert. He placed a cup of tea on the table, kissed her on the cheek and turned to leave.

"Bye, love, have a nice day, let me know what the doctor says," said Carol.

"I will. Bye, love," replied Albert as he picked up his viewer tablet and headed out the front door.

Albert sat in his driverless car and looked at himself in the purposely lowered – to reflect him rather than the road behind – rearview viewer. "Call office," he said.

"Good morning, Diamonds Time-Share Estates, Toni speaking."

"Morning, Toni," replied Albert with an uncharacteristic low tone.

"Oh, hello, Mr Diamonds, happy Monday to you, sir. Did you have a lovely weekend away?"

"Yes, I did, darlin', thank you. Just calling to let you know I won't be in first thing. I'm on my way to the hospital this morning. Can you book a flight to Manchester for tomorrow afternoon, an overnight stay near the meeting for Wednesday and a flight back Wednesday evening?"

"Hospital, Mr Diamonds, again? Déjà vu! Everything all right?" asked the worried Toni.

"Yes, Toni, I'm ok. Just going for a bit of a check-over. I'm still a bit under the weather since I had that blood test on Friday. I'm sure there's nothing to worry about," reassured Albert.

"Well, I hope not, Mr Diamonds, and don't worry, I'll get your flights and accommodation booked," said the ever-helpful Toni.

"Actually, Toni, book the return for Thursday early morning instead, just in case the meeting runs over, or we go for celebration drinks," said Albert, his inner voice telling him it was best to err on the side of caution in case he didn't have enough time to fit everything in.

"No problem, sir, see you soon," said Toni.

"Thanks, Toni. See you soon."

Albert arrived at the walk-in centre of St Thomas' Hospital. He stepped out of the car and sent it off to park. *Right, let's get this done.* Albert looked to the windows to catch his reflection, but rather than observing how good he looked, a sense of unfamiliarity washed over him. He looked up to the signage and followed the arrows to the third floor, then along the long corridor until he reached the walk-in centre. He momentarily paused to look around the crowded waiting area then walked over to the women at the desk. He held his finger to the bio-scanner, pulled out his private medical card and showed it to the receptionist who then scanned it into her system and matched the finger bio-scan details with the card details.

"Good morning, Mr Diamonds, how can we help you today? Have you come for your blood test results?"

"Good morning, love, I've been feeling a bit under the weather. Just wondered if it's possible to get a quick health scan," said Albert.

"Let me see… Ok, Mr Diamonds, I see that you have platinum healthcare membership. If you take a seat, Dr Marner will call you in shortly."

"That's great, thank you, darlin'," said Albert, giving her a wayward smile. She returned the smile and changed the Time-Share settings on the waiting area part of the room. The crowded room vanished, and Albert sat down in the private platinum-cardholders' waiting room.

No sooner had he sat, a calm, well-mannered voice called him via the tannoy, "Mr Albert Diamonds, door two, please."

Knock, knock, knock.

"Come in," called the even-voiced Dr Marner. "Good morning, Mr Diamonds. I've just had a look at your blood test results, and everything looks fine, so no problems there. How else can I help you today?"

"Good morning, Doctor. I've not had a good weekend, to be honest. Since I came in on Friday for my blood test, I've not quite felt myself, bouts of sudden tiredness, my mood seems to be affected and so has my patience," explained Albert.

"Ok, Mr Diamonds – has anything different happened lately, any extra workloads or pressures in your personal life?"

"Well, nothing different in my personal life, I'm such a lucky git when it comes to home life – my beautiful wife and her kids are my world – but I must admit, a lot is going on in my work life, especially this week. I've got a very big project about to finalise, my wife seems to think that's causing me to feel a bit anxious."

"Ah, ok, well, you know what they say? Wives are always right," joked the doctor. "But I'll tell you what, just to be sure, and so we can rule out any other possibilities, let's give you a full scan anyway, shall we?"

"I was hoping you would do a scan, Doctor, at least that will give me a bit of peace of mind. I must admit I've been feeling like a bit of hypochondriac the last couple of days, wondering what's wrong with me."

"Don't worry, Mr Diamonds, we'll get you sorted and back to your very old self again. Take this over to the scanning department then pop back and see me after." Doctor Marner handed Albert a scan pass.

"Thank you, Doctor, see you soon."

Albert walked out of the doctor's office, through the empty waiting room, exited its bubble to face the same receptionist. The room he'd come out of disappeared, and the real-time, people-packed waiting room reappeared.

"Hi, love, which way to the scan department, please?"

"Just follow the blue line on the wall, Mr Diamonds," replied the helpful women behind the desk.

"Thank you, love." He smiled at her then turned to follow the blue line along the long corridor and read the department names to himself as he passed them. "Wow, this is a long corridor, ENT, Paediatric, Neuroscience, Coronary Care Unit." Albert stopped and turned back around to look at the last department sign. "Coronary Care Unit," he mumbled. A hint of recognition hit him, but he struggled to recall why.

Albert was vaguely aware of someone speaking in the distance. "Sir, are you ok?"
And then again, "Sir?"

Albert looked round to see a man with long grey-hair, walking away along the corridor then refocused on the nurse standing in front of him. "Sir are you ok? Are you lost?"

Albert looked around for familiarity, but couldn't remember walking to the part of the corridor he was standing in. “Oh, I think I am,” he said, disoriented. “I’m looking for the body scan department.”

“You’ve missed it, love. This is the MRI department. If you follow the blue line back that way, it’s two departments up,” said the nurse.

Albert turned to look up the corridor then back again to thank her, but the nurse was scurrying quickly away towards an urgent shout from another nurse inside the MRI department.

He walked back along the corridor towards the body scan department, catching his smiling reflection in the windows as he passed.

*

Tuesday 23rd September 2059

Albert Diamonds’ eyes opened. He was hungry and excited to get the day started and felt in a bright, satisfied mood. He looked to his alarm clock, *6:53, oh yes! Back to beating the alarm!* He leaned over, stretched his hand, and hit the alarm off button on the retro clock.

Albert prided himself on positivity, he was nervous about the Manchester meeting but also had a strange feeling of accomplishment, maybe it was because all his hard work over the last couple of years was about to pay off with the signing of OXO contract?

“Morning, love.” Albert leaned over and gave his wife, Carol, a kiss on her cheek, “I’m gonna jump in the shower, then I’ll get the kettle on.” He leapt out of bed and headed to the bathroom, singing his reworded version of Craig David’s *7 Days*. Carol pulled a pillow over her head.

Albert bounce-stepped out of the shower and picked his towel up from the floor in one sharp movement. He looked into the mirror and saw his right index finger pointing at him in the reflection. He gave himself a wink, went back into the bedroom to get himself suited and booted, packed a suitcase ready for his Manchester trip then headed downstairs to make the tea, still humming *7 Days*.

Carol finished tying her dressing gown as she walked into the kitchen, “Kids are up, and you seem in a much better mood than yesterday,” she said.

“Here you go, love,” said Albert, placing two cups of tea on the kitchen table. “I do declare I feel much better, love. I feel as fresh as a daisy in the mornin’ dew, and I’m looking forward to the rest of the week. It’s gonna be fantastic,” he said, attempting an old southern-American movie accent.

Carol looked at him oddly. She was used to him being a bit strange sometimes, but today, he seemed a bit more quirky than usual. "Are you all ready for your trip? Did you pack the shirts I left on the side for you?"

"Yes, I did, thank you, my suitcase is all packed. I just need to make final checks on the OXO Tower's virtual files. Toni has sent the flight and accommodation reservation details to my tablet, and my flights at twelve-thirty. Lovely jubbly. I've got a few quick jobs to do this morning, and then I'll be all set." A bout of nerves washed over him as he realised how close the meeting was.

Carol picked up her cup and started to sip her tea.

"Oh my, it's really happening, after tomorrow's meeting, we might even be able to afford a new level on the house," said an overexcited Albert.

Carol stifled a laugh as she tried not to spit her tea out, she lowered her cup, "A new level to the house?" She stared at her husband and laughed again. "What are you on about? I think you're losing it, love."

They both laughed as they continued drinking their tea.

*

Ten minutes later

Albert left the house and waved goodbye to Carol and her kids as they waved back at him from the upstairs windows. He placed the suitcase on the back seat and climbed into his car. "Drive to the Elephant and Castle shopping centre, sub-location, Rosa's Pantry. Park outside," he ordered.

The driverless car merged into the unfaltering flow of traffic and steadily made its way to Rosa's Pantry.

"Morning, morning, morning," said Albert as he burst into the café.

"Hey, good morning, Mr Diamonds. Cuppa?" said the jet-black-haired Carmela, holding an empty tea mug up to Albert.

"Oh, that would be heaven, darlin'. Just gonna use your loo first. Oh, and if you get my bill ready, I'll pay you for the breakfast rolls we had on Friday," he replied as he diverted to the toilet.

Albert answered the call of nature then checked the time on his mobile viewer, *plenty of time. Right, sort out Mrs Rosa's bill then get to the airport nice and early.* He moved over to the sink to wash his hands, looked in the mirror, brushed his hair with his hands and watched himself wink.

Albert looked at his reflection in the rear-view viewer, then looked at the time. *11:15, what the...? I don't even remember drinking my tea or leaving Rosa's, I'd better get to the airport. Where has the time gone? Time is flying by this morning,* thought a confused Albert. "Viewer, drive to London City Airport, Time-Share terminal six."

The car pulled up to the terminal six drop-off point. Albert exited the car, grabbed his luggage, took his viewer tablet out from the side of the bag, opened the driverless car app to send the car home, then ran into the airport terminal.

*

Wednesday 24th September 2059

Albert Diamonds awoke in a confident mood, excited to get the day started. He looked at his alarm clock, *7:16*, stretched his hand out and hit the alarm-off button on the hotel clock. He was feeling positive, he was no longer nervous and couldn't wait to get going. He jumped out of bed and headed for the shower room.

Albert stepped out of the shower, the meeting wasn't until midday, so he had a bit of time to get himself ready and relax, *maybe I could visit the hotel's gym?* He picked up his toothbrush, spread toothpaste on the brush, looked at his reflection in the mirror and started to clean his teeth. He spat out then looked back up to the mirror. “You fancy a nice morning swim?” asked the man in the mirror. Albert exited the shower room and sat on his bed. *Mmm, gym or swimming?* He lay back on the bed and stretched his arms and legs out. *This is relaxing.* His eyes started feeling heavy, he closed them and fell back to sleep.

*

A few hours later

Albert woke up and looked over at his clock, “Eleven sixteen, well so much for killing a bit of time,” he muttered. He finished getting dressed, picked up his viewer tablet and the OXO folder and rushed down to the lobby.

“Hello again, sir, back out so soon? How can I help?” said the cheerful assistant, instantly acknowledging Albert’s approach.

Albert momentarily pondered on how friendly the hotel staff were being and wondered why she had commented on his leaving the hotel again so soon. He looked at her name badge. “Hello, Jen, could you call me a TaxiCab to Trafford Park industrial area, please? I’m in a bit of a hurry.”

“No problem, sir.” She looked over to her viewer, swiped at the DRLTaxiCab app then looked back at Albert. “The driverless TaxiCab will be at the pickup area in two minutes, sir. Hope you have a lovely day,” said the helpful Jen.

“Thanks, darlin’, you too.” Albert quickly walked through the lobby and headed to the exit.

*

Four hours later – after the meeting

Albert slumped into the back seat of the TaxiCab. not a fed-up slump, more of a “wow” slump. “Please take me to the Victoria Hotel.”

The driverless TaxiCab pulled away and merged into the traffic.

Albert took out his mobile viewer and called home. Carol’s face instantly popped up on the screen. “How did go?”

“That was quick,” said Albert, taken aback by the speed Carol had answered. “Were you waiting by the viewer?” he said teasingly.

“Come on, don’t keep me in suspense, how did it go?” asked the eager Carol.

"Darlin'... we're in the money. Signed, sealed, and delivered, baby," said the elated salesman.

"Oh, my God! Really? Really? Did they sign? I'm so proud of you, Albert."

"Darlin', open the drawer in the wall unit, have a look in the blue envelope," said the smiling Albert.

Carol did as Albert instructed and shrieked, "Oh, my God! Oh, my God! You got meet-and-greet VIP tickets for Wireless for Sound! Oh, my God, it's Friday night! Oh, my God, we're VIPs!" exclaimed Carol. She could hardly contain herself; she'd not yet had fully absorbed Albert's contract success or their upward turn of fortune. Now, she had VIP tickets to meet her all-time hero, Calvin Wireless.

"Nothing but the best for you, love. I need to quickly pop to the office when I get back, so I'll be home late afternoon tomorrow. How about we have a little celebration at home tomorrow night?" He gave Carol a wink, "And then Friday night, we'll go to the concert and celebrate there as well."

"Oh, my God, I need to go shopping! I need something new to wear. Friday's only two days away. Oh, darling, you're the best! Bye, darling, see you soon," said an overexcited Carol.

She forgot to hang up the viewer and rushed off as Albert watched her scurry away in an excited panic. He hung up and smiled to himself, thinking how happy he had made her. "Viewer, call the office."

"Good afternoon, Diamonds Time-Share Estates, how can I help you?" said Toni in her ever efficient and friendly manner.

"What colour car would you like, Toni?" asked Albert.

His question was met with a short silence followed by a delighted scream. "Well done, Mr Diamonds, well done!"

"A promise is a promise, Toni, so Friday morning, we're going company car shopping," said Albert.

"Oh, Mr Diamonds, you are the best!" replied Toni.

"Any messages for me, Toni?" asked Albert.

"There are a few emails. I've forwarded them to your tablet. There's a couple of property viewing appointments made for tomorrow afternoon – I sent them to your diary app, wasn't sure if you would be up for any appointments after flying back in the morning, but if you're not, I can rearrange them if you like and push them to Friday. Oh, and the police department called, a DS Chang would like to talk to you about something that happened at St Thomas' Hospital. Apparently, they're asking anybody that had been there either last Friday or Monday to pop into the TSM-PD to see if they can help them with their enquiries."

"It's ok, Toni, I'll take the appointments for tomorrow. Not sure how I can help the police though. I don't remember seeing anything out of the ordinary at the hospital, but as you know, I've always been one to help our boys in blue, so give them a tinkle back and let them know I'll be there at nine on Saturday morning. Even though we've just tapped a rich vein here in Manchester, it doesn't mean we've stopped selling Time-Shares. You never know, I might find someone at the TSM-PD looking for a new house," said always-the-salesman Albert, hoping that a pointless visit to the TSM-PD might work to his advantage.

"No problem, Mr Diamonds. Oh, a couple more things, Mr Diamonds. There was a bit of a commotion at Rosa's pantry yesterday, tried to ring her to get the tattle but couldn't get through, and Mr and Mrs Lowe are moving into their new home tomorrow. Shall I arrange some welcome flowers and a nice bottle of fizz to be delivered to their address?"

“That’s a lovely idea, Toni, but get them delivered to the office. I’ll pop round myself, you know, a bit of aftersales care. I’ll try and swing back past Rosa’s after, if I get time, Thanks, Toni, see you tomorrow.”

“No problem, Mr Diamonds. Looking forward to seeing you, and I’m really looking forward to my car-hunting day on Friday!” replied Toni cheekily.

What a day! thought Albert.

*

Thursday 25th September 2059

Albert Diamonds woke up in a relaxed mood. He looked over at his alarm clock, *7:10*, he stretched his hand out and hit the alarm-off button on the hotel’s clock. He felt satisfied and unconcerned, his life seemed like it was really together and was looking forward to getting back home to see his lovely wife. He couldn’t wait to get the day started and get to the airport. His flight was at 10:30. He leapt out of bed and headed for the shower room.

Albert checked into the airport in plenty of time and headed over to the departures lounge to look at the flight information board, “*Boarding now for pilotless flight number 6745 to London City, Airport Time-Share 4, flight time, one hour.*” He pulled out his viewer tablet, opened the driverless car app and sent a message to his private driverless car to collect him at 11:45.

*

Albert exited the airport, immediately spotted his waiting car, and climbed into its familiar confines. “Drive to the office, please, and send a message to Carol to tell her that I’ve landed safely, and I’ll see her tonight.” The car pulled out and merged into the steady traffic. It arrived at Diamonds Time-Share Estates office and pulled up outside. “No parking required, wait here,” ordered Albert.

He had barely stepped through the doorway and Toni was rushing at him, holding a virtual car brochure. “Hello, Mr Diamonds, I’ve chosen my car!” she said, pointing to a picture of a vintage 2015 Bugatti Veyron. “I’d be happy to put a Diamonds Time-Share Estates sticker on the back if it helps?” She let out a small chuckle.

“Well, I think we’d need a few more deals like the OXO contract to get you that as a company car. Anyways, you couldn’t afford the petrol for it – you’d need a year’s wages just to fill it, and the government announced last week that worldwide oil production is stopping next March.”

"Oh, well, I can dream, Mr Diamonds," said Toni. She swaggered back to her desk to pick up her viewer tablet. "Here you go, sir. You have two viewings, one at two-thirty and one at three-thirty, both at the old church nursery school conversion in Bromley Street. And here are the flowers and bottle for the Lowes. Mr Lowe will be there all day."

"That's fantastic, Toni, I'll go straight home after. So! I will see you in the morning for a bit of..." Albert strategically paused, waiting for Toni to finish his sentence.

"Car shopping!" said Toni excitedly.

Albert's car pulled up to number twenty-four, Gospel Oak Avenue. Just as he was about to leave the car, his viewer started to ring. He looked up to see his wife calling, "Hello, darlin'."

"I'm so looking forward to you getting home. I've taken the kids to my mum's, and we've got the whole evening to ourselves. I've got a special dinner planned," she said.

"Lovely jubbly! Just got one last call to make then coming home, I should be back within the hour, love."

Carol stepped back from the viewer to show her wearing her new dress, then walked forward to refocus the viewer on her face as she blew Albert a kiss. “Well, don’t be too long. You can see what you’re missing, can’t wait to start celebrating, see you soon!”

Carol hung up, and Albert saw his reflection in the blank viewer screen. He paused, gave it a wink then daydreamed about Carol. *Maybe I’ll go straight home instead*, he thought, convincing himself to just leave the flowers and bottle by the door rather than waste time giving them to the Lowe’s personally. Carol, in her sexy new dress, had given him a new priority. He jumped out of the car, placed the wine, flowers and his business card by the front gate and returned to his car. He stared back into the blank viewer screen and paused for thought, *what if one of the other Time-Share residents pick the flowers up first?* He looked back at his reflection, watched it wink back and started to daydream again, shook his head to snap himself awake and decided to go straight home.

“Drive home,” instructed Albert. “Get there as fast as you can,” he added, smiling as the image of Carol in her new dress popped back into his mind.

*

Friday 26th September 2059

Carol Diamonds woke up in a happy and excited mood, she was eager to get the day started and was looking forward to seeing her singing hero later, she looked over at Albert's retro clock, *6:30,* she leaned over Albert, making him moan groggily, stretched out her hand and hit the alarm-off button.

"Morning, love," she said as she kissed Albert on his cheek, she returned to his side and cuddled in for a quick hug. "I'm going to jump in the shower, then I'll get the kettle on." She leapt out of bed and headed off to the bathroom. She stopped short of going in, turned back round to Albert and winked, "Fancy joining me?" Albert wasted no time in following her.

*

"Here you go, love," said Carol, placing two cups of tea on the kitchen table.

"Hope my mum's ok with the kids."

"Well, she's got them for another night, love, and I think it's more appropriate to say, are the kids ok with your mum?" said Albert, laughing.

"Cheeky," said Carol, playfully hitting Albert on his hand. "What do you have planned for today, love?"

Albert took a sip of his tea. "Well, I've given myself a bit of an easier day, moved most of my appointments to Monday. I'm taking Toni to order her company car, finish off a bit of paperwork at the office then coming home to pick up my beautiful wife and go out to celebrate," replied Albert. "What about you?"

"I've got such a busy day," said the smiling Carol.

"Let me guess, more shopping, hairdresser's, nail bar and getting ready for tonight?"

"Right, I'm off," said Carol. She sassily stuck her tongue out, turned and walked away.

*

Friday 26th September – 6:46 p.m.

A long, black, driverless limousine pulled up outside Wembley Stadium's VIP entrance. The suited-and-booted Albert and the stunningly dressed Carol exited the car and were instantly welcomed by a porter.

"Good evening, folks, my name's Hayden. Can I see your tickets, please?"

Albert pulled a virtual ticket from the inside of his jacket pocket and handed it over to the porter. "Thank you, sir. Ah! I see you have meet-and-greet."

Carol gave a slightly excited squeal.

"And I can see madam is very excited," continued Hayden. "If you would like to follow me." He turned and guided them through the main VIP entrance. "Sir, madam, if you can place your bags on the security scanner then walk through the detecting ring, we have a slightly heightened security tonight. One cannot be too careful."

"No problem at all," said Albert. He lifted his side bag onto the scanner and walked through the scanning ring. "It's nice to see you're looking out for our safety," he added. The scanner showed the contents of Albert's bag: keys, a pen, sunglasses, and his viewer tablet.

"Thank you, sir, thank you, madam," said the security porter, handing the items back to them.

"If you would like to follow me, I'll take you to the VIP dining lounge," said Hayden. He led Albert and Carol to a large candlelit dining area and took them to a table near a large viewer screen backdrop. Carol stopped short of the table, her jaw dropped, and she squeezed Albert's hand. She had recognised the table setup and the images on the screen, which were showing an outside view from the window of the Castle pub, the same Castle pub and the exact same view from the table near the window where

Carol and Albert had had their first dinner date about eight years ago.

"Here you go, folks," said Hayden, pulling out a chair and gesturing Carol to sit. "Is this the correct view you requested, sir?"

Carol stared, starry-eyed at Albert, and wondered at her amazing good fortune in having such a wonderful man after the tragedies of her earlier life.

"It's perfect," confirmed Albert.

"Your server will be over momentarily. While we're waiting, I'll run through a few timings. The concert starts at eight with support act, Dry Till Friday. The main act, Wireless for Sound, will come on at around nine. After the concert, there will be a short meet-and-greet with the band then back here for the after-party. Unfortunately, the band will not be attending this as they will be heading straight out to Germany for their next concert. But don't worry, we have a few other surprises in store for you," said the very professional Hayden. A waiter approached the table and stood to the left of him.

"Ah, this is Thomas. He will be your exclusive waiter and escort for the rest of the evening. I will leave you in his very capable hands."

"Thank you, Hayden," duetted Carol and Albert.

"Good evening," said Thomas, smiling at his table guests. "Can I start you off with some drinks?"

The meal was perfect, the set-up was faultless. A complete replica of that first date. Carol was in awe of the evening, and the best was yet to come.

"Was everything ok with your meal?" asked Thomas.

"Yes, thank you," said Carol.

"Perfect, ten out of ten," said Albert.

"It's nearly eight, the support act is just about to go on. Would you like to follow me, and I will take you to your private box," said Thomas. He stepped back, bowed his head slightly and bent his arm outwards to the direction he wanted his guests to walk. He led them to a private Time-Share viewing box close to the stage, in fact, it was so close that Carol wondered whether, if she stretched out her hands, she might even be able to touch Calvin Wireless. It was the perfect view for the perfect evening. Albert looked proudly at the stunned Carol. He wasn't overly into Wireless for Sound, not his type of music, and he'd always found the bright lights hurt his oversensitive eyes, but it was worth it. He'd be happy just to prolong the closing and opening of his eyes and partially daydream the concert away, content in the knowledge that Carol was so happy.

What a perfect week it has been. I've completed so much, thought Albert as the drums thundered, the screams of the crowd echoed and the blinding spotlights lit up the stage, indicating the start of the concert. He closed his eyes to protect them from the glare and started to daydream about the crazy but best week of his life.

Albert opened his eyes as a fine spray of wetness hit him. The screams were different, Carol was hysterical. Speckles of red covered them both. His disbelieving eyes focused to the stage, where a giant African elephant was standing on the flattened remains of Calvin Wireless.

*

Saturday 27th September 2059 – present day

Carol and Albert Diamonds lie on their backs, wide awake, motionless in their bed, their eyes fixed into the blankness of the white ceiling.

Albert looks round to his retro clock, *7:38 a.m.* He turns to a shocked-looking Carol.

"Are you ok? Sorry love, silly question. I'll go and put the kettle on." He awkwardly eases himself out of the bed, trying hard not to move the mattress and covers too much, walks out of the room and heads to the kitchen to make the tea, but unlike most other days, Carol doesn't follow.

He carries the two cups upstairs. Carol is sitting on the side of the bed, silently crying. He walks over, puts the two cups on the bedside cabinet, sits next to her and gives her a side-on hug.

"That was awful, just awful," she cries and turns to face him, tries to speak but lets out a more audible, inconsolable cry. Albert hugs her even tighter.

"I'll cancel my diary. I didn't have much on, just a couple of appointments and a quick visit to the TSM-PD."

"It's ok, don't worry, I'll be ok. Mum's bringing the kids back at ten, I've got to pull myself together before then, I can't let them see me like this. You go about your day, love, it might be easier if you're not here," she says, sobbing gently onto Albert's shoulder. He can feel the fabric of his top getting wetter.

"Oh, I'm sorry, love, I've completely soaked your shirt," says a teary-eyed Carol.

"Don't be silly, love, it's ok. Are you sure you don't want me to stay?"

"It's ok, Albie, I'll be ok. It's just that the last time I felt like this was nine years ago. Last night just brought back some painful memories. Maybe, I just need a bit of time by myself before the kids come back."

"Ok, love. Just call me if you need anything, and I'll come straight back." Albert kisses Carol on the cheek as she lets go of the hug.

*

8.45 a.m.

Albert pulls up to the barrier of the police headquarters secured car park. The barrier guard pops her head out of the cubical window. "Good morning, sir, how can I help you today?"

"Good morning, darlin'. I've got an appointment to see a DS Chang?" says Albert. Handing her his identification card, he notices a sudden frown on the security guard's forehead and decides it might not be a good idea to call her darling again.

The guard scans the card. "Ok, you're expected. Drive through when the barrier opens, go to the left, park your car and take the lift to the third floor. There's been a change on the system. You're now meeting Detective Inspector Mirror," says the guard tersely.

She sets the Time-Share to the Time-Share-Misuse Police Department's time bubble, and Albert instructs his car to enter the car park, smiling at the frowning barrier guard as he passes.

"Detective Inspector Mirror," repeats Albert. He gets out his car and heads over to the lifts while the car self-parks. He stares at the reflective metal as the lift climbs, to catch his reflection and wonders how Carol is.

The lift opens to the view of the impressive and shiny reception counter of the TSM-PD. Albert cagily walks up to it and watches his reflection in the highly polished counter getting bigger as he approaches, behind it, there is a glass partition. Albert feels hypnotised by the buzz of the large desk and personnel-filled office on the other side. His gaze refocuses to catch himself again in the glass.

"Good morning, sir, can I help you?" says the Glaswegian-accented receptionist. Albert snaps himself out of his gaze and smiles. "Oh yes, sorry, my name is Albert Diamonds. I'm here to speak to a DI Mirror."

"Oh yes, he's just over there, talking to DS Bailey. He's been expecting you," says Elaine. She looks over to her left and calls out to DI Mirror, standing further along the corridor. "DI Mirror, this gentleman is here to see you."

Mirror walks over, closely followed by DS Bailey.

"This is Mr Diamonds," says Elaine.

Mirror puts out his right hand to Albert, "Mr Diamonds, thank you for coming in. I'm DI Mirror, and this is DS Bailey."

Albert pauses, looks directly into DI Mirror's eyes then over to DS Bailey's then extends his arm to shake Mirror's hand.

Chapter 10

Nine Years In The Hide

Meaning of "hide" in the English language:

i) to put something or someone in a place that cannot be seen or found

ii) a place from where someone can watch without being noticed

iii) to remain out of sight or secret

iv) the skin of a mammal

*

Friday 19th September 2059 – 8:31 a.m.

"Ahhhhhhhhhh!" Maddison Bartel screamed as the sharp sledgehammer-to-the-head-like pain sped through his skull then as quick as it came on disappeared... *What was that?* he thought as he surveyed his surroundings and gathered his bearings. *I think I'm in a waiting room.* He started taking stock of all the sheep waiting and spotted a bearded man with long grey hair staring at him, the man smiled when he saw Maddison looking then pointed down a corridor. *Wonder what's so interesting? Wait a minute, I recognise those two... is that? That's the... yes, that's two of those bastard jurors from the courtroom, found me guilty. I'd love to show them just how guilty I am.* Maddison's happy thought was cut short by a tap to the shoulder.

"WHAT?" he snarled, turning to see the old hag who had just touched him. His head shook as his thoughts pondered how lovely it would be to put her on one of his lists.

*

A few minutes later

Maddison's head felt fuzzy, his eyes were shut, and he tried to recall the court proceedings. *Right, I was found guilty, taken to the transport. Then it gets hazy. Why am I thinking of kids and a house? The jurors? I'm seeing images of some of the jurors, but they aren't sitting in the courtroom, they're sitting in an office opposite me.* The confused Maddison opened his eyes and tried to make sense of his thoughts. *Why aren't I in handcuffs? Why aren't I surrounded by coppers, and what's that twat smiling at*, he thought angrily as he looked over to a soft drinks machine and caught the reflection of someone in the waiting room smiling at him. "I don't know what you're smiling at, sunshine," he muttered. He shut his eyes to buffer his confused thoughts then quickly opened them again to stop himself passing out. He got up, looked around cagily then walked out of the waiting room, wondering when the police would show up to arrest him. He made his way along the corridor where a doctor and nurse were talking to each other and slowly walked past them to catch their conversation and a glimpse of their name badges.

Dr Anthony Chand looked lovingly into Nurse Ophelia Schmidt's eyes, "Honestly Ophelia, you can. I was up there yesterday; I could see it."

"Well, I certainly did like the look of it. Maybe we'll call the agent after our shift and put an offer in," said Ophelia.

Dr Chand looked at his vintage wristwatch, "Tell you what, it's quarter to nine, I've got a quick round to make on the third floor. How about I meet you on the roof in half an hour, and I'll prove you can see the house?" said Anthony.

"Deal," replied Ophelia, smiling, then with an increase in urgency, "Well, if I'm gonna meet you in half an hour, I'd better get these samples over to the labs."

With his back to the wall, Maddison stood in earshot and watched the two newly listed names walk away from each other.

Two names. Which to cross off first? Mmm, the doctor. Maddison followed and watched as his list-topping doctor entered the coronary care unit. His eyes scoured his surroundings for an area, for a toy, something that would help him play with the doctor. *A walking stick, a pen, an open window? None of these toys are suitable. They would feel rushed, not enough artistic integrity*, thought Maddison. *It must be something fun, more special, more creative, just more.*

His other lists had been ticked off with pride. He had used his knowledge of Time-Share manipulation to create dark-share bubbles, dark rooms – off-grid and unmonitored Time-Shares that allowed him all the time in the world to play with his list entry, the time needed to create art without the worry of being disturbed or being overheard, even when they screamed or shouted, he would carry on and play his games. Should he leave it today, until a better playtime opportunity presented itself? No, he couldn't. He'd already decided and already mentally crossed the doctor's name off the list. Maddison desperately looked around. He walked further along the corridor and spotted the same bearded, long-haired man that he'd seen in the waiting room. The man was talking to a nurse in an office. The nurse followed the man out and walked away along the opposite corridor. A possibility! An empty office! Inside the empty office, a viewer screen. Maddison grinned as a sadistic idea hit. *Instead of creating a dark share bubble to play, maybe I could use the Time-Share bubble to tick them off. Oh, how creative of me. Only a genius like me can change the time of a bubble within a bubble,* thought Maddison. He entered the office, he sat at the desk, easily hacked into the hospital's viewer camera system and then into the hospital's Time-Share management systems. *Art creates art... the doctor and the nurse, the lovers die together.* Maddison looked up at the office clock, *9:14 a.m.* He tapped away at the viewer, then with a final press of the enter key, he got up, left the office, walked back to the blood-test department, entered the waiting room, sat down and looked over to the clock. *9:20.* Then, in the essence of accomplishment, closed his eyes to relive his soul-satisfying past few minutes.

*

Forty minutes later

Two police cars were driving up to the front of the hospital as Maddison exited. With urgency and panicking to avoid them, he quickly jumped into a car pulling up next to him. *How did they not see me?* he thought as he faded out of consciousness.

*

A little while later

Maddison's eyes opened; *how did I get here? What was I just dreaming about? It must have been something interesting,* he thought as he looked around the unfamiliar yet familiar room. *How did I get here?* he wondered. *These hazy spells are starting to annoy me.* A mixture of irritation and reality detachment washed over him. *I can't even remember getting out of the car, let alone walking into this office.* Images flooded his head, they seemed recent, people he had met, familiar faces and places in his mind but not making any chronological sense. He shook his head, got up and walked over to the door. Opening it slightly, he peered through the gap and saw a tall brunette sitting at a desk, talking on a viewer.

"Hello, Mr Lowe, it's Toni, just calling to let you know the contracts have now exchanged… That's right, the keys are ready for you to collect… yes, that's right… Both of you need to sign… twelve-thirty, that's perfect… then the house is all yours… Congratulations, guys!" Toni ended the call and instantly answered another incoming ring.

Maddison closed the door, sat back at the desk and swiped at the viewer. *Maybe it's time to get some answers to all these questions in my head.* "Viewer, find details, Maddison Bartel, trial and juror names."

The viewer listed its search results, "Viewer, expand the third result."

The viewer screen enlarged a newspaper article dated 20th October 2050, the headline read "*JUROR NAMES REVEALED, EXCLUSIVE*". He looked back at the date, *20th October 2050, that's two days ago.* "Viewer, return to results, expand article seven," said the confused Maddison.

The viewer expanded a media file from a television talk show dated 11th November 2050, the headline read "*THE MADDISON BARTEL JURORS, THE INTIMATE INTERVIEWS*".

His head started to spin as he read the article, its wording and more significantly the date, *it makes no sense.*

"Viewer, show jurors' names and locations from the article, cross reference names with current locations and print copy." Maddison watched with fascination as the digital pages printed and sat on top of the existing virtual paperwork, then turned his head back to the viewer screen to focus on the information scrolling at the top of the screen. *TIME – 13:09 – DATE – Friday 19th September 2059 – Diamonds Time-Share Estates.*

2059?

The brightness of the viewer screen became more intense and blinded Maddison, and along with the overload of new information, he became dizzy.

*

A little while later

Maddison opened his eyes; he looked at the door glass and spotted a familiar face looking back at him. *I know you, you're Albert Diamonds*, thought Maddison. He wondered why he knew the name of the man staring back at him, he gave him a wink and a smile, turned, and spotted another familiar face. It was another juror. He mentally matched the face against the list of names he'd printed out. *Christopher Lowe, nice to finally know your name.* Maddison looked into Christopher's eyes and wondered when he would get the chance to play, how would he tick him off his list. *I think that I…* "Would kill," he said out loud, then back to his thoughts, *you with Time-Share art.*

*

Sunday 21st September 2059 – 9:25 p.m.

Maddison's eyes opened to catch Albert's reflection in the shutting fridge and gave him a wink. Was he in a dream, was he going crazy, or was he a ghost? Albert seemed to be there every time he woke up. Albert seemed very familiar and at the same time, unfamiliar. He'd only met him a couple of days ago, and never seen his face before that, but it seemed that he'd known him long enough to know everything about him. *Could Albert become a potential playmate? Could I put him on a new list?* As Maddison pondered about his new potential playmate, a spider crawled past him, he instantly cupped it. He slowly unclasped his hand, picked it up with his opposite hand and started to pull its legs off, one by one, to the tune of *He Loves Me He Loves Me Not – On the list – PULL – off the list – PULL – on the list – PULL – off the list – PULL – on the list – PULL – off the list – PULL – on the list – PULL – off the list – PULL. That's a shame*, thought Maddison as he squashed the legless trunk. *Maybe next time?*

*

Monday 22nd September 2059 – 1:30 a.m.

Maddison couldn't sleep. He was wide awake and had a sense of urgency, he jumped out of bed. *It's already Monday*. He desperately needed to get on with his list. He'd always prepared the week's list over the weekends; it was the way it had always worked. Monday to Friday he'd play, and the weekend was for work, preparing and organising the following week's playdates. *I need to find names and locations of this week's playmates so I can tick them off my list.*

"Where are you going?" asked the sleepy woman from the other side of the mattress. A wave of joy washed over Maddison as he spotted another potential list candidate. He moved back closer to the bed, then stopped as he caught a reflection in the dressing table mirror. It was Albert, and he was shaking his head. Maddison smiled back, nodded, and turned towards the door. "You're right, finish one list before starting another," he muttered to the reflection as he left the bedroom. He walked along the upstairs corridor, looking in two other bedrooms as he passed, mentally adding the sleeping candidates to his next list. He walked downstairs, he didn't remember coming into the house or ever being in it before, but he seemed to know where everything was. He walked through the living room and into an office area. *Albert's home office* confirmed Maddison. *And his viewer.* He opened the second drawer down and took out the OXO tower folder, opened it and took out one the of the virtual sheets, his juror's name list. A list of names and locations that he'd found earlier from a simple search.

1. *Carmela Rosa – Rosa's Pantry – Unit 2, Time-Share 17, Elephant and Castle Shopping Centre*
2. *Lindsey Clark-Carter – Senior investment manager, AXA Investment Managers, Newgate St, London*
3. *Lucy Victoria – Lifeguard, Bank Street Flats, Floor 5, Time-Share 12, Central Manchester*
4. *Ravi Binning – Retired, Time-Share 4, 1178 Grange Avenue, Edgware.*
5. *Michael Craven – Michael's Cycles – Daltons Road, Wandsworth*
6. *Christopher Lowe – Hairstylist, 24 Gospel Oak Avenue, Time-Share 74, Greater London*
7. *Calvin Wireless – Musician, Malibu, California*
8. *Jade Andrews – Robotics Engineer, Queen Mary University, Bethnal Green, London*
9. *Betsy Thorn - 20/20 Vision Optometrists, Unit 27, Time-share 11, High Holborn*

10. *Michele Esteves – Musician – New London Theatre, Drury Lane, London*
11. *Anthony Chand – Doctor, St Thomas' Hospital, Gassion House Lodge, Time-Share 43, Residential Block*
12. *Ophelia Schmidt - Nurse, St Thomas' Hospital, Gassion House Lodge, Time-Share 12, Residential Block*

Maddison picked up a pen, digitally ticked numbers eleven and twelve, then worked through the information on the list, searching for addresses and locations of the remaining names. Hacking into government servers, cross-referencing data, planning, prepping and mentally sketching how his artwork was going to come together. Like any good artist, he would only need to plan the who and where, an idea of where to find his playmates would do, that was all he needed, the art could wait until the moment he was there and ready to play. He would get inspiration from his surroundings and create art in the moment.

Lucy Victoria lives in Manchester – wasn't Albert going to Manchester this week? Maybe I can tag along? Maybe I can ask Albert to help with my list? His lists had always been personal – he wasn't yet sure why, but something inside was telling him he could share his lists with Albert and it would be ok. Maybe he had the same dark desires, maybe he was a fellow list-bearer, maybe a kindred spirit? Maybe Albert hadn't yet realised his true self, and Maddison could help him to awaken.

Maybe I can teach him, I've always believed I could be a good teacher. The thought of taking on a student to help him on his dark journey sent a tingle of joy through Maddison's body. He wondered how else Albert could help. Or had Albert already been helping?

He opened Albert's work files. "Viewer, cross reference juror list with Diamonds Estates company files, find matches."

The viewer revealed several files. Maddison clicked on Mr and Mrs Lowe. "Christopher's just bought a house from Albert. I have his address and its Time-Share date information, thank you, Albert. What else?" muttered Maddison. "Viewer, return to search, expand the next file."

The file showed details of Carmela Rosa's Unit-2 purchase. "Thank you, Albert," said Maddison.

- *Monday – Ravi Binning*
- *Tuesday – Carmela Rosa*

- *Wednesday – Lucy Victoria*
- *Thursday – Christopher Lowe*
- *Friday – Calvin Wireless*

Maddison gradually put order to his list. The first part was ready, the week's diary was now full. He knew who was next to play. All the information he needed was there, either thanks to Albert or hacked with his very capable knowledge of viewer technology and genius brain. *What a coincidence, finding an MRI appointment for Ravi Binning at St Thomas' in the morning...* thought Maddison as his ear-to-ear smile turned to a yawn and he felt a sense of accomplishment. He printed the updated list, digitally tagged it to the back of the original list and placed it back into the OXO tower folder. He yawned again and shut his eyes. He was ready for the coming week.

*

Monday 22nd September 2059 – 9:30 a.m.

Maddison's eyes opened, he felt confused. He'd fallen asleep in Albert's house then awoken somewhere different again. He looked up and recognised the sign "*Coronary Care Unit*". He was back at the hospital. He turned around, spotted the familiar office, and smiled, *it's empty again.*

He entered the office, sat at the viewer, and hacked back into the hospital's Time-Share and viewer camera system.

"Viewer, show patient file, Ravi Binning – 1178 Grange Avenue, Edgeware." The viewer displayed Ravi Binning's patient file, showing him as attending the hospital and booked into Time-Share MRI suite five at 9:45 a.m. Maddison looked to the wall clock. It was 9:33. "Viewer, show me why Ravi Binning is having an MRI." The viewer expanded the results. "*Mr Binning has been diagnosed with emphysema, and as such, needs an oxygen cylinder with him at all times to aid his breathing. He is attending an MRI on his lungs as a prelude to cloned lung surgery.*" Maddison laughed out loud as his insidious thought process worked out a play theme for Ravi Binning. He hacked into the MRI suite Time-Share mainframe to see which bubbles had active MRIs then merged Time-Share suite five to appear at the same time frame as Time-Share suite four.

Now to watch my art unfold, thought Maddison. He jumped up excitedly and exited the office just in time to see an old Indian gentleman heading towards the MRI department, pulling an oxygen cylinder behind him.

*

Tuesday 23rd September 2059

Maddison Bartel awakened in a dark, soul-satisfied mood. He was hungry for his next play date and excited to get the day started. He looked at the alarm clock, *6:53*. He felt himself lean over, then watched as his hand stretched out to hit the alarm-off button on the retro clock.

Maddison was proud of his lists and so obsessive about completing them that being on-track made him happy. He felt himself lean over to give the sleeping woman next to him a kiss on her cheek. *Don't worry, you can be on my next list,* he thought.

As the woman pulled a pillow over her head, he jumped out of bed and headed to the bathroom, singing his own version of Craig David's *7 Days*.

"*I played with a man on Monday.*"

"*Going to pay an overdue bill at a café on Tuesday.*"

"*Then play a game in Manchester on Wednesday.*"

"*Play again on Thursday and Friday then chill on Saturday and Sunday.*"

Maddison bounce-stepped out of the shower and picked up a towel from the floor in one sharp movement. He looked into the mirror, pointed his right index finger, and watched the familiar face wink then went back into the bedroom to get himself suited and booted while continuing to hum *7 Days*.

Maddison walked out the front door and turned to look at the upstairs windows to watch the future list candidates waving and smiling – they couldn't wait to be on his next list. He put the suitcase on the back seat then climbed into the driverless car. He heard himself tell the car where to go and smiled. "Drive to the Elephant and Castle shopping centre, sub-location, Rosa's Pantry. Park outside."

The car merged into the unfaltering flow of traffic then steadily made its way to Rosa's Pantry.

*

Maddison looked straight into Albert's eyes, *this list is mine. Maybe I'll let you help with the next one*. He left the café toilet, stared at his playmate then smiled as he noticed the black, stained skin around Carmela's hairline from where she had recently self-dyed her hair.

"Here you go, love," said Carmela, placing a mug of tea and an invoice on the counter.

"Thank you, Mrs Rosa," said Maddison. He picked up the tea and invoice then sat by the café's front window, facing inwards towards Carmela. He took out Albert's viewer tablet, hacked the shopping centre Time-Share

codes then hovered his finger over the tablet's return key. The return key was eager to be pressed, eager to execute its command, but he needed to be precise, he needed to be exact. Maddison watched Carmela as she served, watching her steps, and waiting for that critical moment to change the Time-Share date, that circumscribed moment when Carmela would be standing in the exact position to…
"Now!" cried Maddison with excitement, as the press of the return key was met by a thunderclap, The moment was perfect – *BANG!* – a deafening sound. Maddison had sat directly below the blast. Shattered glass rained down out of nowhere, outwards from the untouched and completely undamaged front window. Maddison's eyes followed the swarm of lead pellets as they made their way through the air above his head. He let out a joyful scream as he watched the tiny balls find little resistance as they travelled through Carmela Rosa's neck and head then lodge themselves into a blood-speckled wall and the newly appeared hanging picture of a ballerina.

Maddison was chuffed with himself, his warped mind transforming the screams of the café's customers into cheers and hails for his masterpiece, an ode to his genius. "Thank you, thank you, I know it was, and I know I am, but I really must go now. I have another performance to prepare for," he told his fans as he left the café and headed back to Albert's car.

"Drive to London City Airport, Time-Share terminal six," Maddison heard himself say.

*

Wednesday 24th September 2059

Maddison woke up, "What a lovely day, I fancy a nice morning swim." He got up, got dressed, picked up the viewer tablet and headed to the lobby.

"Good morning, sir, you're up nice and early," said the polite assistant, instantly acknowledging his approach.

Maddison looked at her name badge, "Good morning, Jen, I fancy a bit of a swim this morning, and a little birdie told me that there's an Olympic standard pool near here. I'm dying to try it out – can you point me in the right direction, please?"

"I can do better than that, sir. I can order you a driverless TaxiCab, and it will take you straight to the Manchester Aquatics Centre," said the helpful Jen. She swiped at her viewer and hailed the TaxiCab. "There you go, sir, it will be here in one minute and waiting for you by the pickup area in front of the hotel."

“Driverless TaxiCabs,” repeated Maddison. “I miss the old days when you could have a chat with the cabby as you drove, they always had the best stories. Thank you, Jen, I will see you later.” He headed outside, and impressed by the speed of the TaxiCab’s arrival, he climbed on board. The TaxiCab acknowledged his entry and destination. “Thank you, passenger, your journey to Manchester Aquatics Centre will take nine minutes. Please sit back, fasten your seat belt, relax and enjoy the scenery. If you would like a commentary of your journey, please press the blue tab on the viewer in front of you.”

Maddison laughed to himself as the TaxiCab pulled up to the swim baths, then chuckled to himself as he considered whether putting the TaxiCab on one of his lists would give him any kind of satisfaction.

“Thank you, passenger. Your taxi fare has been charged to your hotel room account, please dismount the car and take all of your belongings. If you would like TaxiCab to pick you up, please press the red button on the viewer and state time for pickup.”

Maddison paused as he started to dismount the TaxiCab. He never liked putting time on how long it would take for his artistic inspiration to manifest once he’d met up with his playdate, but it would be nice to get a lift back to the hotel after. *8:45.* He pressed the red button, "Pick up at ten forty-five a.m. please."

Maddison exited the car and made his way to the swimming baths'. Sitting with her back to the entrance, a long-black-haired receptionist was busy moaning to a co-worker about how her manager had refused to let her leave early on Tuesday so she could go and watch her son's performance in the school play.

"That's terrible, Angela," replied the co-worker, all too ready to agree with her black-haired colleague.

"I know, right, and I was only asking to finish half an hour early. And to make things worse, I had sorted cover – Graham said he would cover for me, but that arsehole wouldn't even listen. I actually think he's got it in for me since I turned him down at the Christmas party," said Angela, laughing.

The colleagues were completely oblivious to Maddison's presence. He waited at the desk and listened to the duo's comical conversation of management-slaying and justification on how useless everyone seemed to be compared to them. He was happy to stand back, listen and look around the foyer for anything interesting, and as he did, he noticed a staff family tree on the wall. *That's handy*, he thought. He looked for his play date's name – there she was, with a photo. He looked back round to the woman talking to the receptionist and smiled.

"Anyways, Lucy, what you doin' here so early? I fort you was on lates today?" said Angela, pausing momentarily as she finally spotted Maddison. She partially turned round, "With you in a min, sir," then, not being one to be stopped mid-flow from a social conversation, even for a customer, she turned back round to continue her conversation with Lucy.

It's her! Maddison couldn't believe his luck, finding his play date waiting for him on arrival. He knew she worked at the pool from finding her social media profile earlier with a viewer search, but to have Lucy Victoria waiting like a gift was enough for him to overlook how rude the receptionist was being, she would never know how lucky she was that his list entry had taken priority this morning.

Lucy looked dismissively at Maddison then continued her conversation with Angela. "Well, you know me, Angie, I want to get a few good dives in before my shift starts, practice, practice, practice as coach always says."

"Well, should have guessed, babes, I really fink you're gonna nail it this time. That gold's coming home. Anyways, are you goin' to Sean's party this Saturday?"

Maddison, uncharacteristically happy waiting, listened to the girls as their important social-life conversation continued. He was ahead of schedule, and he would allow his artistic flair to take over in working out how the date was going to play out.

"Anyways babes, chat to you when I start my shift, I'd better get some dives in," said Lucy, and she headed off towards the changing rooms.

"Yes, sir, can I help you?" The unapologetic Angela finally turned her attention to the smiling Maddison.

"Yes, one for entry to the main pool, please, my dear." Maddison looked at the wall behind her and grinned as he noticed the pool's emptying and cleaning schedule and a Time-Share control unit logbook.

"There you go, sir," said Angela with a shiver.

Maddison's mind had conjured a perfect and poetic way to cross another name off his list. As he walked away from the desk, he heard the receptionist mutter, "That was a creepy guy," under her breath, and he decided Angela would be a perfect candidate for a future list. Walking straight past the changing rooms, he diverted towards the spectators' area and sat in perfect view of the diving boards. He took out his viewer tablet, hacked into the swimming pool's Time-Share unit, then watched as Lucy Victoria climbed the ladder to the ten-metre dive platform. Lucy walked to the edge of the platform, her toes parallel with the edge, then looked straight ahead, her face solid with a concentration of the dive ahead. She turned around, foot-shuffled backwards so her heels cleared the edge then jumped back. She tucked her body into a tight ball, her hands held her shins and her toes pointed out as her body shape changed through a series of twists and somersaults as she rotated downwards, finally opening out her body position vertically. One of her hands grabbed the other, her arms perfectly extended forward in line with her ears, her elbows locked and her stomach and back tightened as she disappeared beneath the surface of the water without a splash, accompanied by the characteristic ripping sound, like the tearing of paper. Maddison was in awe of how majestically elegant she looked as she rehearsed her routine. But something was missing, and maybe, he could be the one to take her to the next level and give her the dive of her life.

Lucy climbed back out of the pool, walked back round to the steps and restarted her ascent to the top. Maddison was ready to help, his finger hovering above the enter key. Lucy reached the top and walked towards the edge, unaware that this would be the last time she would ever be at the top of that platform. She walked to the edge, her toes parallel to it, looking straight ahead, totally focused on the dive ahead. Like the first time, she turned, shuffled back, heels clear of the edge and jumped back. Maddison pushed enter on his viewer. She tucked her body into a tight ball, her hands held her shins, and her toes pointed. She changed her body shape through a series of twists and somersaults as she rotated downwards, finally opening to vertical, one hand grabbed the other, her arms perfectly extended forward in line with her ears, her elbows locked, her stomach and back tight, it was the perfect dive. But there was no rip, no tearing-of-paper sound. The water depth was low, four meters lower. Her body kept rotating, hitting the water flat with a thud. The extreme deceleration, along with hitting the bottom of the pool causing severe bruising internally and externally, straining the connective tissues that secured her organs and haemorrhaging to her lungs – none of which were immediately life-threatening. Maddison watched with delight as a stunned Lucy struggled to lift her head out of the shallow water. “And now, the final brushstroke,” said the excited, but outwardly calm Maddison as he cancelled the change he’d made to the swimming bath’s Time-Share system, the water instantly reverting to its original five-metre depth, the struggling Lucy still at the bottom of the pool. Maddison laughed as moments later, a lifeless body floated to the surface. “Perfect!” he shouted, springing out of his seat with excitement, then slowly sat back down and watched as the emergency services arrived to the chaos he’d unleashed.

*

Maddison left the spectator area, walked out through the foyer, turning to the crying receptionist as he passed, “Thank you, Angela. See you soon, dear.” He jumped into the waiting TaxiCab and headed back to the hotel.

The assistant at the front desk instantly acknowledged Maddison as he walked back into the hotel. “Good morning, sir, did you have a nice time at the swimming baths?” “Hello, Jen, it was relaxing, very relaxing, just what I needed, dear.” He looked at the nearby clock, the time was 11:05. "Have you got a pen I can borrow, please? I just need to cross something off my to-do list?"

"Here you go, sir, you can keep that one," replied Jen, handing him one of the hotel's souvenir pens.

"Thank you." Maddison walked towards the lifts, headed back to Albert's room, and throwing himself on the bed, he stretched out, closed his eyes, and let the feeling of achievement wash over him...

*

Thursday 25th September 2059

Maddison woke up looking straight into Albert's eyes – it was a reflection in the car's rear viewer. He turned round to look at the back seats, then got distracted as he noticed the car was outside Christopher Lowes' house. He looked back at the mirror and gave Albert a wink, "Thank you, friend, I'll take it from here." He picked up the viewer tablet, exited the car, walked to the gate of number twenty-four, picked up the flowers, a bottle of champagne and a card and pressed the buzzer to the Lowes' Time-Share bubble.

"Hi, come on in, I'll open the doors," said Christopher's voice over the intercom.

The gate automatically opened. Maddison walked up the garden path. *How welcoming, Christopher,* thought the smirking Maddison as he entered the house.

"Won't be long, just in the loo, make yourself at home," called Christopher from the back of the house.

Maddison walked through following the voice towards the downstairs toilet. *How perfect,* he thought and laid his tablet on the kitchen table. He'd had most of the week to plan this one; he'd searched the history files, he'd looked at blueprints, and he'd come up with a perfect sketch of how his latest piece of art would look. The only improvisation or hurdle he might have had to face was how to get Christopher into his ground floor toilet, but he was already in there, and to make things all the sweeter, he'd gone there of his own accord, it was all too perfect. Maddison hacked into the house's Time-Share unit and changed the bubble settings of 24 Gospel Oak Avenue from Time-Share 9:35 a.m. on June 20th, 2025, to Time-Share bubble 2:27 p.m. on May 29th 2023, which just happened to be the exact same day and time a train derailment occurred in the exact location where a toilet would be built at 24 Gospel Oak Avenue…

Maddison went back into the first of the living rooms and picked up a digital pen from a desk. He turned back to face the direction of the downstairs bathroom and waited and listened… *There it is!* His eyes widened as heard a distant rumble. He looked over at a half-drunk glass of wine, the contents trembling against the sides. A gentle breeze was breaking through from the gap under the toilet door, increasing in pace and getting stronger as the rumble got louder and louder until it became deafening. Maddison smiled as the door and part of the wall disintegrated to make way for the front of a train as it appeared and obliterated everything in its path, a path which, of course, included an ex-juror named Christopher Lowe.

Maddison's jaw dropped as he watched his artwork take a life of its own. "Perfection," he said. He looked at his hand, it was still holding onto the pen but shaking with excitement. He took out his list, ticked another name then casually turned to slowly walk out, absorbing and cataloging as many of the sights and smells as possible as he left the late Christopher Lowe's house.

*

Friday 26th September 2059 – 10.15 p.m.

Maddison struggled to open his eyes, closing them quickly as the bright stage lighting pierced through his eyelids. He turned his head to avoid the direct glare. Finally able to open them, he saw the now familiar face of the woman next to him. *Oh, I wonder if Albert is here as well. I'd love for him to see what I've planned for tonight!* Maddison shivered in anticipation of the impending high note to finish the week. He looked over to the woman; she wasn't paying any attention to him; she looked hypnotised by the terrible sound coming from the stage. He took out the viewer tablet, bypassed Wembley's Time-Share system with ease, set the new time and date for the stage and waited to press the enter button, it needed to be pressed with split-second precision. If he hit that perfect moment, he would have an audience of nine hundred thousand fans witness his best art to date. He looked back towards the woman, she was singing.

"*Take it with ice, take it or leave it.*"

Maddison sat upright; the moment was drawing closer. Calvin stopped singing and threw himself to the floor. Maddison pressed enter on his tablet to complete his masterpiece and was instantly rewarded with a mist of red liquid as the once was Calvin Wireless exploded under the weight of a six-thousand-kilogram African Bush Elephant that had arrived to share space with him. The crowd's screams translated to him again as cheers. *Perfect,* he thought as a tear of joy ran down his cheek.

*

Saturday 27th September 2059 – 8.45 a.m. – present day

Maddison wakes to the feeling of unrivalled accomplishment. How is he going to top this week's playdates, especially after such a monumental evening? He doesn't know, but it will be fun to find out. *Work to do, let's prepare the rest of the list— Wait, I'm in a car.* A confused Maddison spots Albert's eyes staring at him in the rear viewer.

Where are you taking us, Albert? he asks. He watches Albert's reflection in the car's windows, *why is he pulling into a police station?*

Maddison uncontrollably follows Albert over to the lifts and stares at him in the shiny reflective metal as they ascend.

The lift opens fully to the impressive and shiny counter of the TSM-PD. Maddison and Albert walk over towards the receptionist. Maddison watches Albert's reflection getting bigger as they move closer to the counter. *Wait,* thinks Maddison, slowing his pace, *Why's there only one reflection?* An element of fear engulfs him.

"Good morning, sir, can I help you?" says the Glaswegian receptionist as she acknowledges their arrival.

Maddison looks past her into a glass partition separating them and the main TSM-PD office and refocuses to catch Albert's reflection then watches as Albert's mouth moves, and he hears himself answer the women.

"Oh yes, sorry. My name is Albert Diamonds, I'm here to speak to a DI Mirror," says Maddison.

"Oh yes, he's just over there, talking to DS Bailey. He's been expecting you." She looks over to her left and calls out to DI Mirror. "DI Mirror, this gentleman is here to see you."

DI Mirror walks over, followed by the woman.

"This is Mr Diamonds," says the receptionist as she introduces Maddison to Mirror. *Why did she call me Mr Diamonds?*

Mirror holds out his right hand. "Mr Diamonds, thank you for coming in. I'm DI Mirror, and this is DS Bailey," he says.

Maddison looks up at the two detectives, then stares in turn at their reflections in the counter and the glass partition but sees only three people: the two detectives and Albert.

Maddison stares in turn into Mirror's and DS Bailey's eyes, then watches as his arm extends and shakes Mirror's hand. The room spun as his head processed the pieces and suspicions of the last few days, why he can only remember parts of his day. Why Albert seems to always be there. Why he has memories of Albert's life and places Albert has been. Maddison finally starts to comprehend what has been so obvious, the reality that—

I am Albert Diamonds.

Chapter 11

Meeting Albert Diamonds

Saturday 27th September 2059 – 8.40 a.m.

Mirror steps out the elevator into the TSM-PD foyer, he feels like he's only just left and wonders if he's really been home or if had he fallen asleep in the lift and has only dreamt that he'd been home to sleep a futile couple of hours. He quickly snaps out of his thoughts as he spots DS Chang walking away up the corridor. "DS Chang, wait!" He quickens his pace towards him, walking straight past the reception. "Morning Elaine," he says, glancing over as he hurries past.

"Och, guid morning, DI Mirror," says Elaine in her natural Glaswegian accent.

Mirror looks back round to face her, "Ah, Elaine, a gentleman called Albert Diamonds will be coming in this morning to see DS Chang – change of plan, I will be interviewing him instead, so please call me when he's here."

"Will do," replies Elaine.

"Good morning, sir – disaster of an evening last night. Didn't you want me to interview Mr Diamonds?" enquires DS Chang, reacting to Mirror's request.

Mirror ignores DS Chang's comment about last night. "DS Chang, I'll take care of Mr Diamonds. I want you to follow up on the solicitor, Harrison Mann. Locate him, see if he can come in to talk to us this weekend. If he doesn't want to or can't for whatever reason, insist it's important that I talk to him before Monday, so if he can't come here, we will go to him. Find out where he'll be."

DS Chang looks confused and wonders why Mirror would be so interested in talking to the solicitor, considering he's already added all the information that was available into his report. "Ok, sir, I doubt he will come here at short notice, considering he's in Cornwall. Are you sure about going to see him? I could set up a viewer call. It's a long old trip, sir."

"Yes, Chang, I'm *sure* I want to speak to him in person," Mirror snaps as Chang's quizzing twangs a nerve. "And Chang, after you've done that, there's a sealed file on shared drive forty-two. See if you can do anything with it, get it open if you can. If you have any luck, call me straight away – and Chang, it's best you tell no one, report to me only. When you see what type of file it is, you'll understand. My eyes only, Chang, ok?"

"No problem, sir," replies DS Chang, deciding it best to just do and not ask as he turns and heads away up the corridor.

Mirror pauses for thought, then, just as he is about to follow DS Chang towards the main department, the lift doors open, and DS Bailey comes out.

DS Bailey waves hello to Elaine, who chooses to ignore her, pretending to be engrossed in a viewer conversation. Unfazed, DS Bailey walks past her towards Mirror. He wouldn't have been concerned that Elaine had purposely ignored Bailey, had it been last week Mirror might have readily agreed, he'd often felt like ignoring her as well, but the last couple of days, DS Bailey has been different. Her overconfidence has vanished, and she is showing humility. More importantly, her voice isn't bothering him anymore. He looks away from Elaine and greets the inbound detective sergeant.

"Morning, Bailey," he says.

"Morning, sir. Did you get any sleep?"

"Not much, Bailey, how about you?"

Before DS Bailey can answer, a loud Scottish voice calls out, “DI Mirror, this gentleman is here to see you.”

“I’ll carry on finding information on the solicitor, sir,” says DS Bailey.

“No Bailey, I’ve asked DS Chang to look into that. I would like you in the interview room with me, please.”

DS Bailey’s first instinct is to question DI Mirror as to why she is no longer allowed to investigate the solicitor. Has he reverted to not wanting her involved? Last week, she would have instantly reacted, but a pause is all she needs to realise he’s just said he wants her to take part in the interview. DI Mirror is involving her more on the frontline of the case. She turns and follows him back along the corridor to the reception.

“This is Mr Diamonds,” says Elaine introducing Albert.

Mirror extends his right hand to welcome the visitor.

“Mr Diamonds, thank you for coming in. I’m DI Mirror, and this is DS Bailey.”

Albert pauses, he looks into DI Mirror’s and DS Bailey’s eyes in turn, then slowly extends his arm out to shake Mirror’s hand.

“We’ve invited you in to see if you can help tie up a few loose ends we’ve encountered during our investigations of some incidents this week,” says Mirror. He is still firmly holding onto Albert’s hand, but quickly releases his grip as a cold chill runs through his body, concluding as a tingle in his toes.

“Shall we use interview room two, sir?” says DS Bailey, attempting to restart Mirror from his handshake.

Mirror snaps out of his momentary pause, “Err, yes, please, DS Bailey, this way if you would, please, Mr Diamonds.”

DS Bailey leads them to the interview rooms, presses the Time-Share panel to select interview room two, then stands aside, allowing Mirror and Albert to enter.

“Please take a seat, Mr Diamonds,” says Mirror as he and DS Bailey walk through the grey-walled police interview room to sit on the opposite side of the table and face Albert.

Maddison watches the two detectives sit, then starts looking around the room. It is bare, consisting solely of some chairs, a table and a video-recording viewer.

“Mr Diamonds, once again, thank you for coming in, just to let you know this interview will be videoed and lie-detector monitored,” explains DS Bailey.

“Lie-detector monitored? I thought this was a ‘pop in and help with our enquiries’ type of chat,” replies Albert.

“It’s just routine, sir. It’s so we can keep everything in order,” replies DS Bailey in a friendlier tone.

“Mr Diamonds, this interview is voluntary, but at the same time, it will help to eliminate you from our enquiries. As you may or may not be aware, you have been in the same place as some unfortunate incidents this last week,” says Mirror.

“Oh, I know, tell me about it. I’ve had the strangest of weeks – my other half is in bits this morning. These Time-Share accidents aren’t going to do my business any favours,” says Albert.

“Sorry, sir? What do you mean your other halves in bits this morning?” enquires DS Bailey.

“The concert! I mean what happened there was bizarre, so I assumed you were going to ask me about that as well?” replies Albert.

“You were at the concert?” says a surprised Mirror, glancing at DS Bailey.

"Yes, like I said, my wife loves Calvin Wireless, or should I say loved? We were in VIP seating, right next to the stage. The tickets cost me an arm and a leg, and I nearly got covered in his arms and legs. Sorry, was that was bad taste."

"Mr Diamonds, that puts you in the same place and at roughly the same time as all seven of the suspicious deaths we are investigating this week," says DS Bailey.

A wide-eyed Mirror turns to look at DS Bailey and sharply shakes his head, making DS Bailey realise that she has just fed unreleased information to Albert.

"Suspicious deaths!" repeats Albert, taking in what he'd just heard, "I thought they were all accidents?"

"Mr Diamonds we are still investigating all the incidents and have yet to conclude our findings," says Mirror, covering the tracks quickly. He knows he needs to push forward with the interview now that DS Bailey's extra information has rattled Albert.

"Unfortunately, Albert, as DS Bailey has just said, that does place you at every incident this week. So, for the record and the lie-detector viewer, I'm going to ask some sensitive questions to eliminate you as a suspect. My apologies if the questions make you uncomfortable, but you understand, we need to ask."

"I'm a suspect?" says Albert, taken aback.

"Mr Diamonds, please answer the following questions truthfully with either a 'yes' or a 'no'," continues Mirror.

A gobsmacked Albert looks in turn at the two detectives. He'd thought he was coming in to help, not to be eliminated from a murder enquiry, "Err, yes, ok," he replies nervously.

"Ok, Mr Diamonds, again to make you aware, this interview is being recorded, and you are also being monitored by a lie detector. Please answer the following questions with either 'yes' or 'no'. Do you understand?"

"Yes," replies Albert.

"Were you at St Thomas' Hospital at any time this week?" asks Mirror.

"Yes."

"Mr Diamonds, do you know Doctor Anthony Chand?" Mirror brings a picture of Doctor Chand on the viewer.

"No," replies Albert.

"Mr Diamonds, do you know Ophelia Schmidt?" Mirror brings up a photo of the victim to the viewer.

"No," replies Albert.

“Did you kill, or do you have any reason to kill either Anthony Chand or Ophelia Schmidt, or are you involved in any way in the deaths?” asks Mirror.

“No, and no, I’m most definitely not involved,” replies an agitated Albert.

“Sorry, Mr Diamonds, just ‘yes’ or ‘no’, please,” says DS Bailey.

“NO!” replies Albert loudly.

“Do you know a Ravi Binning?” asks Mirror, putting a photo up.

“No.”

“Do you know Lucy Victoria?” asks Mirror.

Albert looks at the photo of the pretty young woman and thinks what a shame if she has died. “No.”

“Did you kill, are you involved in the deaths in any way, or do you have any reason to kill either Lucy Victoria or Ravi Binning?” asks Mirror.

“No,” replies a calmer Albert.

“Mr Diamonds, we know that you know who Calvin Wireless was,” says Mirror. “Did you kill, are you involved in the death in any way, or do you have any reason to kill Mr Calvin Wireless?”

“No,” replies Albert, feeling a lot less anxious.

Mirror has purposely left the next two victims to last, to gauge Albert's reaction.

"Mr Diamonds, do you know these two people?" He puts two pictures up on the viewer.

Albert's mouth falls open as he stares at the viewer, "What the? Why are you showing me pictures of my clients? Are they involved?"

"Mr Diamonds, did you kill, are you involved in the deaths in any way or do you have any reason to kill either Carmela Rosa or Christopher Lowe?"

Albert sinks back into his chair, his view tunnelled as he looks in turn at Mirror, DS Bailey, and then back at the pictures of Carmela Rosa and Christopher Lowe, and his chin drops further, unable to lift it back up.

"Are they dead? I was talking to them both this week, are they dead?"

"Mr Diamonds, I'm sorry, but please answer the question. Did you kill, are you involved in the deaths in any way, or do you have any reason to kill either Carmela Rosa or Christopher Lowe?" repeats Mirror.

"No," replies the subdued Albert, in shock from what he'd just heard.

Mirror looks at DS Bailey monitoring the lie detector. DS Bailey shakes her head, "All clear, sir, prelims show he's telling the truth."

"Mr Diamonds, are you ok?" asks Mirror.

"Are you ok?" repeats Albert. "Not really sure how to answer that. What happened to Carmela and Mr Lowe?"

"Unfortunately, until we have more information, we aren't able to release any details other than to say they both died this week," replies Mirror, looking pointedly at a shamefaced DS Bailey. "Mr Diamonds, would you excuse DS Bailey and me for a minute. Would you like anything? A drink maybe?"

"I'm ok, DI Mirror," replies Albert.

Maddison smiles as he watches as DS Bailey and DI Mirror leave. Something is different, he is awake at the same time as Albert. Does he have any control of Albert's body, or is he just along for the ride? He is fully aware of Albert, but as just proved by the lie detector, Albert isn't aware of him.

Mirror and DS Bailey stand just outside the interview room. "What do you think, sir? The lie detector tests are meant to be 99.99% accurate, and it clearly shows he's telling the truth. How can he be linked to what's going on?" asks DS Bailey.

"I think we need to tread very carefully here, Bailey. He might be a target; his wife may be a target or his wife may be involved somehow. I think we need to tell him something close to the truth, but not everything. Follow my lead when we go back in." They head back into the interview room, and Mirror stops before going in. "What if Albert is the reason for the new list?"

"What do you mean, sir?"

"Each of Maddison's lists had something linking them together, right? What if some sick copycat killer is using Albert's link to Mrs Diamonds being the ex-wife of an original Maddison victim as the list link?" Mirror quickly realises how complicated what he'd just said sounded, but knew in his mind, it is making kind of sense.

Maddison concentrates on lifting his right arm and scratching Albert's head. Sure enough, Albert lifts his arm and itches his non-itchy head. He then thinks about getting up and sitting back down. Albert gets up, paces then sits back down. Maddison is fully conscious and is fast learning how to control Albert. He'd seen the pictures on the viewer screen, heard Albert's conversation with the two detectives and had enjoyed reminiscing on the past week's playdates.

Maddison and Albert watch as DI Mirror and DS Bailey re-enter.

"Sorry about that, Mr Diamonds," says Mirror.

"Oh, I think you've got to know me a little bit better now, so you can call me Albert. Am I still a suspect?" Albert leans back in his chair, his hands clasped cockily behind his head. Maddison smiles at Albert's sarcasm towards the detectives. *I'm starting to like you, Albert.*

Slightly unnerved, DS Bailey manages a semi-smile back at Albert, "No, Mr Diamonds."

"Mr Diamonds… Albert," says Mirror, correcting himself, trying to help Albert relax then realising that what he's about to say will far from calm him. "I'll get straight to the point, Albert. We think that you and your family might be in danger."

Albert drops his arms from behind his head and sits up in his chair. "I'm sorry? What do you mean, we're in danger?"

"Albert, we've had seven deaths this week, and they've all happened in suspicious circumstances, and you're linked in some way with every victim, either by knowing them or being in the same area when something happened," explains Mirror.

"Ok, what are you saying then? I've answered all your questions, now it's time for some answers," replies an anxious Albert.

Mirror wonders if beating around the bush has been the best approach. Maybe, if he just came out with what they know so far, it would be more beneficial and less of a time-waste than this tender-footing. "Ok, Albert, the seven deaths this week," he pauses to self-affirm his approach. He is about to tell someone who's not a member of his team his suspicions, and this will make the situation much more real. "Albert, we believe that we have a serial killer."

Albert stares incredulously at Mirror, "What?"

"We believe the murders this week are linked, and we're investigating the possibility that it might be a serial killer."

"Look, you've already said that. Now, what the hell has this to do with me and my family?" demands Albert.

"It's a copycat killer," adds DS Bailey.

Mirror looks over at DS Bailey. He's not sure if he's happy that she has just said that, but at least it has been said, which makes the next part harder for Albert to hear but easier for Mirror to say. Unsure if Albert knows his wife's past link to The Slate Killer, Mirror knows to gingerly drip-feed his words. "We believe that the serial killer is copying Maddison Bartel's kill pattern, and we believe that somehow, you or your family could be on a future list or be a target."

Albert looks stunned as he tries to absorb what DI Mirror has revealed.

"Mr Diamonds, are you ok?" asks DS Bailey.

"Albert, do you know who Maddison Bartel is? Albert… Mr Diamonds?" asks Mirror.

"Yes," whispers Albert. "He's my wife's recurring nightmare."

Albert's reply confirms Albert's knowledge of his wife's past.

"Yes, Mr Diamonds, we know about your wife's link to the original killer," says DS Bailey, relieved to no longer be treading on eggshells, Mirror instantly changes pace to full police officer mode. "We believe that someone is copying The Slate Killer's MO. We believe that the murders this week are linked via the common element that they were all jurors on the Maddison court case. We also believe you are linked somehow, as your wife was the spouse of one of the original victims. We are unsure if the copycat is following you in preparation of his next list or whether the jurors' list will be expanded to include your wife as a possible target due to her connection to the original court case."

"Well so much for coming in to help with your enquiries. I've gone from helping you to being a murder suspect to being a potential murder victim," says Albert. "This is a lot more to take in than a simple 'can I help you with your enquiries?'"

"I'm sorry, Albert, I know it's a freaky situation, but we need your cooperation to help us figure this out," says Mirror.

"No! I can't have this anywhere near my wife or stepchildren, not after all they went through with her first husband and how he was killed. When I first met her, she was in pieces. I've helped her and the kids get their lives back together, it's only been the last couple of years that she's been back to a more normal life, so there's no way, *no way* I'm letting you bring up that bloody Maddison Bartel again to set her back and destroy years of therapy," says Albert angrily as he stands up and makes a beeline to the exit.

“Albert stop… Mr Diamonds, wait,” says Mirror, intercepting and blocking Albert’s path.

“Get out of my way,” says Albert, stopping just short of DI Mirror’s face.

DS Bailey jumps up from her chair, ready to move in and restrain Albert.

Mirror holds out his hand to stop her. “Mr Diamonds, stop, please.”

“It’s back to Mr Diamonds now is it? Am I under arrest? Do I need a lawyer? I’m guessing the answer to both those questions is no, so please get out of the way, thank you.”

Mirror steps aside and puts his hand on the door handle as if about to open the door for Albert. “Ok, Mr Diamonds,” he says, turning the handle, he pulls it ajar then stops. “But what if our suspicions are right? What if you are being followed or your family is being targeted?” He opens the door a little more but still not wide enough to let Albert through. “Now, it would be fantastic if we are completely wrong and way off track, but… what if we’re right? We’re not trying to force you to do anything, but we are asking for your help. Work with us to make sure that you and your family stay safe so we can catch this copycat killer before he kills again." Mirror takes a step back and leaves Albert a fully cleared path.

Albert looks at Mirror as his thoughts play tug o' war with what to do for the best.

As soon as the door had fully opened, Maddison's instinct should have been to force Albert out and leave that police station as soon as possible, but Albert's pause has allowed him a moment to think, it is ok to stay, Maddison the methodical genius is happy that Albert has stopped him. To be honest, he isn't sure if he stopped Albert or whether Albert stopped on his own accord, but he knows if he plays his cards right, Albert could be the perfect hiding place to continue playing with his lists, in the shadows at night and whilst Albert plays the cocky salesman that everybody loves in the sunshine of day. To make things more scrumptious, the police are asking Albert to help them. What could be better than being on-side with the police and being told what they're planning to do? Maybe, just maybe, it will give him the time he needs to figure out how he ended up inside Time-Share salesman, Albert Diamonds, in the first place.

Albert focuses on the cleared pathway, "It can't affect my wife and kids, they can't know what's going on," he says.

"For now, Albert, we will keep an eye on them from a distance. They won't even know we're there," says Mirror.

"Ok, what do you want from me?" asks Albert, turning around slowly and walking back to his chair.

"Thank you, Albert. Firstly, we must stress how important it is that none of this gets out to the media or public. As far as the world should be concerned, for now, the incidents this week were accidents. As you can imagine, if the press gets wind of a serial killer, it will cause panic, and it will make our search harder." Mirror picks up his tablet and sends names and profile pictures of the remaining jurors to the viewer.

1. *Lindsey Clark-Carter*
2. *Michael Craven*
3. *Jade Andrews*
4. *Betsy Thorn*
5. *Michele Esteves*

"Albert, do you know any of these people?"

"I know Lindsey, Michael, and Betsy quite well, and I recognise the picture of Michele Esteves, he's a musician, isn't he? Oh my God! Why? Are they dead as well?" asks Albert.

"No, Mr Diamonds, but we believe they could be on the killer's list," says DS Bailey.

"Why is he killing people I know?" says Albert.

"Albert, remember, this cannot leave this room. We don't know how you fit into this yet. The seven people killed this week and the five people I've just shown you were jurors from the Maddison Bartel trial in 2050, and we believe the copycat will attempt to kill next week. What we don't know is whether that will be the end of the list and they'll start a new list or continue to kill everyone else connected to the court case," says DS Bailey.

"Oh, my God, I can see why you thought I was a suspect," says Albert.

"Albert, you seem to have a link to this copycat, and we don't know why. I think the killer is watching you and your family. It's too much of a coincidence that you just happened to know the victims or be nearby when they were killed. I want to use surveillance drones to follow you and your family. We'll be discreet so your wife and kids can continue their day-to-day lives," says Mirror.

"So, we're the bait," says Albert cagily.

Mirror avoids Albert's question, "And we would like to put a monitor on your business, personal and home viewers."

Albert looks at Mirror in disbelief, wondering how it has been possible for his life to not only be turned upside down, but inside out as well. "This was meant to be the best week of my life. I've just signed the biggest of business deals that was going give my family, after all the crap they'd been through, the lifestyle they deserve," he says, deflated.

"I'm sorry, Albert, I really am. We're going to do everything we can to make sure you and your family's lives are not affected. Albert are you happy with what we're proposing?" asks Mirror.

Albert hesitates then quietly and slowly nods his head, "Ok."

"Thank you, Mr Diamonds," says DS Bailey.

The three occupants of the interview room and Maddison Bartel wait in awkward silence as Mirror swipes at his viewer tablet to call PC Polly Killy to join them.

"PC Killy, please take Mr Diamonds to the surveillance team. We would like a covert surveillance operation to follow Mr Diamonds and his family. Full business and personal viewer monitoring has been authorised. All information and footage to be made accessible only to myself and DS Bailey."

"Yes, sir," says PC Killy.

DS Bailey swipes at her tablet, brings up the surveillance authorisation form then hands the tablet to Albert.

"Albert, please read and sign this form, it will allow us to carry out authorised surveillance of you and your family," says Mirror.

Albert takes the viewer tablet, signs his name without reading the form and hands it back to DS Bailey.

"Albert, thank you for coming in, I promise we will do everything we can to make sure you and your family are safe. If you follow PC Killy to the surveillance team, she will show you what we have in mind," says Mirror.

Albert stands up, walks over to PC Killy, and follows her out.

Chapter 12
The Lizard Points

DS Bailey watches as Albert and PC Killy depart then turns to face Mirror. “How can you trust he won’t tell anyone or go the media? This story would make a nice payday, sir.”

“He won’t do that, Bailey,” says Mirror.

“How can you be so sure, sir?”

Mirror stands from his chair. “Because he wants to protect his wife and stepchildren.”

They leave the interview room and head towards the incident room.

DS Bailey walks slightly ahead to reach the door first and presses number one on the keypad.

“Four, Bailey, we’ve moved operations room.”

“Yes, sir.” DS Bailey presses number four on the keypad.

They momentarily wait while the Time-Share unit unselects one and connects to incident room four.

DS Bailey steps back to invite Mirror to go first. Mirror shakes his head, “Go on, Bailey, in you go.”

DS Bailey looks around the glass-walled room. It is almost identical to the first incident room. The five original TSM-PD team members of DS Chang, PC's Killy, Reeves, Gill and Dragan are all there, but now, the space is much larger, the Time-Share bubble timeline is set to the pre-partitioned original size.

The room is full of officers gathering information on the week's seven "incidents," since they haven't officially been called murders. DS Bailey has never seen so many officers working on a single case. It is the first time in years that any police department has committed so much resource to a single task force. Since the introduction of mainstream Time-Share, the world has generally been a much safer place. More jobs, cheaper production and cheaper goods have all resulted in a vastly improved quality of life for much of the world, which, in turn, has resulted in fewer reasons for people to steal or commit a low-level crime. Serious crime, on the other hand, hasn't really changed much at all, but since such cases are generally few and far between, there still hasn't been this type of an incident-room buzz for a long time.

Bailey follows Mirror over to a desk where PC Dragan and Reeves are working.

"PC Dragan, any news on the five remaining jurors?" asks Mirror.

"Yes, sir, we have them all under surveillance. We've not approached any of them yet, but we are monitoring their movements. They all seem to be getting on with their lives as normal, sir."

"Ok, I want you to stay on surveillance. Don't lose track of any of them, move straight in if you see anything suspicious or a cause for concern. PC Reeves, I want you to work on a new angle. I want you to trace back all the remaining five jurors' movements over the last eight days. Highlight anything that brings them anywhere near Albert Diamonds or the victims we already have."

"Yes, sir."

"You think it might be another juror, sir?" asks DS Bailey.

"No, I don't Bailey, but we leave no stone unturned," he replies, stepping past her. "Come on, Bailey, this way." They head to the far end where Captain Marshall Mason is standing next to a seated DS Chang working on his tablet viewer.

"Sir," says Mirror as he approaches the captain.

"I got your message, Mirror, you've got the full team here, I've looked through your notes. If any of your suspicions are leaked, this will be a media nightmare."

"I'm hoping I'm wrong, sir, but if I'm not and there is a copycat out there, we have until Monday before they kill again. You can guarantee it won't be long after that that the media will start to piece the victims' names together and report their versions of what's going on."

"DS Chang tells me you've asked him to work on opening a judge-sealed file," says Captain Mason.

Mirror stares at DS Chang who in turn lowers his head and eyes to his keyboard.

"No, he hasn't told you, sir, and no, DS Chang is not attempting to open a sealed file, sir," says a straight-faced Mirror, trying to give the captain deniability in case it goes public.

Captain Mason looks at Mirror then at DS Bailey standing next to him.

"I haven't heard a thing, sir," says DS Bailey.

Captain Mason, happy to see DS Bailey becoming a team player, nods at her, walks closer to Mirror and places his hand on his shoulder. "I appreciate what you're both trying to say, but if you're right about this case, I don't care what you do to stop the killer. Mirror, do what you need to do." The captain pats Mirror's shoulder and heads back to his office.

"Thank you, sir," replies Mirror. "What we got, Chang?" he says, quickly redirecting his attention to DS Chang's viewer.

"Working on it, sir," says DS Chang, raising his left eyebrow an inch higher than his right.

"Ok, Chang, maybe try and give me a little more information when I'm asking you what we've got, especially as it's a bit of an important case," says Mirror in a more assertive tone.

DS Bailey is taken aback by Mirror's quick change of tone and temperament.

"Sorry, sir. Yes, I've just started working on the judge-sealed file. So far, it's not accepting any of the usual extracting software, but I've not been beaten yet, I'll get in."

"Ok, good, it's a priority now, Chang. Pull in resources if you need them. What about the solicitor? Any luck?" asks Mirror, calming his tone.

"Yes, sir. I've finally tracked down the elusive Mr Harrison Mann. He lives near Lizard in Cornwall, completely off-grid, running a back-to-basics holiday camp. There are no viewers and hardly any technology – All bookings and enquiries for his campsite are handled by a third-party booking firm called Off-Grid Camping Holidays via the internet, communication is via email which then is forwarded to the campsite via fax, and they redirect any replies. Apparently, it's a bit of a niche market for people who call themselves 'wannabe hippies'. I did, however, manage to get a message out to him via the agency and received responses, and sir, I'm quoting his words here, he said that he's 'far too busy to come up to London', he's 'got chickens to feed'."

"Chickens to feed? Is this guy a bit of joker?" says DS Bailey, joining the conversation.

"After several messages backwards and forwards and another message telling him that it was urgent we talk to him in person, his reply was, 'Book in, we have a cabin, a tent or gipsy caravan still available. We look forward to seeing you.'"

"Definitely a joker," says DS Bailey.

"Book us something for tonight, Chang – two of something, anything, under mine and DS Bailey's names, then get another message to Mr Harrison Mann. Tell him that we are coming, and we will want to speak to him tonight, straight away."

"You and DS Bailey, no problem, sir. "Oh, sir, one thing that did seem odd," says DS Chang.

"What's that, Chang?" asks Mirror.

"Well, it was strange. Not once in all the back and forwarding of messages did he ask why we wanted to talk to him, not once."

"Thank you, Chang, keep working on that file. You're in charge until I get back, send any new information to me as soon as you have anything." Mirror walks away from DS Chang's desk and turns to DS Bailey, "Sorry DS Bailey, I'm assuming you're happy to give up the rest of your weekend?"

DS Bailey smiles at Mirror, "It's ok, sir, I'm treating this weekend like just another couple of days of the week. I've not exactly got any other plans, but I would like to go home, pick up a few things and leave enough food for Charlie first if that's ok?"

"Charlie? Can't your partner sort himself out, Bailey," asks Mirror.

"You're assuming Charlie is a man, sir," replies DS Bailey.

"Ah! Yes, I was, DS Bailey, my apologies, I should have said, 'Can't your partner sort *themselves* out?'" he replies sarcastically, remembering he was meant to be using the most recently approved-and-recommended terminology in his sentencing and thinking maybe Bailey hasn't fully lost that irritating politically correct attitude that had seemed to have been absent over the last couple of days.

"Actually, sir, *she's* my cat," smirks DS Bailey. She walks past Mirror, knowing they've just shared their first bit of banter as he smiles back at her.

"Ok, Bailey, it's a six-hour drive. Go home, get what you need, I'll swing past in an hour, and we'll go." He hopes that type of humour will feature on the drive – it would certainly make for a more relaxed trip.

Mirror walks back to his office. He is ready to go; he has always kept a spare set of clothes and an overnight bag at the office, due to on more than one occasion working late or sleeping in the office. He swipes at the viewer, "Viewer, call Frances."

Frances immediately appears on the screen, she is still in her work apron, a duster in one hand and a bottle of polish in the other. “Hi, Gabriel, this is a surprise,” she says as she continues dusting a bookshelf.

Frances works as a domestic cleaner. Her OCD has made her one of the best around, her clients always rave about how thorough and pristine her work is, yet Mirror would never dream of letting her clean his house. Just the thought of Frances’ over-the-top cleaning and germ phobia in the one place he can usually relax drives him crazy.

“Hi Frances, I’m not coming round tonight, I’m working late. This case is a bit of a bugger.” He sees no point in telling Frances that he is going to Cornwall to interview a witness, he knows how the conversation would go. *Why are you going that far?* and *can’t you send someone else?* and then how she would like to go to Cornwall and her friend had been to Lizard. Usually, he would have been ok to go through all the questions and answers and listen to the story about her friend going to Cornwall, but time is short, and the impending drive is long.

“Oh, that’s a shame love, I was looking forward to seeing you, but it’s ok, it will give me a chance to sort out the garden and the outhouse.”

"Ok, Frances, I'd better go, I'll talk to you soon." Mirror smiles, knowing the garden and the outhouse are already perfect but guaranteeing Frances will still find ways to make it better.

"Bye love, see you soon," Frances replies.

DS Bailey fills up her overnight bag, then walks through to her kitchen, "Charlie, Charlie, where are you, girl?" She hears the familiar buzz and looks towards the back door as a meowing black cat wearing a marble-sized pendant dangling from its collar leaps through the cat flap. The pendant allows the cat flap to set entry to her house's Time-Share bubble. She's only just had the system fitted and is happy to see Charlie has got used to it so quickly. DS Bailey lives in a large Time-Shared townhouse. The original house had belonged to her parents who'd had the Time-Share units installed before they moved out of London to earn extra money by renting out. They had given their daughter one of the Time-Shares as a graduation gift. The house is far too large for DS Bailey's needs, she doesn't use all the rooms, most are still empty. It hadn't made sense for her to furnish areas that she is never going to use. Bailey picks up the cat food and overfills the bowl. She puts down extra water, making sure there is enough so the cat will be happy for a couple of days. Charlie jumps up onto the grey worktop and brushes her head against Bailey's arm then jumps back down as the mobile viewer starts to ring. She gives Charlie a reassuring stroke then answers.

"Come on, Bailey I'm outside," says Mirror.

"Be right there, sir." She turns to the cat, "See you soon, Charlie, be good, and no kitty-kat parties while I'm gone." She gives Charlie one last head stroke, grabs her bag and leaves.

Mirror leans over, presses the passenger lock button, and opens the door for DS Bailey. "In you get, Bailey."

*

It had only been twenty minutes of the journey and it has mostly been travelled in silence. DS Bailey sits awkwardly in the car, wondering how uncomfortable the long drive is going to be. She can't help thinking it wasn't all that long ago that she'd reported DI Mirror to the captain for reasons she'd now come to realise, compared to the events of the last few days, were ever so petty. DI Mirror has, or so it seems, ignored what she'd done. Is it because of the case? Will he, as soon as he has his chance, seek a bit of revenge, or has DI Mirror decided to give her a chance to learn from what she can now clearly see was her being overzealous.

"That's us leaving London, Bailey, onto the first of the motorways." Mirror adjusts his seat closer to the car's dash, "Viewer, convert to self-drive mode." The right-hand side of the car's dash opens, and a steering wheel emerges in front of Mirror. Pedals, gear stick, handbrake and retro-looking dash dials slot into place and Mirror adjusts himself to the newly installed features.

"Sir, you're not going to… are you going to drive?" asks a worried DS Bailey. "Wouldn't it be safer, I mean better to allow the driverless system to be active on such a long journey, sir?"

"Viewer, I'm ready to execute self-drive mode," says Mirror.

The car momentarily slows then speeds back up as Mirror presses the accelerator. He moves the car over to the outside lane and starts to overtake the steady flow of driverless cars in the first two lanes.

"Bailey, if there's one thing I miss, living in London, is driving. Just being able to drive myself somewhere, so there's no way I'm going to be a passenger for the next five hours if I don't have to be, it would drive me nuts."

Mirror smiles as he overtakes the much slower driverless cars.

"But, sir, isn't it safer to use driverless?" repeats DS Bailey, wondering if this is Mirror's way of getting back at her.

"My dad taught me to drive, he loved being in control of a car, especially on longer drives. He used to say the only thing that spoiled the roads was the traffic and other drivers. He once drove across America, following the old Route Sixty-Six, said it was the most relaxing trip he'd ever taken. He would have loved driving on today's roads with the self-driver lanes clear like this. Can you drive, Bailey?"

"I've never seen the point, sir." DI Mirror's sharing of something non-work related has done little to relax her from the unfamiliar self-drive experience, but strangely, she finds herself enjoying the speed, *maybe this journey isn't going to be as awkward as I thought.*

The introduction of driverless cars has improved traffic flow, not just in towns and cities, but also on motorways, primarily thanks to the driverless systems being in control of the vehicles. They can move steadily and fluidly, rarely causing any traffic hold-ups, breakdowns or accidents. The traditional three lanes on motorways are now first and second lanes for driverless vehicles only, and the outer lane exclusively for self-drivers and emergency services. The seventy miles-per-hour maximum speed limit has been removed and replaced with an unlimited speed limit lane. Since the widespread use of driverless, most people don't bother to take their driving test, as there is no need – anyone of any age can own a driverless car without a need for a licence. On-board viewers do all the hard work, which means that hardly anyone uses the outer lane, also meaning clear driving for the minority of real drivers.

*

Five and half hours later – Southwest Road, Lizard Point, Cornwall

Mirror pulls over to the side of the road, stopping just in front of the entrance to Harrison Mann's back-to-basics camping site.

"What's wrong, sir?' asks DS Bailey.

Mirror points to a sign just below the entranceway.

WARNING!

SIGNAL SUPPRESSERS IN USE

NO SIGNAL BEYOND THIS POINT

NO WI-FI – NO VIEWERS

"We'd better check in with Chang before we go in," he says. "Viewer, call DS Chang."

The viewer buzzes once, and DS Chang instantly pops up on the screen.

"Sir," answers DS Chang, raising his right eyebrow.

"Checking in, Chang. We're going to be out of communications range for a while."

"Ok, sir, talk to you soon," replies DS Chang.

"Anything on the file yet? Any other news I need to be aware of?" A hint of frustration tones in Mirror's voice at having to badger for information, information that he should automatically be receiving. "Oh, yes, sir, nothing more than what we already know. PC Killy has sent updates to shared file forty-two, regarding the remaining juror's movements and…" DS Chang pauses and starts to tap his tablet.

"And what about the sealed file?" repeats DS Bailey, sensing Mirror's agitation of having to wait.

"I'm getting there, DS Bailey," says DS Chang. "I've started to extract files. It's going slowly, but we're getting somewhere. I'm sending you the one file we have recovered to your viewer now."

The car's viewer receives a file named "*Witnesses*".

"Viewer, open the file," says DS Bailey.

"It's a small file containing just four names – Harrison Mann, Donald Ayres, Judge Edward C Crowley the Second and a Commander Jacob Lawrence. As you can see, they have all signed the Official Secrets Act for something, but there's no information as yet on what it was they were asked to keep secret sir," says DS Chang.

"Harrison Mann and the judge we are aware of, Chang. Who are the other two? Have you anything on them?" asks Mirror.

"I have, sir, and I think we can eliminate both from the suspect pool," replies DS Chang. "Donald Ayres and his wife emigrated to Australia after winning big on the lottery a few years back. Unfortunately, some time after that, and thanks to his new lavish lifestyle, Mr Ayres had a jet-ski accident, crashing into his yacht, resulting in severe brain damage and amputation of both legs. He's now wheelchair bound. As for Commander Lawrence, he's now Vice-Admiral of His Majesty's Navy intelligence and has been in Washington for the international waters summit the last two weeks. That's all I've got for now, sir, but as soon as I get more files extracted, I'll send them. Oh! One more thing, I've booked your accommodation at the campsite."

"Ok, Chang, thank you," replies Mirror.

DS Chang ends the viewer call.

"The file's called '*Witnesses*', Bailey, and it's dated the same day Maddison Bartel died."

"What do you think they witnessed, sir?" asks DS Bailey.

"Let's go and find out." The car restarts and they enter the gates to Harrison Mann's Back 2 Basics Campsite.

Chapter 13
What Happened the Day They Lied

Tuesday 18th October 2050 – the day of Maddison Bartel's sentencing

Judge Edward C Crowley the Second looked up from his paperwork and addressed a smirking Maddison Bartel. "The court has considered the nature and circumstance of the offences, and I have considered the decision found by the jury. After deliberating all factors, the court finds, as the jury found, the crimes especially cruel. The offences were committed with a series of different weapons and instruments. They involved substantial planning and organisation. The defendant has shown no remorse for his victims, has destroyed evidence at the crime scenes and gone to great lengths to conceal his involvement. I have also considered the emotional and financial harm these offences have caused the victims' families."

Judge Edward C Crowley the Second looked back down to his paperwork, then lifted his head back up, slowly shook it and stared at the defending solicitor, Harrison Mann.

“I acknowledge that the defendant’s counsel has asked for leniency, but he has shown no valid reason as to why this should be granted. It is the court’s ruling that the defendant be given a life sentence and to be imprisoned for the rest of his natural life without the possibility of parole. Bailiffs, please take the prisoner down.”

Two large bailiffs cuffed Maddison then turned him away from the court and led him down the steps at the back of the courtroom.

“Prison’s too good for him, he should be hung,” shouted Carol Christie from the observers’ bench, as she and the other families torn apart by The Slate Killer jeered and hurled abuse at the smiling Maddison being taken away.

“Hang him, hang him, hang him!” shouted the agitated crowd.

Carol turned her attention to the defending solicitor. “You should be ashamed of yourself, trying to defend pure evil.”

Harrison Mann looked dismissively at Carol and continued packing his paperwork into his case. He looked at the growing number of reporters and anti-Maddison crowd at the court's main entrance and decided it best to follow the bailiffs and Maddison via the back exit.

Harrison accepted that taking The Slate Killer case had been a risky move, no other firm would touch it, but it had, at the start, made business sense, or so he had thought. His firm would receive free advertising. He was right, it did; it was now the most searched solicitors' firm on the internet. Had he won the case, he would have become a superstar to every future criminal and murderer out there. I mean, imagine the free publicity that would be gained by the firm that got The Slate Killer off? Even losing the case, his firm would still have earned notoriety, and he could have sold his story to the press. His morals were low when it came to making money. Unfortunately, the gamble had backfired. He hadn't anticipated just how bad the Slate killings were and how much the media and public would be shocked by the case.

Harrison caught up with the slow-moving bailiffs and Maddison.

"You didn't do very well there, did you, Mr Mann?" said the eerily calm Maddison, sensing Harrison walking up behind.

"Err, no but, no, no err, don't worry. I will appeal, and we can…" said Harrison trying to think of something reassuring to say to Maddison.

"I'm sure you will, Mr Mann. Still, it's nice of you to walk me to my transport back to my prison cell."

Harrison had had no intention of walking Maddison to his transport, he'd only gone that way to avoid the crowds. But even cuffed and surrounded by bailiffs, the cold, hypnotic intensity that Maddison's aura gave out to his surroundings made him submissive to his client. "Well, of course, Mr Bartel, you're my client," he said as he followed the little group to the underground secure parking area.

"Well, there's my taxi," said Maddison spotting the plain white prison transport vehicle through the opening at the other end of the corridor. The long-haired driver had propped the door open with a fire extinguisher.

One of the bailiffs held onto Maddison's arm and pulled him sideways, the second bailiff stopped, turned in the doorway and held his hand out to stop Harrison following. "Ok, sir, that's far enough. You will have to wait here until we have loaded the prisoner," said the door-blocking, deep-voiced bailiff.

“Right, of course. Don’t worry, Mr Bartel, I will get you that appeal,” said Harrison Mann, standing on his tiptoes and looking at his client over the shoulder of the burly bailiff.

“Sure you will,” said the bailiff. Turning round in the doorway and taking a step forward at the same time, he brought his back foot forward to take another step and accidentally but firmly kicked into the fire extinguisher, knocking it forcefully to the floor. The fall snapped the plastic hose, pressurised water jetted out of the damaged area, forcing the fire extinguisher airborne. Harrison watched, in what seemed slow motion, as the extinguisher rocketed through the air towards the small group by the prison transport. The long-haired prison transport driver dodged sideways by pushing into Maddison, the sideways push placed Maddison directly into the path of the projectile, hitting him in the back of his head. The impact of the blunt force knocked Maddison’s head forward and into the side of the armour-plated transport vehicle, crushing his face. Maddison dropped, lifeless, to the floor. A painted wash of blood streaked down the white van as he dropped, and the empty fire extinguisher fell to his side.

"Oh, my God!" shouted Harrison. He pushed past the second bailiff and ran over to the blood-covered body on the floor. The bailiffs were stunned and frantic; they had no idea what they were meant to do in this unprecedented situation. "Don't just bloody stand there, call an ambulance!" screamed Harrison to the bailiff closest to him.

Harrison crouched over Maddison, lifted his limp unrecognisable blood-'soaked' head then lowered his ear near to Maddison's mouth to check for signs of breathing. His hand sank into the newly formed dent in the back of Maddison's head. He carefully put Maddison's head back down and checked his neck for a pulse, he spotted bubbles of blood exiting the area of what used to be Maddison's nose.

"It's nothing more than he deserves. It's karma," said the smiling, long-haired prison transport driver knowledgeably.

Harrison's scrupulous business thinking kickstarted as his fingers found a weak pulse. "What's your name? This is my client; he has been seriously injured. He could die whilst in your care, and you make a disgusting comment like that. My client was in the court's care. I'm going to have a field day suing all of you. Now! Where the hell is that bloody ambulance?" he demanded.

"It's on its way, and please, please try and sue me, I'll be seen as a hero, my name's Brian Smale, Brian *Todd* Smale to be exact. Make sure you write it down," said the driver cheekily.

Brian turned to the bailiffs, "I think one of you should ask the judge to join us or at least make him aware of the situation."

*

A few moments later

The ambulance arrived at the secure car park and pulled alongside the transport vehicle. Harrison was crouching over Maddison's near lifeless body. Everyone else, the bailiffs, Brian Smale and the newly arrived Judge Edward C Crowley the Second with his government-appointed security man stood at a distance, none of them inclined to help, as they stared at the man on the floor.

The Maddison case had been high profile, it had drawn worldwide attention and the media circus had inevitably led to the judge and his family receiving death threats and disturbing messages from so-called Slate Killer groupies. The government had stepped in and provided the judge with a military intelligence security detail, for his protection.

The two-person crew jumped out the back of the driverless ambulance, one heading to the injured Maddison, the other towards the bailiffs, driver and judge.

“What we got?” said the ambulance crewman.

“It’s Maddison Bartel,” said one of the bailiffs.

“No, I mean what… Did you say Maddison Bartel?” repeated the ambulance crewman, quickly absorbing the serial killer’s name.

“Yes,” said the judge.

The ambulance crewman called out to his partner, “Jenny, stop, come here.”

The second crewman leaned over the bloodied body, “No, Don, I need you. Come here, this man needs immediate treatment, or we’re going to lose him.”

“Jenny, come here now, please,” reiterated Don.

Jenny, the ambulance nurse, grabbed hold of Harrison’s hand and placed it behind Maddison’s head. “Hold his head up, I’ll be back in two seconds.” She got up and ran over to the distanced group. “What the hell are you doing, Don? I need your help, that man needs your help, both his face and back of the head have been pushed in," she said.

"That man is Maddison Bartel," said Don.

Jenny stopped and slowed her pace as she moved closer to the group. "But we're meant to help everybody without discrimination," she said, doubt quickly making its way to her morals.

"Jenny, I'm not helping that man," said Don. "I'm sure he died before we got here."

Harrison Mann looked over in disbelief at the group gathering and shouted over, "Oi! Can you please come and help me? This man is dying!"

"Who's that?" said Don, turning to the judge.

"That's trouble, he's Maddison Bartel's solicitor," said the judge. Then, in a louder voice, "I think you should take Maddison into the ambulance *as quickly as you can*," he discreetly air-quoted, "then drive *as quickly as you can*," he made the gesture again then lowered his voice once more, "and be careful what you say in front of the solicitor."

"Are you ok with that, Jenny?" asked Don, looking at his partner, knowing exactly what he was asking of her.

Every instinct in Jenny's body was telling her that she was meant to help every human, but did Maddison Bartel classify as a human? "Yes," she replied hesitantly.

The ambulance crew walked over to the body on the floor. Harrison was still holding Maddison's head. "It's ok, sir, we'll take it from here," said Don as he and Jenny crouched next to the man with the crushed face. "I don't think there's much I can do here; we'll have to take him to the hospital."

"Don't you think you should be hurrying along a bit then?" said Harrison as his bloodied hands passed the head back to Jenny.

"Sir, if you can leave this to us, we know what we're doing," said Don.

"Jenny, I'm gonna get the gurney," Don walked slowly over to the ambulance, pulled out the stretcher and walked slowly back.

"What the hell is wrong with you? I've seen faster snails," said Harrison. He took out his mobile viewer and started videoing the ambulance crew.

Jenny and Don realised they had no choice but to do their job at a quicker pace. They placed Maddison on the gurney and carried him to the back of the ambulance as

Harrison continued to record them. They lifted the stretchered Maddison into the back of the driverless ambulance. “I’m coming with you,” said Harrison, attempting to climb into the back. Don stood in front of him, “I’m sorry, sir, we can’t allow that.”

Harrison pointed the viewer camera straight at the ambulance man. “I am his representative, and I’m coming. You seem to be wasting time here. I’m sure your bosses will love the lawsuit I’m going to bring,” he threatened.

Don, the ambulance man, took a step closer and squared up to Harrison. Jenny placed her hand on his shoulder, guessing that the thought of ripping the viewer out of Harrison’s hand and shoving it down his throat was temptingly going through Don’s mind. “Don, don’t, it’s ok.”

The judge and his security detail walked over to the back of the ambulance.

“Sir, I think we should go as well,” suggested the judge’s personal security detail.

“Do you think I should, Mr Lawrence?” asked the judge.

Judge Crowley’s personal security detail, Mr Lawrence, was a military intelligence commander and had been hand-picked by the government due to his impeccable record. “Yes, sir, I think it would be best,” he said, “especially if Mr Mann is insisting on going as well. We are coming too.” He helped the judge up into the ambulance then climbed into the back himself.

Don engaged the driverless ambulance and pulled away. They travelled at speed, with their blues and twos switched on, through the London traffic. All the other driverless vehicles on the road automatically made way, clearing the route. Jenny monitored Maddison’s pulse. “It’s very weak, should we connect life support?”

She looked over at Don who slowly shook his head, “No, I think that will do more harm than good at this stage. We are nearly at the hospital; the surgeons can see what’s best when we get there.”

Jenny knew Don was lying, connecting life support was the obvious situational choice, but she couldn’t bring herself to correct him. “I think we’re losing him,” she said.

Harrison alternated pointing the video viewer between the judge and the two crewmen then back over to Maddison’s blood-messed head.

“His heart has stopped,” alerted Jenny. She stretched over to grab the defibrillator paddles. Don grabbed her hand, stopping her from reaching and before Harrison's camera turned back to them.

"It's too late, Jenny, there's nothing more we can do," said Don, holding Jenny's hand in more of a supporting way as the camera turned back to him. Don felt for a pulse and confirmed there was none. Harrison continued pointing the camera towards him. "Judge, unfortunately, this man has died. Would you like me to call time of death?" said Don, looking at the judge and then purposefully towards the camera as if he was reporting the news.

The judge looked round to Mr Lawrence and received a nod. "Yes, call it, please," replied Judge Edward C Crowley the Second.

Don looked round to the camera, relishing the announcement he was about to make – the death of The Slate Killer. He looked over to the ambulance clock. "Time of death, one thirty-four p.m." He smiled into the camera, imagining how much happiness the news of Maddison Bartel's timely demise would bring to so many people and that he was the one who had called time.

The ambulance arrived outside the emergency department of St Thomas' Hospital. Jenny opened the back and jumped out, eager to escape the claustrophobic confines of the ambulance. She headed straight to the emergency room and waved the standby team of waiting doctors and nurses back into the hospital. "It's too late, guys, we've got a DOA. Don't worry, back in."

"I'm not letting this go," said Harrison, looking at the judge and his security detail.

Don jumped out of the ambulance and waited to help the judge down the steps.

"Do what you think best, Mr Mann," replied the judge as he exited the ambulance, followed by the silent Commander Lawrence.

Harrison turned the camera back to the motionless body, then pointed it back at the judge then started to exit the ambulance. His descent was halted as a tug on his arm made him suddenly stop. He turned to see Maddison's hand gripping his jacket sleeve. He re-pointed the camera back at Maddison, who was not only breathing but regaining consciousness. Commander Lawrence, noticing the resuscitated Maddison, pushed the judge and Don back towards the ambulance and herded them into the back, pulling the doors shut behind him.

“Where am I? What’s happened?” said the croaky blood-gurgling voice from the gurney.

“You’re a free man,” said Harrison, smirking at the judge.

“I don’t think so, mate,” said Don, shaking his head.

“I do, I’ve got it all recorded, and it’s all thanks to you, Mr Ambulance Man. Isn’t that right, Your Honour?” said Harrison, as the realisation dawned that he was on the verge of the greatest of escape acts a solicitor has ever performed, making him feel unstoppable.

The judge shook his head in disbelief. He knew exactly what Harrison was getting at. “Please put this man on life support,” he requested, looking towards the stunned ambulance man.

“You can’t do this, Harrison; it will cause a media storm and public outrage,” said the judge.

“I have it all on video, if it doesn’t go back to court, I will go to the media,” threatened Harrison.

“What the hell are you two talking about? What’s all thanks to me?” said Don.

“I gave him a life sentence without parole; he was to be incarcerated for the rest of his natural life, meaning Maddison would not have left prison until he was dead.”

The judge looked at Don, "And *you* pronounced him dead."

"No way! This ain't happening," said Don, struggling to comprehend what he was hearing.

"Put him on life support now, or I'll make sure your name is given to the media as the man responsible for Maddison Bartel being let go," said Harrison, feeling as if he was now king of the situation.

"What's happening? Where am I?" gargled the unrecognisable pulp of mush that was once Maddison's face.

"It's ok, Mr Bartel. It's Harrison Mann, your solicitor. You've had an accident. We're going to take you straight to surgery."

"Who's Mr Bartel? Who's Harrison Mann? Why do I need a solicitor?" replied Maddison, struggling to talk through the blood.

"Do you know who Maddison Bartel is?" asked Commander Lawrence, pushing Harrison along to lean over the patient.

"I don't know him. Is he the one who did this to me? What's happened to me? Where am I?" asked the body on the gurney as he slowly slipped back out of consciousness.

“Oh, my God, he doesn’t remember,” said Judge Edward C Crowley the Second, realising that the situation had just become even more complicated.

“Don, I am a representative of His Majesty’s Government. My name is Commander Lawrence, do you understand?” said Mr Lawrence to the stunned ambulance man.

“Ye-yes, sir,” said Don.

“Ok, Don. I’m taking charge of this situation, and I’m ordering you,” Commander Lawrence looked at Harrison, “both of you, for this to be kept quiet for now.”

“The public has a right to know, and I have a right to protect my client. Everything I’m videoing is being uploaded straight to my secure server,” said Harrison, seeming to be in automatic mode as he repeated the same words, his viewer still videoing but now continually pointing at the gurgling body on life support.

“Mr Mann, if you want to continue working as a lawyer, shut up and leave this to me, and turn that bloody camera off,” ordered Commander Lawrence, grabbing the mobile viewer from Harrison and switching it off.

“Yes, yes, ok,” replied a suddenly deflated Harrison.

"Don, can you drive this ambulance?" said Mr Lawrence.

"It's driverless, sir."

"I know that Don. Does this vehicle have driver override fitted, and can you drive it?"

"Yes, err, I've been trained to drive it, sir," answered the confused Don.

"Ok, good, Don. I want you to manual-drive this ambulance away from here. I want you to head out of London towards the M1," instructed the commander. "Now! Please, Don."

The judge took out his viewer to make a call. Commander Lawrence stopped him by holding the top of the judge's viewer. "Sorry, Your Honour, no calls for now, please. I will explain everything soon," he said, reassuringly.

"Please, all sit back. It is not in anyone's best interest to attract media attention to this situation until we have had time to assess," said Commander Lawrence.

The commander took out his communicator viewer. A uniformed woman appeared on the viewer screen and saluted, "Sir."

"Afternoon, Sergeant Bunnage, please inform medical I have an injured man coming in. We are in a civilian ambulance, estimated arrival one to one and a half hours, no record to be made of our arrival," ordered Commander Lawrence.

"Yes, sir," replied the woman.

Commander Lawrence moved to the front of the ambulance and handed Don his viewer tablet in navigation mode with a route laid in. "Don, I want you to follow the navigators' directions, please. We are heading towards Chicksands military base in Bedfordshire."

"Ok," said Don. He took the viewer tablet and set it in view on the dash.

The three passengers stared in silence at the steadily breathing patient lying on the gurney as Don taxied them on their surreal journey.

*

One hour twenty minutes later

The ambulance turned into a quiet, tree-lined road as it reached its destination and was waved straight through the heavily armed security barrier to enter the Chicksands base.

Commander Lawrence opened the back of the ambulance and was immediately greeted by the waiting Sergeant Bunnage and a military medical team. "Take the patient straight in, please," he ordered.

The team lifted the patient out of the ambulance and wheeled him away.

"Your Honour, Don, Mr Mann, you are in a high-security area. Please hand your tablets and viewers to Sergeant Bunnage, then please follow her to the waiting area. I will join you and update you as soon I have something," said the commander.

The three unnerved men complied with the request and followed the sergeant into the building nearest to them.

*

Fifty-eight minutes later

Harrison paced and Don sat at a table, frustratedly banging his hand against the wall as they both expressed their impatience of waiting in a cold-walled room. The judge seemed calm and waited patiently. The base gave the impression that it had eluded the Time-Share revolution and had kept its original cold, barracks look from the 1950s.

The three roommates simultaneously turned to look as Commander Lawrence enters.

"What the hell is going on?" said Don, jumping up from his chair, loudly directing his voice towards the commander. "I should have finished work ages ago. My wife will be going mad worrying."

"Yes, what the hell is going on? You have no right to keep us here," added Harrison, moving next to Don to face an unfazed commander.

The judge walked over and placed one hand on each of the irritated men's shoulders, softly beckoning them apart to walk in between them. "What is the situation? Mr Lawrence?" he asked with a much calmer tone than the situation warranted.

"Please sit, gentlemen," requested Commander Lawrence.

The commander walked past the three men and sat towards the top end of the desk, he held out his hand and waved it towards the chairs, re-inviting them to sit. He handed each them a set of virtual paperwork files, each one with the name of the individual receiver on the cover.

Harrison picked up his file. "Ok, what's going on?"

"Your Honour, gentlemen, the patient is stable and has regained consciousness. At present, I believe that he does not know who he is and has no memory recall beyond the last couple of hours. An MRI brain scan has been performed and has shown several brain bleeds that may have caused permanent damage to his memory. The medical team's initial assessment is that he will have permanent amnesia. He doesn't remember who he is or anything that he has done in the past' explained Commander Lawrence.

"What the hell does that mean?" asked Don.

"It means we have a problem, don't we, Mr Mann?" said the judge, looking at Harrison.

"That's right, Your Honour. Unfortunately, you have all placed the government in a very difficult position. As far as the rest of the world will know, Maddison Bartel died on the way to the hospital in that ambulance. The four of us here are the only people to know any different. The team caring for him have only been made aware that they are looking after a 'John Doe' with a squashed face. I have told them that we don't yet know his name either, so they have conducted the self-identity tests 'blind'. Gentlemen, this situation could not have been predicted, but I know the government will demand deniability, and I have been tasked to do what I believe will be for the best," said Commander Lawrence.

"You're going to kill us..." said Don, backing out of his chair towards the rear wall.

"No, they wish they could, but I'm guessing they're going to offer us deals, aren't you, Mr Lawrence?" smirked Harrison, realising his amateur camerawork was about to come in handy.

"What will happen to Maddison?" asked the judge.

"Well, thanks to Mr Harrison and Don here, The Slate Killer legally no longer has a prison sentence. Luckily, the man in there no longer knows who he is, and maybe that's for the best," said Mr Lawrence.

"So, what will you do with him?" asked the judge.

"We will watch him, monitor his progress, rebuild his face, give him some made-up story as to how he got here, and if he continues to show no sign of recall, give him a new identity," explained Commander Lawrence.

"How the hell can that be right?" shouted Don angrily. "That man has killed and ruined lives, and this idiot is defending him. He should be put down; he should be dead!"

"I agree, Don. Apart from this slug of a solicitor, we all agree. The trouble is, and don't ask me as to why or how, but unfortunately, the man in our medical ward is no longer Maddison Bartel," said Commander Lawrence.

"This is ridiculous, you wait till I get out of here. I'm going straight to the papers," said Don.

"Before you do that, please take a few minutes to read the files in front of you. I will then speak to you in turn before you go." The commander stood up and walked out. The three men picked up their named files and started to read.

*

Sergeant Bunnage entered the room. "Mr Ayres, please follow me." Don, taken aback by the use of his surname, looked up from his reading.

Sergeant Bunnage led him along the corridor to an office where Commander Lawrence was sitting behind a desk, waiting. "Please sit, Don. Have you read your file?" asked Mr Lawrence.

"Yes."

"As you can see, Don, we know everything about you. Everything. Including a certain gambling habit that has amassed a very large debt of which I'm sure your wife is not aware. Yet," hinted the commander.

"I'm authorised to offer you something, but in return, we would like you to sign the Official Secrets Act which will legally bind you to not reveal anything that happened after you pronounced Maddison Bartel dead. If anybody asks where you've been, you simply reply that you needed a bit of time out after a long and somewhat traumatic day at work. I'm sure they will understand. In return, we will pay off all your debts and arrange a small windfall from the lottery ticket that you will buy on your way home tonight," said the commander.

"Am I going to win the lottery?" asked Don excitedly.

"Don, do you understand what I'm asking of you? After you sign this form, you will be arrested and charged with breaking the Official Secrets Act if you leak any information," affirmed Commander Lawrence.

Don looked over at Commander Lawrence and smiled. "I think I can forget what's happened today quite easily," he said as realisation dawned that his family's problems were about to be solved. Commander Lawrence passed a form tablet over to Don. "Sign here, please."

Don placed his right hand over the tablet screen and signed his digital signature.

“Thank you, Don. Follow Sergeant Bunnage, she will show you out and arrange your onward journey home – via a newsagent, obviously,” said Commander Lawrence as he buzzed for his sergeant to come back in. “Sergeant Bunnage, please show the judge in next, thank you.”

“Yes, sir. Mr Ayres, this way, please,” instructed Sergeant Bunnage as she led a smiling Don out.

The judge entered the office. “Please sit, Your Honour. I’m sorry for putting you through this, sir,” said Commander Lawrence.

“Don’t worry, I completely understand, Mr Lawrence. If anything, I’m ashamed of the way I’ve behaved. I was ready to let that man die when I should have been representing the law, not deciding who lives and who dies.”

“No one would have blamed you, Your Honour. That was a monster of a man, yet now, we are in a bit of a dilemma as to what to do for the best. The man in there is a blank canvas, he has no memory of what he’s done. If we try to imprison him, it would be like imprisoning an innocent man, and as for that solicitor, he’s like a dog with a bone and will never let it go if he's allowed to get the word out. I know it sounds strange, but we need to protect you and the government from any comeback."

"What would you like from me?" asked the judge.

"Firstly, we need to agree that Maddison Bartel died in the back of that ambulance. Next, if this patient recovers and shows no sign of who he was, we will need to give him a new identity, a cover story. We will need you to sign the seal order to hide the file. I will include in it the truth of what happened today and all the concealed aspects of the case that were not revealed to the jury or public during the trial. You will be the only person to authorise the release of these details once they are sealed if ever that becomes a necessity. Do you understand, Your Honour?

"Yes, I understand," said Judge Edward C Crowley the Second.

"Thank you, Your Honour. Sergeant Bunnage will come through in a short while to arrange your return to London. I've now got to deal with the audacious solicitor." He got up and headed back to the waiting room where Mr Harrison Mann was pacing.

"At bloody last," he said as Commander Lawrence entered.

"Mr Mann, did you read through your file?"

"I did, and it's a bit of a joke, isn't it?" replied Harrison. "Not only do you want me to stay quiet about what I've seen today, but you want me to quit being a solicitor. I don't think so. I've got everything on video. As soon as I'm out of here, the news desk will be my first port of call," he threatened.

"Mr Mann, your servers have been seized, along with any data uploaded today. They, along with your viewer, have been wiped. I have made sure that the judge and Mr Ayres will not be saying anything, so there's only your word about what happened today. In the meantime, a statement has already been issued to the media informing them of his death, and I'm sure we can find a random John Doe's body if we need it as further proof. Mr Mann, you have no close family to speak of, your whole life has revolved around your law firm and making money. We can either make sure you and your business are ruined and ridiculed, or we can allow you to start a new life somewhere else, maybe even help you with a new business venture. Just not in practising law," the commander subtly threatened back.

"Oh, my God, you're blackmailing me," said Harrison.

"Mr Mann, I wouldn't call it blackmail, it's more of a suggestion of extremes with polar opposite endings. All you have to do is to decide whether you sign the Official Secrets Act form and choose a new life or not sign and watch your world crumble. The choice is yours." The commander remained straight-faced.

Harrison was shaking. He'd been plunged into a nightmare and could see only one way to go to make it end.

"What's it going to be, Harrison?" insisted Commander Lawrence.

Harrison looked at the tablet form waiting for his signature, moved his hand closer and looked up at Commander Lawrence. "I want a holiday village in Cornwall, Lizard Point." He had no idea why he'd asked that, it had never been an intention or ever entered his head that he'd want to run a holiday camp, but the stress of the day and the realisation of his situation had thrown his mind back to a happier time and place, to when he was a child and his parents would take him to Cornwall on holiday, more specifically, the day they had visited Lizard Point. He and his dad had stood at the top of the cliff, looking out to the Atlantic Ocean, watching the giant waves as they crashed onto the rocks below.

"Ok Harrison, I will see what I can do," promised Commander Lawrence.

Harrison moved his right hand over to the tablet and signed the form, legally binding him to remain silent about the strangest of days…

Chapter 14

Revelations at the Back 2 Basics Campsite

Saturday 27th September 2059 – evening

Mirror drives along the long, winding dirt road that leads to the campsite. DS Bailey looks at her mobile viewer, then checks the car's viewer. "The sign at the entrance wasn't wrong, no signal, sir."

"Look, Bailey." Mirror points to two masts either side of the dirt path, then moves his finger through the air to follow a series of camouflaged masts through the woods and into the distance.

"What are they, sir?" asks DS Bailey.

"I think they're signal suppressors, Bailey. They've purposely made a dampening field around the campsite, that's why there's no signal."

"Who would want to live off-grid like this? I mean it's not for me, and I can almost understand if someone wants a short break, a getaway to switch off for a bit, but Harrison Mann has lived like this for the past nine years."

"I know what you mean, Bailey. What would make a hotshot lawyer give it all up, move to the edge of nowhere and switch himself off to the world? I'm guessing the answer might have something to do with a form he signed back in 2050."

"The Official Secrets Act form, sir?" says DS Bailey, acknowledging she is thinking along the same lines as her senior officer. Mirror looks at her and nods.

The bumpy, twisting road ends at a large paddock car-parking area. Several large wooden buildings, interconnected by a boardwalk, are at the furthest end of it. A wooden archway with a sign above reading "*Welcome 2 Harrison's Campsite*" stands at the base of the boardwalk steps that lead to the wooden buildings. Behind the buildings, they can see a large, open field containing various types of vintage gipsy caravans, tents and small log cabins scattered throughout and stretching out to the cliff's edge at Britain's most southerly point.

Mirror pulls into a parking bay, and they both exit the car. "Shall we take our bags with us now, sir," asks DS Bailey.

"Let's see if we can talk to Mr Mann first, I'd rather not stay if we don't have to," replies Mirror.

They walk over to the large wooden archway, climb the steps to the boardwalk, then stop to read the signpost at the top. It points to various directions and activities. "That way, sir," says DS Bailey, pointing towards the building directly in front of them.

They enter the reception area. "it's like I'm stepping into a scene from Grizzly Adams. Have we gone back in time?" says Mirror.

"Grizzly Adams, sir?"

"It's a very old TV series, even before my time."

At one end of the reception is a wood firepit. Rough carved wooden tables and chairs surround the crackling flames, something DS Bailey has never seen before because of the open flame in cities ban which was introduced to control air pollution.

Mirror looks around and makes a mental note of not seeing any kind of technology. The furniture, rugs, the ornaments, even the paintings on the wooden walls look handmade.

They approach the desk and are quickly greeted by a tall, long-haired woman wearing a hand-knitted fleece poncho.

"Good evening, folks, my name's Melanie, are you checking in?" she asks cheerfully.

“Hi Melanie, I’m DI Mirror and this is DS Bailey. We were wondering if we could have a chat with Mr Mann. Is he about?”

Melanie looks over her left shoulder to the cuckoo clock on the back of the wall. “Oh no, no chance, my lover, it’s eight-thirty. Harrison will be taking those dogs of his down the cliff path for their walk.”

“Ok, what time does he usually get back from walking the dogs, ma’am?” asks DS Bailey.

“Oh, he won’t be back till morning now, my love. Harrison walks those lucky devils for ages, then he’ll camp up somewhere for the night. He does love his outdoors and early nights.”

“So, he’s not coming back here tonight then? Is there any way you could get a message to him, to see if we could have a word tonight?” asks Mirror.

“Oh, I wouldn’t know where to begin, my love. As you know, we’re all about being retro ’ere, so no viewers. But don’t worry, he’s usually back about five-thirty in the morning to feed the chickens,” replies the laid-back Melanie. “So, did you say you ’ave got reservations, my love? If not, we do ’ave a couple of tents you could hire. I mean, it’s starting to get dark, and we’ve got singing by the firepit in the top field at nine, you won't want to miss that, it's so much fun."

Mirror looks over to DS Bailey to check whether her facial expression matches his feelings. The thought of singing around a firepit isn't for him, and by the look on DS Bailey's face, it's not her cup of tea either. "We should have reservations under Mirror and Bailey," he says.

Melanie picks up her notepad and slowly flicks through by lifting one page at a time over on themselves.

"So, you really don't have any form of technology here?" enquires DS Bailey, her frowned expression saying all it needs to as she watches the women flicking through real paper.

"Oh no, my love, none at all. It's heaven, well, apart from Harrison's old landline in his log shack, he's got it hooked to an old fax machine which he uses to receive our bookings from the agency. Right, let's see, ah! Here we go, that's right, we've got a log cabin and a gipsy caravan reserved for you by a Detective Sergeant Yik Chang." Melanie puts a couple of clip-boarded forms in front of Mirror and DS Bailey then places two feathered quills and an inkpot in the middle. "If you can both sign here, then I'll show you where you're going."

Mirror and DS Bailey simultaneously pick up the quills and stare at the feathered stalks. It has been a while since either of them has held a real pen or a pencil, let alone a used one. Now, they are faced with the prospect of using something from the Victorian age. Everything today is digitally signed, either by a fingerprint or digital tablet squiggle.

Mirror dips the quill deep into the ink then lifts it over to the paper. As the nib touches the paper, the overload of ink stored in the feather's hollow shaft results in his signature merging into a blob of black. DS Bailey, learning quickly, gently dips her quill into the pot then taps off the excess ink and executes a much neater signature.

Melanie picks up their completed forms, places them on a back shelf and smiles at DI Mirror, "Looks like this one might take a bit longer to dry." She heads out to the boardwalk, "Right, follow me."

"Right, my loves if you follow the green-tagged ribbon pathway, it'll lead you to your accommodation. There's only one cabin in the green-tagged field, and it'll be the red gipsy caravan. If you fancy a drink or something to eat later, there's a bar and firepit barbeque in the top field until two in the morning, just follow the yellow-tagged ribbon pathway, and it will take you straight there. If you need anything else, I'll be in reception till about midnight."

"Thank you, Melanie. Where's the chickens?" asks Mirror.

"Oh, you'll hear them in the morning, they're just over there, behind the activities shack," replies Melanie, pointing along the wooden boardwalk to the furthest building.

"Anything else, me lovelies, just ask." Melanie turns and walks away.

"Oh, just one more thing, please, Melanie. Has Harrison Mann left the campsite over the last couple of weeks?"

Melanie carries on walking and laughs, "Oh, my dear Mr Mirror, you don't know Mr Mann very well, do you? He hasn't left the campsite in years; he's got everything he needs right here."

Mirror and Bailey watch Melanie walk back into her reception. "Looks like we're staying, sir," says DS Bailey.

Mirror slowly nods his head, "Yep, guess we are. Let's get the bags, Bailey."

"Yes, sir," both silently agreeing there wasn't much else to be said about where they were.

They walk back to the pathway and follow the lantern-lit, green-tagged ribbon pathway to the green-tagged field.

"There's the red gipsy caravan, Bailey, do you want that or the cabin?"

"I'll take the cabin, sir, it looks safer. I don't fancy the caravan suddenly rolling off over the edge of the cliff in the middle of the night."

"Well, at least it will bring an end to this nightmare case for one of us, Bailey."

"Put your bag in your cabin, Bailey. Meet back here in a couple of minutes. We'll get a quick bite to eat then call it a night. I want us to catch Mr Harrison Mann when he feeds those chickens then get out of here."

*

Sunday 28th September 2059 – 5:20 a.m.

DS Bailey opens the door to her cabin and spots Mirror walking over. "Morning, sir. I can't remember the last time I was up this early. Did you get any sleep?"

"Not much, Bailey. I was worried that the caravan would roll off the cliff."

There is a hint of a smile as DS Bailey stifles a yawn and closes her door, giving Mirror an embarrassing semi-opened mouth stare as she walks over.

“Well, in case you’re wondering, I didn’t get much sleep either, sir. I was contemplating all night if I should take the brakes off your gipsy caravan then come and back to sleep and get a lie-in,” says DS Bailey. DI Mirror gives her an uncharacteristic smile, impressed that she is comfortable enough to banter back so readily.

“Come on then, Bailey, let’s go find ex-solicitor-turned-chicken-feeder Harrison Mann and find out what he knows.”

They walk back along the green-tagged path and head to the main wooden buildings at the front of the campsite. Mirror isn’t superstitious but finds himself looking down at the clover as they walk, hoping to find a four-leaf one that might bring him a bit of luck with the case.

“I think the receptionist said the chickens are over there, sir,” says DS Bailey, pointing towards the furthest building. The familiar sound of clucking grows louder as they walk, confirming they are heading in the right direction. They arrive at a fenced-off chicken paddock. In the middle of the paddock is a man surrounded by clucking hens, wearing an oversized duffle coat and a baseball cap, holding a grey metal bucket in one hand, and using the other to spread chicken feed.

Mirror and DS Bailey walk towards the gate and halt sharply as two white German Shepherds pop out from the overgrown grass then walk over to sit either side of the paddock gate. DS Bailey moves back behind DI Mirror as the sudden appearance of the two large dogs makes her jump. Then, realising it looks like she is putting Mirror in the line of fire, she steps back beside Mirror, "Sorry sir."

The dog on the left lets out a loud but friendly bark to alert the man feeding the clucking chickens.

"Hello, campers," calls the man from the paddock. "Oh, don't worry about them, they wouldn't hurt a fly. Buffy! Thorn! *AWAY!*" The white, wolf-like dogs' ears prick up as they pay attention to their owner's call, then slowly trot back over to the long grass.

"Come in, come in," says the waving man.

Mirror opens the paddock gate and invites DS Bailey to go through first.

"I think that's him, Bailey," says Mirror.

"I think you right, sir, he's got a beard and longer hair, but it definitely looks like him," agrees DS Bailey.

The two police officers greet the man.

"Good morning, good morning. I see you two are like me – early birds. How have you found the campsite so far? Are you booked in for long?"

"We're police officers, sir. We were wondering if we could have a word with you. Are you Mr Harrison Mann?" asks DS Bailey.

"Oh! You're the police officers. I did get a message from someone in Scotland Yard yesterday saying that a DI Mirror would be coming to have a chat with me. I thought you were guests. Still, how are you finding your stay so far?"

"Sir, can you confirm that you are Harrison Mann?" repeats DS Bailey.

"Oh, yes, sorry, didn't I say. That's me, and this is my campsite," replies Harrison. He puts the bucket on the ground and heads over to a chicken coup at the far end of the paddock.

Mirror and DS Bailey look at each other in disbelief at how unconcerned Harrison is being, then follow him to the chicken coup.

"Mr Mann, can you please just stop so we can have a word with you?" says DS Bailey with a slight irritation in her voice.

Harrison picks up a metal bowl by the side of the chicken coup, opens a hatchway and walks inside.

"Yes, yes, of course, carry on. Don't worry, I can hear you from here, best I don't stop, as I really must gather these eggs. Need to get them over to the kitchen so I can get them ready for the campers' breakfasts – they'll all be getting up soon," says Harrison, shuffling along the chicken coup.

DS Bailey looks at Mirror, "Is this man for real, sir?"

Mirror looks down for that much-needed bit of luck in the grass, gently moving the clovers with his foot to distract himself from the growing irritation inside.

"Sir, please can you come out of the chicken coup," asks DS Bailey.

"Yes, yes, be out in a jiffy," replies Harrison.

Mirror shakes his head, looks at DS Bailey as she lets out a defeated, "Huh," and gestures her to go into the chicken coup to get Harrison out.

"Err! No thank you, sir!"

They follow Harrison along the outside of the coup, watching him collect his eggs through the chicken-wire-covered windows.

“Sir, as I have said, we are police officers and would like to ask you a few questions. Have you left the campsite any time over the last couple of weeks?”

Harrison holds an egg up to the light then slowly places it in his basket. “Oh no, I can’t remember the last time I left home, apart from roaming the surrounding countryside with the dogs.”

“Why did you give up being a solicitor nine years ago, Mr Mann?” asks DS Bailey.

“For the quiet life, my dear,” replies a laid-back Harrison.

“This is getting us nowhere, Bailey,” says Mirror, close to breaking point. “Why did you and three others have to sign the Official Secrets Act the day Maddison Bartel died?” asks Mirror abruptly, hoping that his curt manner will prompt a more rewarding reply from Harrison.

Harrison pauses momentarily, then continues collecting his eggs, “Well if I told you, it wouldn’t be a secret anymore, now, would it?”

Mirror picks up on the slight delay in Harrison's response and realises he has, at last, got a reaction – something he can exploit. "Has the signing of the Official Secrets Act got something to do with Maddison Bartel's death? And what have Donald Ayers and a Commander Lawrence got to do with the same secret?"

Harrison stops collecting eggs and stares through the opposite chicken-wired window, away from where Mirror and DS Bailey are standing.

"Shall I tell you what I think, Mr Mann? I think you were forced to quit. I think there was something about the case and Bartel's death that the public was never meant to find out about." Mirror could tell he'd hooked his target. Harrison's body language has changed, he is less comfortable, and his egg-hunt has come to a complete stop. "Mr Mann, I'm going to be straightforward with you, we believe that someone is copying the Maddison Bartel killings, and they have started targeting people involved in the court case. Now! As you were involved, and as you could be a potential target, we thought you might want to help. We were hoping that you might be able to shed light on any possible suspects or any reasons why the killer is targeting these individuals. But since you don't have anything helpful to say or, indeed, seem at all bothered with us being here, or at all bothered that you could be a potential target, I'm guessing you'll be ok to deal with any encounters you may have with this copycat. Come on, Detective Sergeant Bailey, we've wasted enough time here. We need to get back to London." Mirror turns to walk away then stops as he spots a five-leaf clover on the ground and bends over to pick it up.

"Wait!" calls Harrison.

Mirror carefully places the five-leaf clover inside the flip cover of his mobile viewer. "Come on Bailey," he says as he puts it in his pocket, "let's start walking away, I think our luck with the unhelpful Harrison Mann is about to change," he says, heading towards the gate.

Harrison exits the chicken coup, "Wait! What makes you think there's a copycat?" he asks, his voice suddenly sounding official and rushed.

Mirror and DS Bailey stop, turn back around and allow Harrison to catch up. "What makes you think it's a copycat?" he repeats.

"Maybe there's somewhere we could sit and talk, Mr Mann?" says Mirror.

"Follow me," replies Harrison.

Mirror and DS Bailey move slightly apart, allowing him to walk between them. Harrison opens the gate to the paddock and is instantly joined by his two white German Shepherds. "We can talk in my office. *Later*, I have to get these eggs to the kitchen and get breakfast on the go for the rest of the guests first, your welcome to have some."

*

They leave the canteen and make their way to the wooden boardwalk's second building and enter a door labelled "*Office*".

"Come in, please sit." Harrison points over to a floor area, furnished with scattered beanbags circled a hand-carved wooden table made from a tree trunk. The dogs walk past and head through to another room.

"Once again, what makes you think it's a copycat?" Harrison repeats, with renewed eagerness to get an answer. Mirror and DS Bailey awkwardly fall into the beanbags. "That's the question you ask?" says Mirror.

"Sorry?" says Harrison.

"We've been trying to talk to you the last couple of days, messaging and now in person, we've wasted over two hours while you gather eggs, cook, and serve breakfast then watched you do dishes, and not once have you asked or seemed bothered as to why or given us a sensible reply to our questions. Now, you're asking why we think it's a copycat? We have our reasons to suspect it's a copycat. Maybe, after you've answered our questions properly, we can then answer yours."

"Ok," says Harrison. "What do you want to know?"

DS Bailey takes out her tablet viewer and starts to record the interview.

"Now, once more for the record, have you left the campsite at any time in the last two weeks?" asks Mirror.

"No, apart from walking the dogs and popping to my shack to check the fax machine" answers Harrison.

"Why did you quit practising law after the Maddison case?" asks Mirror.

"There are two different answers to that question – the reason that the general public knows and the real reason," replies Harrison. "The first answer I have already given you – because I wanted a quiet life, which, in a way, is not that far from the truth. The second depends on why you think there's a copycat."

"What do you mean it depends on why we think there's a copycat? You're not making much sense, sir, and we haven't got time for riddles," insists DS Bailey.

Harrison chuckles to himself, dismissing DS Bailey's comment. "Well, as you have already guessed, I quit practising law because I was rudely told, by the loveable Commander Lawrence, that I had no choice in the matter, but unfortunately, I am in the very awkward position of not being able to tell you why. You see, I signed the Official Secrets Act, meaning I can't reveal that… are you following, DI Mirror and DS Bailey?" says Harrison with a sarcastic tone to his voice.

Mirror and DS Bailey look at each other, wondering how much more useful information they can get from Harrison or whether they are just going to go around in circles.

"So, you see, unless you give me a life-or-death reason to break the very official document I signed and risk prosecution, maybe you could tell me something that would make it all worthwhile, like why do you think it's a copycat?" he asks again.

Mirror takes a moment to think, weighing up the risks of sharing with Harrison the information of an active investigation, an investigation that has, so far, been kept under the media and public radar. He looks round to DS Bailey. "Bailey, I don't see we have many choices. If we don't get a break in this case before tomorrow, the chances are we will have another murder, then it won't be long before the media find out and then all hell will break loose.

"What do you mean by 'another murder tomorrow'?" asks Harrison.

"Tell him, DS Bailey," says Mirror.

"Mr Mann, over the last couple of weeks, we have had seven deaths. All the deceased are on a list. What list, you may ask? All the seven deceased were jurors in the Maddison Bartel trial. Each one was killed by a so-called Time-Share accident. The murders, or should I say *suspected* murders, have happened on consecutive weekdays. Now, Mr Mann, does any of that sound familiar to you at all?" says DS Bailey.

Although unnerving, it was the first time Mirror had been happy with the level of sarcasm DS Bailey's voice.

"Yes, I, I guess it does sound very familiar." A slight tremor appeared in Harrison's voice.

"Now, Mr Mann," Mirror pauses, looks at Bailey then back to Harrison, "Harrison, is there anything you can tell us that might give us a clue as to who we are looking for? Was there anybody else involved in the case that we should know about? Did Maddison Bartel have any helpers or followers?"

In a fluid movement, Harrison rises from the beanbag and walks behind Mirror and DS Bailey. The look on his face has changed to match the hint of fear in his voice. "No, DI Mirror, DS Bailey. Maddison Bartel was a very, very clever man, a genius, a manipulator, but he worked alone. What makes you so sure they weren't accidents? The people who died, what makes you sure?"

Mirror and DS Bailey both pick up on Harrison's mood change and turn slightly in their beanbags to face him.

"We have no solid proof that they weren't accidents, and we have nothing to prove that they were, but I'm guessing even you, Mr Mann, are thinking that it's too much of a coincidence that seven of the twelve jurors have been killed over the last week and a half," says DS Bailey.

"Harrison, my guts telling me that you're hiding something, something that can help. Tell us. We know you've signed the Official Secrets Act, but there are lives on the line, lives that you can help us to save. We have located the sealed file which we believe contains everything you know. It can only be opened on the judge's authority, but that's no longer possible, as unfortunately, the judge has since passed away. By the time we get it open, we might be too late. So, please, if you have anything that could help, tell us," says Mirror.

Harrison gives himself a moment to absorb the conversation "Follow me, we're going to my shack." He walks through to the other room where the dogs are.

DS Bailey quickly stands up then offers her hand to offer help to the beanbag-swallowed Mirror. He gives her a friendly frown and awkwardly gets up to follow Harrison.

The two dogs are settled on a bedded area at the top end of the room, and Harrison is already sitting at his office desk. He opens a cupboard, takes out a small security-sealed box and places it on the desk. "What's in that?" asks DS Bailey.

Harrison opens the box and takes out a key. "Do you have your mobile viewers with you?" he asks.

DS Bailey takes out her viewer and waves it in front of Harrison. "I thought there was no communication on this campsite?"

"There isn't, and this is the key to my shack, I had it built just outside the signal suppressor field. You can call your office in London from there. I'm assuming you have a team back there still working on finding links between the murders. Call them, and then I can ask them."

"Ask them?" repeats DS Bailey.

"What do you mean, ask them? What are you asking?" demands Mirror.

Harrison lifts out of his chair and walks back over to the boardwalk door.

"What are you talking about?" asks Mirror.

"Let me ask my question to your team. Depending on the answer, I will tell you what you need to know. The shack is a short walk past the green-tagged field. *you coming*?"

Mirror turns to look at DS Bailey. "What do you think, DS Bailey, shall we let him?"

"I guess we don't have much choice, sir, unless we want to leave here with nothing but a wasted trip," she replies, trying not to show her surprise at DI Mirror asking her opinion.

*

A slightly longer walk than Harrison made in out to be later.

Harrison invites DS Bailey to enter first as he unlocks the shack, he follows her in, and an annoyed Mirror joins them. The inside was a replica of Harrison's office, furnished with similarly scattered beanbags circling another hand-carved wooden table made from a tree trunk.

“Ok, dial it up. Call DS Chang, and set it on conference call, please, DS Bailey.” Ordered Mirror

“Yes, sir. You do realise it’s barely nine on a Sunday morning? He might not be up yet?”

“Don’t worry, Bailey, he’ll be up, and he’ll answer. Like Mr Mann here, Chang’s an early riser”

DS Bailey dials DS Chang and places her mobile flat on the office desk. A holographic virtual screen projects from the viewer. The viewer rings twice, and DS Chang’s face appears in the projection.

“Hello, sir,” says the wide-awake DS Chang.

“Morning, Chang. Sorry to call so early. Have you anything else from the judge’s file?” asks Mirror.

“That’s ok, sir, I was already up. I’ve been working on the file all night. I’ve decoded a few more fragments of mixed files. Nothing that we’ve been able to make sense of yet, it’s going very, very slowly. One thing we did get – there are details of the murders that were kept from the jurors and were never revealed in court. What these details are, unfortunately, we won’t know until the whole file decodes. I've sent what we have got to your mobile already."

"Thank you, DS Chang." Mirror motions Harrison to join him in front of the projection.

"DS Chang, this is Harrison Mann, Maddison Bartel's solicitor. He would like to ask you something."

"Hello, DS Chang. Do you have access to the Time-Share accident logs for all the murders this week?" asks Harrison.

DS Chang turns his head to look at DI Mirror, seeking his approval to carry on, Mirror nods. DS Chang then looks down and taps away as his image moves along the screen to a shared view with the seven Time-Share incident reports. "Ok, now what?" he asks.

"DS Chang, are you able to show the Time-Share frequency string code for each of the seven Time-Share bubbles, together in listed format? You only need the first ten lines of code for each Time-Share log," says Harrison.

"Sir?" DS Chang's viewer image turns back to DI Mirror, his eyes fully rounded, and his eyebrows lifted further than they have ever been as if indicating their dislike of this ex-solicitor and possible suspect telling him what to do. Mirror nods his head again to complete his part of the silent conversation.

DS Chang taps away again and brings up seven sets of ten Time-Share codes next to him on the viewer.

“Now, if you don’t mind telling me what we are doing?” asks DS Chang.

“What *are* we doing, Harrison?” asks Mirror.

Harrison moves closer to the viewer screen. “We are looking for something, something the same, a signature,” he mumbles.

“What the hell is he on about, sir?” says DS Chang.

Mirror looks round to DS Bailey as she moves closer to the viewer, in line with Harrison. DS Chang continues tapping on his viewer, searching for more information that might be relevant.

DS Bailey points to a string of code in one of the files. “That code doesn’t belong in the string, it’s binary.”

DS Chang stops his typing and looks at the string of code DS Bailey has pointed to.

“What do you mean, Bailey?” asks Mirror.

“This, sir.” She points at a series of 1s and 0s in the first Time-Share code on the list. “Binary hasn’t been used since we moved to quantum processing. In fact, sir, it has never been used in Time-Share technology."

Harrison points to the exact same string of binary in the next line down and then again in the next five separate Time-Share files.

01001101 01000010

"How's this possible?" asks a surprised DS Chang. "Why is it there? It's not doing anything, it's not part of the program."

"Is this what you're looking for, Harrison? What does it mean?" asks Mirror.

Mirror and DS Bailey sense the fear emanating from Harrison as the colour drains from his face and he nods his head.

Harrison turns away from the viewer and walks towards the back of the Shack. "That's the same string of code that was found in all the Maddison Bartel Time-Share murders. It's how they linked other murders to him after the trial. It was never made public or shared with the jury, and it's one of the things I swore never to reveal when I signed the Official Secrets Act," he says fearfully.

"Harrison, what is it?" asks Mirror.

"It's Maddison Bartel's digital signature," replies Harrison.

Mirror starts to follow him, but DS Chang calls him back. "Sir, wait, those two sets of digits in the binary alphabet translate to the letter's 'M' and 'B'."

Mirror turns to DS Bailey, and they both turn to look at DS Chang.

"Maddison Bartel," say all three in unison.

"Oh, my God, sir," says DS Bailey.

"Thank you, DS Chang. We will be heading back as soon as we can. I'll contact you for another update when we leave," Mirror moves to catch up with Harrison.

"Sir," calls DS Chang, trying to again catch Mirror's attention, but Mirror is already out of view.

"Bailey," says the superior-sounding DS Chang.

"That's DS Bailey to you, DS Chang," says DS Bailey, emphasising the "D" and "S". She grabs her mobile from the table, causing the viewer image of DS Chang to shift sideways and switches it off. The projection beam returns into her mobile viewer, and she follows Mirror.

Mirror and Harrison are standing either side of the tree-stump table, Harrison with his back to Mirror, staring blankly at the wall. DS Bailey walks over to join Mirror.

"Harrison, what was that? What do those numbers mean?" asks Mirror. Bailey gestures to Mirror and points towards Harrison's hands, straight at his sides and visibly shaking.

"What's scaring you, Harrison?" asks DS Bailey.

"That's Maddison's digital signature," replies Harrison.

Mirror walks around the table and stands in front of him. "Explain, Harrison. Tell me about the signature, who else knew about it?"

Harrison turns slightly to the left, avoiding eye contact with Mirror then refocuses to stare at another part of the cabin wall. "Only four people knew about the digital signature, myself, Judge Crowley, Commander Lawrence and the person who told me, Maddison Bartel." Harrison's voice has joined his hands in shaking.

"You're not making sense, Harrison. If there were only four of you, then one of you may be responsible for the latest victims," reasons DS Bailey.

"The judge is dead, Maddison is dead, Commander Lawrence is confirmed to be out of the country and has been for the last few weeks. That leaves you. Are you admitting to something, Harrison? Do you want to confess anything?" asks Mirror, simultaneously gesturing to Bailey to go round to the other side of the table to block the renewed suspect from attempting to run.

“You see, like many serial killers, Maddison was proud of his kills. He treated them like pieces of art, and an artist tends to sign his work,” says Harrison.

“Harrison, I think you should come back to London. There are a few questions we would like to ask in more official surroundings,” says Mirror.

“I’d rather not come back to London, if that’s ok, please. I wouldn’t be safe with him back out there.” Harrison continues staring at the cabin’s blank wall.

DS Bailey looks towards Mirror, shrugs her shoulders then taps the side of her head, indicating that Harrison may have lost a few of his marbles.

“Maybe you already know, but if not, did you know Maddison Bartel is a genius? He was part of the original Time-Share discovery team working right alongside Professor Lukvinder Joshi. Quantum computing just came so naturally to him. Maddison once told me that he could hack into any Time-Share. Each time he did it, he would leave a digital signature in the Time-Share diagnostics – his initials in binary. No one understood how he did it, but if you knew what to look for, you would be able to confirm

Maddison had been responsible because the same digital signature was found in each Time-Share incident. He would keep the Time-Share program logs as kill trophies."

Mirror removes a holo-cuffs disc from his pocket, walks behind Harrison, grabs his hands, pushes them together and places the holo-cuff disc onto one of Harrison's wrists, the disc emits its laser cuff, tying Harrison's wrists together.

"Harrison Mann, I'm arresting you on suspicion of murder. You do not have to say anything, but anything you do say may be used as evidence against you in a court of law. Do you understand what I have just told you, Harrison?" asks Mirror.

"He would continually boast about how there was a back door to the Time-Share engine program. He'd actually installed a back door at the source the day it was discovered, apparently not even Professor Joshi knew about it," Harrison continues, seemingly oblivious to the fact he has been cuffed and arrested.

"Mr Mann, Harrison, do you understand what I have just told you? You are under arrest on suspicion of murder," repeats Mirror.

"Of course, the manipulation of the Time-Share and the digital signature was kept secret because of Maddison's situation. I mean, you wouldn't want the public to hear about Maddison Bartel's situation, would you?" Harrison's hands stopped shaking and his voice adopted a more serious tone.

"What situation, Harrison?" asks DS Bailey.

"Harrison, you have become our primary suspect, you have just shown us a digital signature that only you and one other person alive know about, and it can't be the other person as they have an iron-clad alibi. I think it's time you started making sense. You're coming back with us to London," says Mirror.

"Harrison, what's the situation with Maddison Bartel? What are you trying to tell us?" asks DS Bailey.

"I think he's lost his grip on reality, DS Bailey. Let's get him to the car, it's time to head back." Mirror moves Harrison through the room as DS Bailey leads the way to open the door.

"I'd rather not leave the camp, DI Mirror. It's safer here, no technology, he can't get me." Harrison stops firmly, making himself solid.

"Mr Mann, please don't make this any harder than it needs to be," says DS Bailey.

"What are you so scared about, Harrison? Who will get you? What's the situation with Maddison Bartel?" asks Mirror.

"Oh, didn't I say? Maddison – Maddison will get me, the same way he will get the rest of the jurors, the same way he will get the next list of people."

"Maddison Bartel is dead, Harrison, he died back in October 2050, straight after the court case, so please start moving," says DI Mirror.

"No, DI Mirror! Maddison Bartel did not *die* back in October 2050. In fact, from the Time-Share files your DS Chang just showed us, The Slate Killer is still very much alive."

A chill streams through Mirror's body; his head numbs as Harrison's last sentence forces its way into his reality.

DS Bailey's jaw drops, her words failing to come out.

Mirror grabs hold of Harrison, spins him back around then pushes him into one of the beanbags.

"What the hell do you mean Maddison Bartel didn't die back in October 2050?"

DS Bailey walks back into the room, shutting the door behind her.

"Sir, what do you think he meant?" asks DS Bailey.

"Harrison, what do you mean Maddison didn't die back in 2050?" asks Mirror more forcefully.

Harrison awkwardly lifts himself into a more comfortable position, his hands laser-cuffed behind his back making it difficult.

"Oh, you see, that's another reason I had to sign the Official Secrets Act. Maddison Bartel, as far as I knew, didn't die that day, he was just knocked out."

"Sir, he can't be telling the truth, can he? We would have heard something, wouldn't we?" questions DS Bailey.

"Harrison, what are you saying?" Mirror calms his voice, desperately trying to regain an element of self-control.

Harrison turns slightly to reveal his cuffed hands, then gestures for Mirror to un-cuff him. Mirror places his finger on the cuff control, the disc confirms the finger scans, and the laser retracts to free him.

"I was there, in the ambulance, there were four of us, the judge, the ambulance driver, the commander and me.

You see, Maddison had indeed been hit by a fire extinguisher. His head, nose, face – all caved in. He was just a bloody, unrecognisable pulp and he did die. We were all there, we witnessed him dying. That ambulance man even pronounced him dead, so we all thought he was."

"So, Maddison is dead?" questions DS Bailey, confused by Harrison's story.

"He was! And then… he wasn't. He started breathing again. Of course, straight away, I was thinking like a hotshot solicitor. I saw the path to fame and fortune. Maddison had died, his sentence had been life in prison – well he'd died, so that meant I could argue for his freedom. I would have got Maddison released less than a day after the judge had given him a life sentence. Not even Houdini could have performed that kind of magic trick. I was going to be famous, or so I thought. I look back on it now and ask myself, what was I thinking? We should have finished him off right there in the back of that ambulance, he was pure evil. But instead, my stupid arrogance pushed, and I guess I left them no choice. We were all taken to a secret location. The last thing I heard was that Maddison had woken up but couldn't remember who he was. He had no idea he'd done anything wrong, let alone that he was the most notorious serial killer of our time."

"How the hell are we supposed to believe that Harrison?" says DS Bailey.

"I don't know, Bailey, but my gut's telling me this might not be too far from the truth," replies Mirror.

"Harrison, I'm sorry, but until we clear you and your story, I'm still going to need you to come with us. Let's go." Mirror holds out his hand, and Harrison grabs it to help lift himself from the beanbag.

Mirror gestures DS Bailey to lead the way and for Harrison to follow. They leave the shack and start their walk back to the car.

*

Mirror unlocks the car door, then opens it for Harrison to get in just as a random question falls into DS Bailey's head. "Harrison, have you ever heard of Diamonds Time-Share Estates?"

Harrison lowers himself into the car as DS Bailey watches him, trying to gauge his reaction and see if there is any recognition of the name.

"No, I've never heard of them. Why do you ask?"

Mirror looks at DS Bailey, impressed that she had asked that question.

“Just wondered,” replies DS Bailey.

Mirror starts the car and drives back along the dirt road leading out of the camp.

“Funny though,” says Harrison.

“What’s funny, Harrison?” asks Mirror, looking at him through the rear-view viewer.

“The word ‘Diamonds’. It’s an anagram of ‘Maddison’,” replies Harrison.

A weight push on Mirror’s shoulders, then a sickening feeling washes over him. “Oh, my God! Bailey, the whole name’s an anagram – Albert Diamonds and Maddison Bartel. We had him in the office, and we let him go!”

Chapter 15

Bringing Albert In and Letting Maddison Out

A preoccupied DS Chang walks over to his desk, momentarily pausing for thought before sitting down, he spots PC Killy at the opposite end of the room giving him the “do you want a cuppa?” gesture. He places his paperwork on his desk, lifts both his thumbs up, then nods emphatically to her.

Just as PC Killy walks over, holding two mugs of tea, DS Chang’s viewer illuminates to show an incoming call from DI Mirror, “Sir?”

“DS Chang, we are on our way back and should be there by five. We’ve got Harrison Mann with us.”

“Ok, sir, I’ll be here. Is Harrison Mann under arrest? I can’t see it logged in the system yet, do you want me to update the log, sir?”

“No, Chang, Mr Mann isn’t under arrest. He’s coming back to help us with our enquiries. Have you still got Albert Diamonds under observation?”

“Yes, sir. The last update, he was still at his house.”

"I want you to go pick him up and bring him back in for questioning. It's imperative that I talk to him as soon as I get in."

"You want me to get him today, sir? It's Sunday, and we promised him we would keep it low profile in front of his wife. I'm not so sure he'll want to come today, sir," says DS Chang, showing empathy for Albert Diamonds, but mostly trying to save himself a journey across London.

"I need to talk to him as soon as I get in, Chang. If he won't come in willingly, arrest him, but only as a last resort. It's imperative you keep it as low key as possible and must absolutely be under the media and public radars."

"Arrest him, sir? Why we are bringing him back in, and what would we be charging him with?"

"Charge him with obstructing an ongoing investigation. Take a fully armed team with you but keep them out of sight unless absolutely necessary. Be careful, and message me when you have him. And Chang, make sure you get him before I return. We need him where we can keep an eye on him before tomorrow. I'll explain everything when I get back. Remember, DS Chang, keep it low profile, only use force as a last resort," enforces Mirror.

“We are arresting him for obstructing an investigation?” A look of confusion shows on DS Chang’s face as he repeats Mirror’s words.

“Yes, DS Chang, we have new information that could mean Albert Diamonds is not all he’s making himself out to be. Anything else from the judge-sealed file or on the remaining jurors?”

“The sealed file is still decrypting, sir. There was a locked file within the locked file, but we should have it broken soon. With regards to the remaining jurors, all stakeouts have been reporting in as scheduled.”

“Thank you, Chang, we’ll see you soon. Be careful with Diamonds, take a full team, don’t take any risks, and keep it low profile,” repeats Mirror.

Mirror’s image disappears from DS Chang’s viewer. PC Killy, still holding the two mugs, places one on a coaster to the left-hand side of DS Chang’s desk.

“Wow, sir, is Albert Diamonds a suspect? He seemed so nice.”

“It’s a surprise to me as well, PC Killy. I’m not sure what the DI has found out, and I’m not sure why he would want me to take a fully armed team to pick him up. It all seems a bit overkill to me.”

*

Albert sits in his home office staring at his reflection in the switched-off viewer screen. Conflicted, clouded and confused, he tries to make sense of what has been happening to him over the last week or so. This should have been the best week of his life, he should have been on the highest of highs, but instead, he's been brought crashing down by witnessing the death of Calvin Wireless and then being told by police that he and his family could be in the crosshairs of a serial killer. Overwhelmed he shuts his eyes tight.

*

Maddison opens eyes and stares back at Albert's reflection in the switched-off viewer screen. *How the hell did I end up inside you?* he thinks. *It's funny, it seems I can remember everything Albert has ever done, it's like I was always there. What's the first thing I remember about Albert?* Maddison tries to recall his past. *The first thing Albert remembers is being in the back of an ambulance and a face, whose face? It's a face that Albert has never seen before, but as I look up at him now, it's a face I recognise,* Maddison chuckles to himself. *Harrison Mann, my solicitor. The first face Albert saw was my solicitor. I had plans for dear old Harrison Mann, how I would have loved to have put him on one of my lists*, reminisces Maddison. *Maybe I can look him up? I'm sure he would be pleased to see me again. So, let's think back. Albert woke up in the back of the ambulance, after that, he remembers the hospital, but it wasn't a normal hospital, an army hospital, there were soldiers around him, around me. The nurse, I remember the nurse. She told Albert that he had had a forklift accident, a pallet had fallen on his head and caused memory loss, but I can access all of his memories now, and I know Albert didn't exist before that day. I remember everything Albert remembers. There was no forklift, there never was! It felt like I was in the back seat of a TaxiCab behind soundproof glass and Albert was the taxi driver. I would shout at him, give him directions, giving him orders, but he couldn't hear me, or could he? Hold on! Every so often, something would slip through, wouldn't it, Albert? I would suggest, and you would listen. Your aggressive "I'm a nice guy" selling tactics, getting yourself close to the jurors, even choosing the widow of one of my previous playmates, there must have been something, part of me that had existed in you all along. Who else was there? There was the judge's bodyguard, he wasn't just a bodyguard though, was he? He was an army officer, he questioned Albert, asking him questions about me! Questions Albert couldn't answer, but that officer knew the truth about me, and I guess it's obvious: Albert woke up when I didn't. "I'm Albert and Albert is me, we are the same person,* confirms Maddison. *But now, I'm waking up, feeling stronger, something's cracked that soundproof glass, and I've been more and more in control every day after. Hold on, when did that crack first show? That other hospital. Yes, ever since the hospital when I saw those two jurors. The nurse and the doctor, my first playmates in such a long time. Albert looked at them – he didn't recognise them, but I did! I screamed out so loud when I saw them that my head – or was it Albert's head – either way, it felt like bursting.* Maddison has pinpointed his moment of reawakening. *I guess it won't be long before the police figure it out. There must be someone who knows. The solicitor, the judge, that officer. I think it's time to get to work, make sure my list gets finished. Just in case, I guess setting a few insurance policies at this point won't do any harm either.* Maddison smiles to himself, he switches on the viewer screen and sets to work on the next part of his list and his insurance policies.

*

A little while later

Carol Diamonds opens Albert's office door and walks in holding a cup of tea. "Hi, love, you've been working for hours, I thought you might need a cuppa, lunch will be ready soon."

Albert shakes his head to wake himself out of his solid gaze towards the viewer screen. Confusion hits him as he tries to recall either the act of switching the viewer on or doing any work and why there is a status bar showing "*time until upload*" on his screen. Albert questions himself, then, as if it didn't matter or as if being told by an inner voice to ignore it, he looks up at Carol and smiles at her. He switches the screen into sleep mode, "Thanks, love, how are you feeling?"

"Oh, Albert, I keep thinking about that awful moment. Poor Calvin – no one deserves to go out like that."

Albert reaches out and holds her hand to comfort her whilst wondering how she would react if he told her what he knows. Would the knowledge they were being secretly observed by an undercover police team to protect them against a possible killer who was copying the killer of her first husband and might be targeting them go down well?

He guesses she would be less worried about Calvin Wireless and a lot more worried about herself and her kids if he did.

"I know, love. It's been a bit of a bittersweet week, but things will get better, a lot better. The only way is up for us now, my love, trust me." Albert stands up to hug Carol, but before he does, the doorbell rings. "I'll get it, love." He lets go of Carol's hand and leaves the office.

Albert opens the front door to a man and a woman holding police identification badges. Behind them, seven more officers in black tactical dress, armed and looking as if they were ready to storm the house.

"Who is it, love?" shouts Carol from the office.

"Yes, who is it? And why are you here?" asks Albert.

"Mr Diamonds, my name is PC Killy, and this is DS Chang. We would like you to come back to the station with us, please."

"Has something happened? Why have you bought armed officers with you? Is my family in danger? Shall I get them ready to go?" asks a worried Albert.

"Carol, Carol get the kids, were leaving," shouts Albert, deducing that the only reason the police are there in such numbers is that his family is in immediate danger.

"No, sir, we only need you. It's best if your family remains here, we will keep an eye on them, don't worry," says PC Killy.

"What is it, Albert?" says a panicked Carol as she appears beside Albert in the hallway.

"I'm not sure, Carol. I think they want me to go back to the station with them."

"That's ridiculous, it's Sunday. Can't it wait till the morning?" argues Carol.

"Sir, I'm sorry, but we need you to come with us now," insists DS Chang.

"It's ok, Carol. I'm sure they just want to ask me more questions about the concert since we were so close to the stage. I'm sure it won't take long," says Albert, trying to make light of the situation.

"No, Albert. We are having our family lunch soon. I'm sure their questions about the concert can wait till the morning, I'm sorry, we are going back in. You can call us again tomorrow." Carol moves in front of Albert, making him step back, then holds the door to shut it. DS Chang pushes back, forcing it to fully open, which in turn forces Carol to domino into Albert who then stumbles onto the entranceway table backwards, trips and falls to the floor, banging his head.

“I’m sorry, Mr Diamonds, but we are going to have to insist you come with us. Please do not make it more difficult than it has to be,” says DS Chang.

“What the hell are you doing?” shouts a furious Carol.

PC Killy looks past her and Albert to see her children peering from the bannisters on the stairway, frightened looks on their faces. “Sir, maybe this isn’t the way we should be approaching this.” She points towards the two children. DS Chang, ignoring PC Killy, attempts to sidestep past Carol. Albert finds himself unable to move as the confusion makes his head spin.

Maddison stands up. Spotting the armed police officers, he quickly turns to run back up the hallway to the office. DS Chang and all seven armed officers give chase. PC Killy holds the now frantic Carol back from following them. Maddison enters the office, managing to shut and lock the door behind him just before DS Chang grabs the outer handle. Maddison runs behind Albert’s desk and swipes at the viewer, switching it on.

“Albert Diamonds, open this door, you have nowhere to go,” orders DS Chang.

He steps back and looks towards his backup team. “Break it down.”

Two of the team move forward with a battering ram. Within seconds, the door swings open, splintering the wooden frame around the lock.

DS Chang enters, and the armed officers surround Maddison. “Albert Diamonds, stop what you’re doing and put your hands flat on the desk,” demands DS Chang.

Maddison momentarily continues to tap frenziedly on the viewer then looks up at DS Chang, gives him a wry smile, laughs and presses the enter key.

“I won’t say it again, Mr Diamonds, put your hands flat on the desk,” shouts DS Chang.

Maddison places his hands on the desk, DS Chang moves round behind him, roughly grabs both of Albert’s hands, puts them behind his back and laser cuffs him.

“What’s going on? Why am I being arrested?” asks a terrified Albert Diamonds.

DS Chang looks at the viewer screen, swipes and it lights up to show a locked screen and an enter password box. He turns to one of his colleagues, “We need to find out what he’s been doing on that viewer. Search through the office, seize that viewer bring it and anything else you find back to the station."

"You can't just force me to come to the police station, I have my rights!" shouts Albert.

"You're right, Albert," says DS Chang.

"So, why are you taking me in by force?"

"I can't just force you to come in unless you're under arrest, that's why I'm arresting you. Albert Diamonds, I am arresting you for the suspected murders of Calvin Wireless, Lucy Victoria, Carmela Rosa, Ophelia Schmidt, Anthony Chand, Christopher Lowe and Ravi Binning. You do not have to say anything, but anything you do say may be used as evidence in a court of law. Do you understand what I have told you, Mr Diamonds?"

"I have no idea what you are talking about. This is a nightmare; I didn't kill anyone!" shouts Albert.

DS Chang leads Albert past the screaming and very angry Carol, "What are you doing? Why are you taking him? I will make you so sorry for this, I'll sue your department and make sure you all lose your sorry little jobs!"

"I'm sorry, Mrs Diamonds, he's being taken to the TSM police department. This card will give you all the details and contact numbers you need," says PC Killy in her calmest of voices but unsuccessfully relaxing Carol.

"What is going on? Why have you taken my husband?" she asks tearfully.

"I'm sorry, Mrs Diamonds, I can't say much more than I have already. If you have any questions, please call the number on the card." PC Killy guiltily turns her back and leaves the heaped, crying and wailing Carol Diamonds on her doorstep. PC Killy lowers her head and starts to make her way back to her police car and the awaiting DS Chang, through a gathering of neighbours, inevitably some of whom have their mobile viewers videoing the recent excitement in their usually quiet cul de sac. "So much for keeping a low profile, DS Chang. And why did you charge him with murder?" asks PC Killy as she lowers herself into the driverless car. "Not sure this is gonna go down well with DI Mirror, sir."

DS Chang huffs. "Viewer, drive to the station, blues and twos speed."

"New heading TSM-PD, emergency speed and lights, commencing," the viewer confirms the destination, and the two police officers, the laser-cuffed Albert Diamonds and his yet unrealised passenger drive off at speed.

Chapter 16

Interview With an Innocent Man

Mirror and Bailey exit the elevator with the terrified Harrison Mann sandwiched between them. They walk past the empty counter and are instantly greeted by a very nervous DS Chang.

"Where is he?" asks Mirror abruptly.

Mirror has already been informed of Albert Diamonds' less than low profile pickup by a PC Killy's viewer call on the drive back from Cornwall.

"I've, err, got him in the interview room, Time-Share four, sir," replies DS Chang, wondering at what point DI Mirror is going to lay into him about his very unprofessional approach to picking Albert up.

"DS Chang, this is Harrison Mann. Please take him into the witness's waiting lounge. Make him comfortable, we'll need to speak to him again later. DS Bailey and I are going to talk to Mr Diamonds."

"Yes, sir. Do you want me to join you in the interview room after I've taken Mr Mann to the waiting lounge?" he asks hopefully.

"No, it's ok, DS Chang, stay with Mr Mann. Make him a cup of tea. He must be hungry, see if wants something to eat. Oh! And while you're at it, DS Bailey and I could do with something. Please ask the canteen to send something up to the interview room."

There it is! thinks DS Chang. DI Mirror hasn't said in so many words but giving him jobs like that told him exactly how DI Mirror felt about the mismanaged pickup.

"Yes, sir, no problem, sir," replies the head-lowered DS Chang as Mirror and DS Bailey walk past.

"Mr Mann, if you can follow me, sir," says DS Chang, gesturing the direction with his hand.

Harrison stares at the backs of Mirror and Bailey as they walk away along the corridor, then turns to follow DS Chang to enter the main TSM-PD office.

DS Chang spots PC Killy and calls her over. "Ah, PC Killy, have you got a minute?"

PC Killy walks over, "Yes, sir?"

"This is Harrison Mann. DI Mirror has asked if you can make him a cup of tea, also, see if he wants something to eat and make him comfortable. And if you can ask the canteen to send something up to the interview room, please?"

“Sir?” PC Killy spots the slight smile on Harrison’s face, a look that tells her DI Mirror hasn’t asked DS Chang to ask her to do any of this.

“Thank you, PC Killy. I’m going to continue working on the sealed file,” says DS Chang, desperately trying to avoid direct eye contact with her as he walks away, hoping that opening the sealed file as quickly as possible will put him back in DI Mirror’s good books.

DS Bailey walks slightly faster than normal to keep up with the quickening pace of DI Mirror as they head for the interview room.

“I’m not sure what the best way to approach this interview will be sir. Nothing we’ve seen about Albert Diamonds screams he is a murderer, let alone that he might be Maddison Bartel in disguise, and as for the way he was brought in, sir, I think we could land ourselves and the department in serious trouble if we’re not careful,” she says nervously.

“Noted, Bailey, but my gut is telling me there is more to what Harrison has said than just a good story.”

They enter the interview observation room. On the right-hand side is another door. A Time-Share control panel flashes on the wall next to it. In front of them is an observation control desk above which stands a wall of viewers. Each of the viewers' screens is split into eight boxes, labelled one to eight. Each of the boxes shows a view of the same table and three chairs at eight different Time-Share points. All the rooms bar one were empty. Sitting at the table in Time-Share four, opposite two empty chairs is Albert Diamonds, his hands laser-cuffed together then laser-tethered to a hook in the centre of the table.

"He looks terrified, Bailey," says Mirror.

"Yes, sir. I'm really not looking forward to this," she replies.

"Come on, DS Bailey, let's get it done."

They walk over to the door, and Mirror selects Time-Share room four from the control panel. It unlocks, and they both walk in.

Albert stands up and moves back as far as the laser-cuff tether will allow him. "Why am I being kept here? Why haven't I been able to call my solicitor? What the hell is going on?" he shouts.

"Mr Diamonds, please sit back down. We need to ask you a few more questions," says DI Mirror.

"Questions, why on earth do you need me to answer *more* questions? Considering your fellow officer has already charged me with murder, you should already have all the answers. It should be me asking questions, like why? Why have I been charged? I wouldn't dream of harming a fly, let alone killing another human being," he says, still partially standing.

"Viewer, commence interview recording. Sir, please sit." DS Bailey gestures Albert back to the chair.

"Mr Diamonds, what do you remember before your forklift accident?" asks DI Mirror, ignoring Albert's rant.

The question catches Albert off guard, stopping him from hurling a new barrage of abuse to his would-be captors. "My accident? What has my… why? Why the hell are you asking about something that happened nine years ago?" he says with a calmer tone. He moves back towards his seat. "And what the hell has it got to do with this?" His tone rises again as he sits with a thud.

"Please, Mr Diamonds, just try to remember. What do you remember before your accident? We think it may be connected with the incidents we've had this week."

DS Bailey looks at DI Mirror, impressed with how he has linked Alberts's past and present together without bringing up their suspicions.

Albert leans back in his chair and looks down in annoyance at his cuffs and the laser dragging across the table, restricting his movement. He holds his hands up to DI Mirror.

Mirror looks to DS Bailey and nods. DS Bailey takes out the cuff controller from her pocket, she presses her finger to the scan button, and they watch as the cuff beam retracts back to the laser cuff disc on the back of Albert's right hand and circles itself around Albert's right wrist.

"I have semi-released your cuffs while you're in here, but just to be clear, they will fully engage if you attempt anything that we deem dangerous to yourself or others," says DS Bailey.

Albert looks down to the snake-like tether, "I don't!" he says.

"What's that, Albert? 'I don't' what?" asks Mirror.

"I don't remember anything. I remember waking up in the ambulance then again in a hospital where I was told I'd had a serious accident."

"You remember nothing before that?" asks Mirror.

"No. The only thing I know about my past is what they told me at the hospital and from the bits, I've pieced together after that. I remember they were proper good to me in the hospital. There were always loads of people around, keeping an eye on me, making sure I was ok. They were really concerned about my memory loss. I was there such a long time. I had operation after operation as they tried to reconstruct my face to the way I looked before my accident. I was then moved to rehab for another few months. That's where I met Carol. She'd been through a traumatic time, as you well know. I guess we just clicked. I found a familiarity in her I'd never had with anyone else. We got on straight away." Albert pauses as the mention of Carol makes his temperament change again. "Carol, oh, my God, she must be in bits, bloody terrified, thanks to your heavy-handed officers dragging me out of the house in front of her and the kids!"

"Albert, please calm down. We promise you, Carol is fine. The situation has been explained to her, and she's being looked after by one of my team. Believe me, Albert, the sooner you help us get answers, the sooner we can clear this up, and you can get back to your life and normality," says Mirror.

"Well, come on then, ask away, let's get this over with."

Mirror feels slightly relieved that he has somewhat calmed Albert, but also apprehensive as to how to approach the subject of "you might be a serial killer, but you don't know it". Just as he is about to start, a knock pauses the interview. DS Bailey gets up and opens the door. "It's the food, sir," she says. She takes the trolley from the canteen staff member, thanks him, and wheels the trolley in.

"Would you like a tea, Albert, or a sandwich maybe?" says Mirror.

Albert looks up and nods his head reluctantly.

DS Bailey pours three teas, picks up the milk, sugar and tray of sandwiches from the trolley and places them all in the middle of the table. "Here you go, Albert. There's a choice of sandwiches, please help yourself," she says.

Albert looks to the tray and solemnly shakes his head.

Mirror decides it's best to carry on with the interview. "Albert, we've looked into your past from before the accident, and there's very little. In fact, you left such a small footprint on society that we'd be forgiven for thinking that you never existed until nine years ago…"

"Well! I'm sorry I've not always been a superstar, DI Mirror. Your point?"

DI Mirror looks to DS Bailey for support in finding an easier line of questioning. DS Bailey stares blankly back at him, wanting to help but unable to find the right words.

"My point, I guess is… Albert, your accident happened the…" Mirror looks at DS Bailey then brushes his unusually sweaty palms on his trouser legs, "the same day that Maddison Bartel died."

Albert looks at DI Mirror with fear in his eyes. He jumps back up from his chair and backs away from the table. "What are you trying to say, DI Mirror? Are you trying to fit me up? What? You can't find the person responsible for the murders, so, to look good to the media, you pin it on me?" he shouts.

"Sir, sit back down, please," insists DS Bailey.

Albert backs further from the table, shaking visibly, tears running down his cheeks. "No way, you're trying to fit me up. I want my solicitor!"

DS Bailey turns to DI Mirror, leans in and whispers, "Sir, I'm very troubled with this line of questioning. I really don't think he knows what we are talking about. I don't think it's him."

DS Bailey's whispered words barely have time to sink into Mirror's thoughts when a loud bang emanates from the door. They look round, as it swings open. DS Chang bursts into the room, holding a laser cuff disc controller and points it towards Albert. The beam around Albert's right hand instantly extends around both his wrists, stretches over to the metal cuff loop in the centre of the table and quickly shortens to drag Albert by his hands towards it.

*

Fourteen minutes earlier

"Nearly there," said DS Chang, talking to his viewer. "One per cent to go… come on…" He talked out loud as he watched the estimated time bar move slowly and painfully towards that magic hundred per cent. He spotted PC Killy walking towards him and lowered his head, anticipating she would be riled after ordering her to look after Harrison.

"Mr Mann is *comfortable*, DS Chang, he's been *fed* and *watered*, oh, and Mr Diamonds' wife, Carol, is at the front with her solicitor and a media reporter, and they are demanding to speak to someone in charge. I guess since DI Mirror and DS Bailey are busy, I was wondering if you would like to speak to them," she wasn't happy.

"Thank you, PC Killy." DS Chang's eyes remained fixed on the viewer screen.

PC Killy huffed, turned to walk then glanced back at DS Chang's viewer screen as the bar hit one hundred per cent and the words "*file decryption complete*" flashed up. "Is that the judge's file?" Her attitude mellowed and was replaced by her usual more inquisitive tone.

"Yes, it is, PC Killy. Have a seat. Since DI Mirror is busy, we might as well take a look."

PC Killy was well aware that DI Mirror had said to call him as soon as the file's decryption had completed, and that standing in reception was an impatient Carol Diamonds with an impending media shit storm, but her curiosity overtook as she chose to temporarily forget reminding DS Chang of either. She pulled a chair from the desk nearby and sat next to DS Chang.

"Viewer, open decrypted file," ordered DS Chang.

The viewer opened the file and listed two folders, the first of which was the smaller one they had previously part-accessed, containing the four names and the yet unseen in full Official Secrets Act forms each had signed. The second folder was entitled "*Maddison Bartel/Albert Diamonds*".

PC Killy and DS Chang glanced at each other and observed the same look of confusion on the other's face.

"Why is Albert Diamonds' name on that folder title?" asked PC Killy.

"Viewer, open file entitled Maddison Bartel/Albert Diamonds," instructed DS Chang.

The file opened, and they both started to read, then simultaneously jumped up from their chairs as they reached the same sentence at the same time, an expression of pure shock replacing their confusion.

"PC Killy, please show the guests in reception to waiting room two. I will go and warn DI Mirror and DS Bailey." Chang started running towards the interview rooms.

"Yes, sir," replied the visibly shaken PC Killy.

DS Chang burst into the interview observation room, looked up at the viewer and saw Mirror and DS Bailey in conversation with Albert. He looked at the "occupied" light on Time-Share interview room four. The thought of knocking or calling first wasn't a priority given what he was about to tell DI Mirror.

DS Chang turned the handle, forcefully pushed the door open and walked into the room to see a highly agitated Albert backing away from the table. He grabbed his laser cuff disc controller from his pocket and aimed it towards Albert.

The beam instantly extended around both Albert's wrists', stretched over to the metal cuff loop in the centre of the table and dragged Albert back towards it.

*

"What the hell are you doing DS Chang?" shouts DI Mirror.

Albert cries out as he is dragged towards the table, his hands thumping tight against the centre, tears streaming from his eyes. "Why are you treating me like this? I've not done anything wrong!"

DS Bailey picks up her laser cuff controller to loosen Albert's cuffs.

"Do not loosen those cuffs, DS Bailey. Sir, you need to come and see something before you continue with this interview." DS Chang's breathing is slowly recovering from the running.

"What is it, DS Chang? We are in the middle of an interview with Mr Diamonds," says DS Bailey.

"Sir, I'd rather you step outside for a minute, please," insists DS Chang.

Mirror was still annoyed with DS Chang, but the one thing he's sure of is that he would never have burst in like that without a very good reason. "DS Bailey, loosen Mr Diamonds' hands so they are not so tight against the table, then come outside with us."

"Yes, sir," replies DS Bailey. She loosens the laser cuffs and follows Mirror and DS Chang.

"This had better be good, Chang," warns Mirror.

"Sir, I've opened the file, the judge's file. You're not going to believe this, that man in there, that's not *just* Albert Diamonds…"

In that fraction of a moment, Mirror realises that everything Harrison Mann had told him is true. "It's Maddison Bartel!" he exclaims.

DS Chang is taken aback that Mirror already knows. "Yes, sir, how did you…?"

"He's been lying to us," says DS Bailey.

"Well, he's a bloody good liar, Bailey. He's even managed to fool the lie detector. Ok, Bailey, let's get back in there and help him wipe those crocodile tears away."

"Sir, you don't understand," says DS Chang.

"Understand what, DS Chang?" asks DS Bailey impatiently.

"I said that man in there is not *just* Albert Diamonds, I've sent the open file to your mobiles."

Mirror and DS Bailey take out their mobile viewers and bring up the file. It shows details of Maddison Bartel's injuries, his amnesia, his facial reconstruction and his new identity and life as Albert Diamonds.

"Oh, my God, he doesn't know," whispers DS Bailey.

Mirror looks up at DS Chang.

"I know, sir. It's a bit messed up. I'm guessing the man in there really does believe that not only is he Albert Diamonds and innocent, but he also has no idea he used to be The Slate Killer," explains DS Chang.

"The scary thing is, sir, I think Maddison Bartel might have reawakened and Albert Diamonds is not the least bit aware of it, a split personality, sir," adds DS Bailey.

"I'm not going to pretend I understand what the hell is going on, but if there are two personalities in there, the question, DS Bailey, should be, is Maddison Bartel aware of Albert Diamonds?" says Mirror.

DS Chang adds, "Something else, sir. Carol Diamonds is here with a solicitor and a media reporter she has brought in with her. PC Killy is dealing with them and has managed to calm them a bit, but I suspect it's not going to be long before they demand to see Mr Diamonds."

Mirror shakes his head. They are either on the verge of breaking the strangest case any of them has ever worked on or about to cause the biggest media frenzy that will result in all-round suspension, in Mirror's case, the second in as many weeks.

"What are we going to do, sir? We could be questioning a man that honestly thinks and believes that he is innocent, and in some strange aspect of the law, he is. Also, we still haven't honoured his right to a have solicitor present," says DS Bailey.

"I think I need to take a risk. We need to find out if there's any part of Maddison still there inside Albert. We need to bring him out. What I'm about to do will lead to suspension or possibly being fired if am wrong, so, DS Bailey and DS Chang, I would like you both to go back to the main office. There's no point in all of us getting into trouble."

DS Chang nods his head in agreement; he is always available to take any glory, but equally happy to avoid punishment. "No, sir," says DS Bailey. "I will come in with you. It's a protocol that at least two officers are interviewing at any-one 'time," she says with a wry smile.

Mirror looks at DS Bailey. He knows she isn't quoting protocol because she's being awkward. Quite the opposite, she is letting him know she's backing him. "Thank you, DS Bailey." He turns to DS Chang, "In exactly ten minutes, I want you to bring Harrison Mann here. Knock first and wait for me to answer."

"Yes, sir," says DS Chang.

Mirror opens the door of the interview room, walks in, and DS Bailey follows.

Albert looks broken. He is sitting back on his chair, his hands tethered, hovering over the table, unable to pull away any further.

"I want my solicitor, and I want him now!" he shouts tearfully.

Mirror and DS Bailey walk to their chairs and sit down in silence.

"Why aren't you saying anything? I said I want my solicitor!"

Mirror looks at DS Bailey, then looks back over to Albert and stares directly into his eyes. A terrified man looks back at him. "Who's asking for the solicitor?" he asks, continuing to look at Albert's eyes, in search of that something that might tell him Albert is lying but only getting an expression of confusion and fear returned.

"What?" asks Albert.

"Who's asking for a solicitor? Is it Albert Diamonds or Maddison Bartel?"

Albert's eyes momentarily change from that of a frightened man to a solid cold stare projecting outwards all the fear Albert feels and sending a chill through Mirror, forcing him to look away.

The unnerved Mirror quickly looks back to Albert's eyes, they are back to a frightened tear-glazed stare.

"Did you see that, Bailey?" asks Mirror quietly.

"Y-yes, sir," she replies with a quiver to her voice.

"What are you saying? This is a nightmare! I've not done anything wrong!" wails a distraught Albert.

Albert's crying almost masks the sound of knocking. Mirror gets up and opens the door to DS Chang with Harrison Mann standing next to him. "Thank you, DS Chang," says Mirror. He turns to look at Harrison, "Mr Mann, I'm going to ask you a big favour, which is not strictly protocol."

"What is it, DI Mirror?" asks Harrison.

“We have someone in here, I would like you to meet him. I want you to tell me if you recognise him.”

“Ok,” replies Harrison uneasily.

“Sir, do you think that’s a good idea?” says DS Chang.

Mirror gives DS Chang a hard stare. “Thank you, DS Chang. If you can wait here until we are finished, we shouldn’t be too long, then you can escort Mr Mann back.”

Mirror steps aside, allows Harrison to enter then closes the door. Harrison cagily walks towards the handcuffed man, Albert, with his head down, weeping. “What’s going on?” he asks.

“Mr Mann, do you recognise this person?” asks Mirror, unnecessarily pointing towards Albert.

“No, DI Mirror, I do not. Why are you asking?” says Harrison.

Mirror walks around the table nearer to Albert. “Mr Diamonds, please look at this man. Do you recognise him?” Albert sobs uncontrollably, his head stays lowered. “Please, Mr Diamonds, do you know this man?” asks Mirror again. Albert looks up, wipes his tear-filled eyes on his shoulders as best as his tethered hands will allow and waits for his eyes to focus. “You were in the ambulance,” he says.

A confused Harrison moves closer to the table and looks Albert up and down.

“Ambulance? I don’t recognise you. I’ve never seen you before in my—” The air around him freezes, and a shiver runs through his body as Albert’s tear-filled eyes change into a cold, reptilian stare. “Oh, my God!” He stumbles backwards into DS Bailey.

“Hello, Harrison, have you come to be my solicitor again?” says the smiling, lizard-eyed killer.

Chapter 17

The Trapdoor In The Trap At The End Of The Day

A deafening silence hits the room. the audience watched as Maddison chooses a sandwich from the platter, the laser tethered hand allowed just enough slack for the sandwich to get to his mouth if he lowered his head at the same time to take a bite.

The hypnotic emergence of Maddison has frozen Mirror, DS Bailey and Harrison into doing nothing more than stare as he eats. Even though it is Albert's face they can see, the unnerving malignant aura emanating from the re-emerged Slate Killer makes it obvious that Albert is no longer in front of them.

"I don't think much to these sandwiches. Then again, considering I haven't *personally* eaten anything for the past nine years, I guess they will have to do," says Maddison casually.

"Maddison Bartel?" quizzes Mirror, his question sounding surreal.

Maddison looks up over his sandwich. “Hello, Gabriel, I’ve read so much about you.”

DS Bailey grabs Mirror’s arm, Harrison backs towards the exit.

Mirror grasps hold of DS Bailey’s hand with his opposite hand and gently releases her grip on his arm. He walks back towards the table, pulls out the chair and sits.

“Jana, Harrison, come join us, there’s plenty of sandwiches,” says the unruffled Maddison.

Mirror looks round to DS Bailey, “DS Bailey, see Harrison out and hand him back to DS Chang, please. Then come back and join us if you're up to it.”

DS Bailey opens the interview room door. Harrison eagerly pushes past her to get out. “DS Chang, can you take Mr Mann back to the waiting area, please?” She momentarily pauses, her fight-or-flight impulse pushing her to follow them and leave DI Mirror to conduct the bizarre interview alone… Resisting her urges, she steps back in, closes the door, and returns to sit at the table next to DI Mirror. Completely unfazed, Maddison continues picking away at the sandwiches.

“Where is Albert?” asks Mirror.

Maddison exaggerates his chew, swallows, then casually answers, “Oh, that sappy sod! He’s in here somewhere.” Maddison laughs then leans forward to take another bite of a sandwich.

DS Bailey turns to Mirror and leans in, “He’s aware of the other personality, sir.”

“Jana, Jana, Jana, it’s rude to whisper,” says Maddison between chews.

DS Bailey grips her hand tight to a fist, purposely making her nails dig hard into her palms, in the hope that the pain will either wake her from a bad dream or give her the adrenaline rush she needs to combat the electrifying fear running up her spine.

“That’s DS Bailey to you, Mr Bartel,” she says with renewed authority in her voice.

“Touchy,” says Maddison, giving her a seductive smile.

“Maddison, how long have you been aware of Albert Diamonds?” asks Mirror.

“I’m not *exactly* sure, Gabriel, oh, or would you rather I call you DI Mirror?” Maddison leans in towards Mirror as much as the tether allows, “since DS Bailey wants to keep this more formal.” He winks cheekily at DS Bailey.

"Either is fine Maddison," replies Mirror.

"Well, to answer your question, DI Gabriel Alex Mirror," trying to unnerve Mirror further, "I guess I only figured it out a few days ago. But then again, somehow, I've always known about Albert, ever since that day in the ambulance. Any chance you can release these a little, please, Jana. Oops! I mean, DS Bailey?" Maddison holds up his cuffed wrists.

DS Bailey looks wide-eyed at Mirror who nods back, "Just a bit, DS Bailey."

Maddison stretches his arms as far as the new beam length will allow then casually leans back in his chair.

Mirror has no idea how to approach the interview. He forcefully searches his mind, questioning his years of experience on the force to see if any past case can guide him, but this situation is unique. The only thing he can do is what he's always done when faced with an unknown situation: follow his gut.

"Maddison, I have to tell you the truth. I have no idea how to deal with you. I mean, you're supposed to be dead. You died nine years ago, and now, suddenly, you pop back up."

"I know! Exciting, isn't it?" says Maddison.

"Well, I'm not sure I'd go so far as to say it's exciting, Maddison. I'd use the word 'scary'."

DS Bailey turns to look at Mirror, wondering how he can be talking to Maddison so openly.

"Don't worry, DI Mirror, you're not on any of my lists, nor you, DS Bailey. Well, not yet anyway." Maddison laughs again then leans further back into his chair.

DS Bailey grips the cuff controller tighter, ready to reel Maddison back towards the table the instant he became a threat.

"Actually, Maddison, I'm glad you've mentioned your lists. Have you ticked anyone off any of them lately? Maybe some jurors, to name a list that comes to mind," asks Mirror.

"Oh, DI Mirror, you know I have! I've had nine years' worth of catching up to do," Maddison laughs. "Tick, tick, tick."

"Ticks on your lists are people you've murdered, it's nothing to laugh at," says DS Bailey, her sense of anger overriding her fear as Maddison's comment hits a nerve. "Is Albert aware of your lists, Mr Bartel?"

"Hello, DS Bailey, I'd almost forgotten you were there, you've been so quiet. No, Albert doesn't know a thing, completely unaware, a totally innocent, silly fool. Amazing, isn't it? I just borrow his body for a while each time. Oh, hold on! Or is it my body and he's been borrowing from me? I just don't know anymore, gosh it's a bit confusing, isn't it?" laughs Maddison.

"Ok, Maddison, so Albert isn't aware of you or your lists, but would you share with us? Tell us what you did and who you've ticked off recently. Maybe you could start with a why? Why did you choose them?" asks DI Mirror.

"Why? Gabriel, you're asking why the jurors? The *why* is easy, the *why* is because I can, because they were on the jury, because it was the best place to start, a ready-made list for me, that's why," explains Maddison.

A disoriented DS Bailey had followed the rules all her life and had always, always done things according to the letter of the law, but right at this moment, in this situation, she was conflicted. What she wanted to do to Maddison would go against all the principles she had ever lived by and very much against the law she has always preached. But the more Maddison talks, the more she wants to kill him, get rid of his smile, his laugh, his evil aura.

Mirror senses the tension coming from DS Bailey, and although in any other situation, it would have been highly inappropriate, he puts his hand on her knee, under the table, out of Maddison's line of sight. DS Bailey puts her hand on Mirror's and squeezes. She breathes in and out deeply, "I'm ok, sir."

Mirror lifts his hand and looks towards Maddison, "Ok, I can see how a ready-made list would be tempting, Maddison. Tell us about the jurors, how many you have ticked," asks Mirror with his voice and tone matching Maddison's calmness.

"Gabriel, you're testing me, aren't you? You want to see if it was definitely me. You want me on record admitting it, don't you? DI Mirror, you cheeky boy, you! Well, I've nothing to hide apart from, well, from myself inside this body. I'm proud of my playmates and very proud of my art. Here we go, DS Bailey, I hope you have remembered to press record on the viewer." Maddison sits up straight in his chair. "Let's see, first, there was the doctor and the nurse, easy peasy, one in a lift and one caught a flight to heaven in a helicopter. Next, one of my favourites, Ravi Binning, was magnetically attracted to an MRI machine, I tried to tell him those sorts of relationships don't last long. Carmela got a shot in her coffee house, the swimming athlete who drowned, Chris caught the train or was it the train caught Chris? Oh! And then my pièce de résistance, Calvin Wireless. Oh! Come on, you have got to admit, the timing on that was perfect…" boasts Maddison.

"Maddison Bartel are you admitting that you are responsible for the murders of Anthony Chand, Ophelia Schmidt, Ravi Binning, Carmela Rosa, Lucy Victoria, Christopher Lowe and Calvin Wireless," asks Mirror.

"Duh! Yes! Of course, I am. Who else could create art like that?" replies Maddison sarcastically.

Mirror gives DS Bailey a frowned smile. They have a confession, and they have it late on a Sunday, so maybe, just maybe, they have prevented the deaths of the five remaining jurors.

"Maddison Bartel, I'm arresting you for the murders of Calvin Wireless, Lucy Victoria, Carmela Rosa, Ophelia Schmidt, Anthony Chand, Christopher Lowe, and Ravi Binning. You do not have to have to say anything, but anything you do say may be used as evidence in a court of law. Do you understand what I have told you Mr Bartel?" says DI Mirror.

Maddison laughs uncontrollably, "You can't arrest me, I don't exist, I died nine years ago!"

“Mr Bartel, do you understand the rights I have just read you?” repeats Mirror.

Maddison’s head drops and then lifts back up. “What happened? Did I pass out? Where is my solicitor? Why am I not getting to see my solicitor?” says Albert, his voice rising in panic.

“Oh, my God! Sir, it’s Albert. What do we do?” says DS Bailey.

“I have no idea, Bailey,” replies Mirror.

Mirror looks into Albert’s eyes. Maddison has gone, and there is only the scared, crying man staring back at him.

The tearful Albert looks sorrowfully back at Mirror. “Please, why are you treating me like this?” A new stream of tears floods his cheeks, his head drops back down and Maddison’s lifts back up. “See, DI Mirror, I don’t exist, and Albert is innocent. Now, you wouldn’t put an innocent man behind bars, would you?”

“Well, Maddison, you certainly have given us a dilemma. One thing I can promise is that neither you nor Albert is going anywhere today, and unless we sort this out, you won’t be going anywhere for quite a while. At least the rest of the jurors and any other list victims you had planned to murder are safe."

"Well, Gabriel, I wouldn't say that! You see, I learned a lesson. I was a bit disappointed that when I got caught back in 2050, I never got to finish my list. It was horrible, my work was unfinished. It got me thinking, maybe I could take out an insurance policy this time, you know, just in case. Make sure that if I got caught, at least my list will have a chance of getting finished." A huge smile appears on Maddison's face.

"What are you talking about?" says DS Bailey.

"You see, DS Bailey, Gabriel never let me finish what I was saying earlier. He interrupted before I got a chance to finish my list ticks, far too eager to read me my rights. You see, I haven't told you about this coming week's art. Monday, we tick Jade, Tuesday, we tick Michael, Wednesday, we tick Betsy, Thursday, we tick Lindsey and Friday, we tick Michele. Then my list will be complete."

"I don't think so, Maddison. Unfortunately, or should I say, fortunately, you will not be getting out of here to complete your list, will you?" says DS Bailey with conviction.

Mirror stares at Maddison, his gut wrenching with warning. “He’s already set them up.”

“Well done, DI Mirror. That’s right. As I said, I’ve set myself an insurance policy,” Maddison laughs. “If you don’t believe me, ask your DS Chang to show you. Connect the viewer he stole from Albert’s house earlier today. The password is 1666, the year London burned.” He laughs again.

Mirror jumps up from his chair and rushes out, “DS Bailey, tighten his cuffs, tight!”

DS Bailey gets up to follow Mirror, turning quickly to press the cuff controller. Maddison’s hands dragged him back to the centre of the table.

Mirror is ready to run to the incident room but is stopped in his tracks. The observation room is full, officers staring at the viewers, all of them enlarged, showing Time-Share room four. As DS Bailey catches up, she shares Mirror’s surprise as she spots, amongst the group, Captain Marshall Mason. “Sir,” she says.

“You should have called me straight away, Mirror. Instead, I get a call from the commissioner telling me he’s been called by a media reporter asking why we have forcefully arrested Mr Albert Diamonds in front of his wife and kids," says Captain Mason.

"Sir, you're right, no excuse other than if I had called you, especially on a Sunday, you probably wouldn't have believed me. I was having trouble believing it myself until I saw it with my own eyes. If that can all wait, sir, we need to check on the remaining five jurors straight away." Mirror moves towards the exit, desperate to get to Albert's laptop viewer.

Captain Mason holds his hand out to block Mirror's path "I've already asked DS Chang to get field teams to report in. PC Gill is collecting Albert's laptop viewer, and Mirror, you're right, I wouldn't have believed you."

"Sirs, look," says DS Bailey, pointing back at the viewer screens. Albert has reappeared. Over the speaker system, his agonised cries for help and pleas for a solicitor are deafening.

Mirror looks at the captain's expression as he views the screens. Will Albert's cry for a solicitor persuade him to follow protocol and allow him a solicitor?

"Sir, we can't let him see a solicitor, not yet, not while Maddison has so much control."

"Turn it down," says Captain Mason to the officer nearest the control desk.

"Every man has a right to a solicitor, I've always believed that no matter how much the scumbags don't deserve one," says Captain Mason. Mirror's face fills with tension, and he is about to burst into a justification of his point of view, but the captain continues, "This is a hard one, Mirror. If the media were to see that man in there, the way he is now, shouting out for a solicitor, insisting that he's innocent, we would be hung out to dry for not allowing him representation, but I've been watching and have seen enough to know that Albert Diamonds isn't the only man in there."

"No, sir, he most definitely isn't, we can't let anybody else in to see him yet," says DS Bailey.

The captain turns to look towards DS Bailey, "Glad to see you two are on the same page at last."

DS Chang and PC Gill enter at the same time. Captain Mason walks towards them, "PC Gill, set up the viewer over there, DS Chang, news on the jurors?"

"Nothing, sir, nothing at all," says DS Chang, looking whiter than normal.

"At least they are all ok," says Captain Mason.

“Captain, I don’t think that’s what DS Chang means,” says Mirror, picking up on DS Chang’s wording. “DS Chang, what is it?”

“There’s nothing from any of the remaining jurors. We can’t contact any of them, it’s like their Time-Shares don’t even exist anymore.”

An eerie silence falls, only to be broken by PC Gill. “It’s ready, sir.” PC Gill has plugged the laptop viewer from Albert’s house into the observation room control panel and mirrored the screen onto one of the larger viewer screens. The display shows an enter password box in the centre of the locked display.

“1666,” says Mirror.

“Sir?” questions PC Gill.

“The password, 1666,” repeats Mirror.

PC Gill enters the numbers; the screen unlocks to display six numbered mini-screens. Screen number one is locked and has another enter password box displayed, the other boxes show live feeds of five rooms, each of them with a similar-looking person, panicking in a confined space.

“That’s the remaining jurors, sir,” says DS Bailey.

"What about box one? Shall I try the same passcode, sir?" asks PC Gill.

Captain Mason nods. PC Gill keys in 1666 and presses enter. The whole screen goes blank then resets. The words, "*Wrong password! One attempt remaining!*" flash above the enter password box on mini-screen one. The other five screens now display weekdays as titles, Monday through to Friday. In addition, each of the screens has a timer counting down to midnight of their relevant titled day of the week. Mirror and the captain step closer to the viewer. Before either has time to comment, the volume from mini-screens two to six unmute, for all in the observation room to hear the sounds of panic and screaming as the individual rooms confine even more to restrict the occupants to a coffin-like amount of movement space.

PC Gill turns to the captain and Mirror in distress. The thought that entering the wrong password has caused harm to the jurors is unbearable.

"Sirs," DS Bailey draws her senior officers' attention back to the interview room viewer. They look to see the silenced laughing man laser cuffed to the table. Maddison has re-emerged.

Mirror looks at the timer on the mini-screen labelled Monday. A petrified woman stands in the centre of what looked like a lab. The timer on the top of the box is counting down the minutes to midnight.

Mirror looks at the clock on the wall; the time is 10:33 p.m. "One hour, twenty-seven minutes till twelve, till it's Monday. Don't try anything else yet," he orders, looking at PC Gill. He turns to Captain Mason, "Sir, I need to get back in there." The captain nods in agreement. Mirror hurriedly walks back into the interview room, closely followed by DS Bailey.

"Hello Gabriel, hello DS Bailey… do you like my little insurance policy? I simply can't wait to finish this list and get started on a new one," says Maddison with a chuckle and a smile which immediately turns into a serious, cold, hard stare towards the two officers. "Shall we talk about letting me go then?"

Mirror leans forward, a wave of anger flowing through him as Maddison stares. He grabs hold of Maddison's head, pushing it sideways into the table. "What have you done to the jurors? How do I set them free?" he asks forcefully.

DS Bailey disconcerted that her reaction isn't to immediately pull Mirror away and stop him from using the strong-armed approach, knows it is necessary to get as much out of Maddison and as quickly as they can.

"Ahhhhhhhhhhhhh!!!!!!!! Why are you doing this?" screams Albert.

Mirror quickly lets go and jumps back into his chair, "I'm sorry, Albert, I'm so sorry." He is startled by the sudden re-emergence of Albert.

Albert's screams turn to laughter as Maddison lifts his head back up off the table. "Now, now, Gabriel, why are you trying to hurt an innocent man? This is so much fun! Every time you do something I don't like, I'll just let poor old Albert take the frontline. You really can't touch me!"

In the past, by hook or by crook, Mirror had been able to find a solution to anything he's ever come across, but this is different. In front of him is the evilest manipulator he has ever met, yet whenever he tries to get anywhere, he ends up torturing an innocent man, and that's just wrong…

"What have you done with the jurors?" asks DS Bailey, her voice giving the impression she is calm, but she is shaking inside.

"Thank you for asking so kindly, DS Bailey. You see, Gabriel, manners maketh the man, or should I say, woman."

Mirror sinks back into his chair. "Ok, Maddison, please tell us, what have you done with the jurors?" He is trying hard to contain his anger.

"Oh, that's the clever bit, guys. I've trapped them inside their Time-Shares by shrinking their bubbles. And the best bit is, as each of the timers reaches zero, the bubble collapses. Bye-bye! I get another tick. I mean it's not the best piece of art I've ever created – to be honest, I was a bit rushed, what with your DS Chang showing so up rudely – but a tick's a tick, and a tick a day for the rest of the week until the list is finished makes me very happy."

"That's not possible, is it, sir? Time-Shares have built-in safety systems to prevent bubble collapse," says DS Bailey.

"And yet, DS Bailey, it *is* happening!" says Maddison. "Don't forget who worked on the original Time-Share creation. I might just have added a few back-door programs in the early days, just in case, you know what I mean, DS Bailey?" He is confident, knowing he has full control of the interview.

Mirror's mobile viewer rings as a message comes through from the captain. "Are they your insurance policies?" asks Mirror, reiterating the question on the message.

"Now you're getting it, Gabriel, yes, of course, they are my insurance policies. Now, let's talk about letting me go."

"We can't let you go, Maddison, it won't happen," says DS Bailey.

"DS Bailey is right, Maddison, but I have to admit we have no idea what we are going to do with you."

"What's the time, DS Bailey?" asks Maddison, looking directly into DS Bailey's eyes. She averts her gaze and looks round to Mirror for confirmation. Mirror nods. "It's ten fifty-five," she says.

"Just over an hour to go until Monday's tick, I must confess I have some theories on what will happen to poor old robotics engineer Jade Andrews. I can tell you them if you like, but I'm sure you wouldn't be interested right now. One thing I do know, and as far as you need to be concerned, she won't be here tomorrow."

"What do want, Maddison?" asks Mirror.

"I guess, DI Mirror, there are three choices. Choice one, I release the jurors and you let me go. Now, I'm not going to promise that I won't get them another day, but they will be safe for now. Choice two, you don't let me go, I let Albert back out, the jurors get ticked and you try to take an innocent man to jail."

"And choice number three?" asks Mirror nervously.

"Well, choice number three, Gabriel, or should I say, mini-screen number one?" A devious smile grows on Maddison's face.

Mirror and DS Bailey look at each other, both wondering what on earth could be hiding behind the passcode-protected box on Albert's viewer.

"What is it, Maddison?" asks DS Bailey.

"There you go, DS Bailey, now it's sounding like a game show – 'What's behind box number one?' you ask!" says Maddison, imitating a game-show host. "The passcode for box number one releases the five jurors and restores each of their Time-Share bubbles, saving their lives. Well, for now anyway…" smirks Maddison.

"Ok, Mr Bartel, I'm guessing you're not just going to give us the code then?" says DS Bailey.

Mirror's gut has been sending him a barrage of warning signals since the interview took its surreal twist and now, it is increasing in pace. "What's the catch, Maddison?"

"A catch, Gabriel? Why should there be a catch? ...Well, yes! to be honest, there *is* a catch," Maddison laughs.

"You see, Gabriel, the password needs to be entered in an active Time-Share. The person entering the code will activate a program that releases the other five traps... but! Drum roll, please... here's the good bit, it also activates another program that traps that person in a collapsing Time-Share bubble. And here's the best bit... there is no release password. So..." He pauses for effect and looks to Mirror and DS Bailey in anticipation, as if he were a teacher waiting for his star pupils to give him the correct answer to a question, "So... so someone has to be trapped forever in Time-Share bubble-land. Yay! My version of a dead man's switch, if you like. Now, that's the art." Maddison proudly takes a mini bow but doesn't get the round of applause that his narcissism believes he deserves. Instead, his moment of glory is interrupted by Captain Mason' "Hello, who's this?" asks Maddison.

Captain Mason ignores Maddison. "Forty-five minutes left, Mirror. Do you believe anything this scumbag is saying?"

"Unfortunately, sir, yes I do."

"That's not very nice, calling me a scumbag. I can guess you're the man in charge here. Can I at least have your name?" says Maddison calmly.

Captain Mason continues to ignore Maddison, "I've asked DS Chang to look into finding another way in. I can't order anyone to do it, Mirror, I can't justify a life for a life, even if, in this case, it's five lives against one. We can't rely that he's telling the truth or that it will release the other traps."

"How rude!" says Maddison.

"I'll do it, sir," says Mirror.

A stunned DS Bailey looks at Mirror, "No, sir! We don't know if he's telling the truth."

DS Chang enters the room, "I'm sorry, sir. I don't know how he's done it, but there's no way we can recover the juror's bubbles, they just don't exist anymore."

Maddison chuckles to himself, amused by their futile conversation.

"We are running out of time, sir, there are five lives at stake here," says Mirror.

"No, Mirror! It's not happening. We may have to take the loss on this one," says the captain.

"Err! Excuse me!" calls Maddison.

They simultaneously turn to look at the smiling Maddison, "What?" snarls Captain Mason.

"It's pardon, not what!" says Maddison in superior tones. "I've got the passcode, so I guess I'll have to do it. I mean, it makes sense, doesn't it?"

"What have you got in mind, Maddison?" asks Mirror.

"Well, it's the easiest of solutions, I want to be set free, you want to keep me in jail, blah blah blah, this is a Time-Share room, blah blah blah, bring the viewer in here, and I'll put the passcode in, your precious jurors will be set free, I will be trapped in here, and as an added bonus, to me, I'll be free from all your moaning. Sounds fair, don't you think."

"Somehow, I think you've been taking us down this path from the beginning, Maddison," says Mirror.

"Maybe, Gabriel, maybe, but we're here now, aren't we? So, I guess you don't have much of a choice if you, at least, want to try and save the jurors, do you? But don't worry though, once I'm trapped in here, you can keep an eye on me and Albert via your observation viewers – even though the bubble door won't exist, the video feed will remain active. I can be your prize ship in a bottle," says Maddison smugly.

Mirror turns to leave, "Sir, Bailey, Chang, please come outside."

The four officers returned to the observation room.

"It's twenty minutes past eleven, we have forty minutes to decide or come up with something else," says Mirror.

"There's nothing we can do about the Time-Share traps. We have no idea how he's done it, it's never been done before, and there's no way we should even be able to view the rooms if we can't find them," says DS Chang.

"Ok, so it's we do nothing, or we put a viewer in the hands of a serial killer genius in the hope that he is telling the truth and gets caught in his own trap," says DS Bailey.

"Sir, we can't let five innocent people die if we have any chance of saving them," says an agitated Mirror.

"Do you think we should give him the viewer, Mirror?" asks Captain Mason.

"Sir, the chances are Maddison is a step in ahead of us already and giving him the viewer, we could be giving him the means to escape or set more traps. But what if it does release the jurors?" says Mirror, not committing himself to a straight answer.

Bailey has a sudden thought, "Sirs, we could set up a dampening field around the room. Once Maddison enters the password and the jurors are released, we switch it on, hopefully, immediately stopping him from connecting to any Time-Share servers."

Mirror turns to DS Bailey, "Will that work, Bailey?"

"I think so, sir, well, in theory, it should, but then again, in theory, Maddison shouldn't have been able to set traps as he has," replies DS Bailey.

"Ok, let's do it. PC Gill, give Albert's viewer to Mirror, but keep the live feed to the jurors mirrored on the viewers in here," says Captain Mason.

PC Gill walks over with the viewer, the captain points to Mirror. Mirror takes the viewer from him and turns to the interview room. DS Bailey follows, ready to go back in with him. Mirror holds out his hand and stops her. "Not this time, Bailey, just in case. It will be reassuring to know that there's someone out here with enough brain cells to get me back out if Maddison enters the code before I manage to get out."

"Ok, sir. Good luck." DS Bailey's respect for Mirror has grown massively over the last couple of days. She would have put her fear aside and gone with him but is also thankful that her senior officer has asked her to stay out. "Sir! Wait!" she calls. Mirror looks back around, and she hands him the laser cuff controller. "Use the cuffs, and release him when you're back at the door, sir."

"Good thinking, DS Bailey, thank you."

Mirror enters then closes the door behind him. "Ok, Maddison. Let's see if you're telling the truth." Mirror places the viewer laptop in front of Maddison. Maddison holds his laser-cuffed hands up as far as they can go.

"Not yet, Maddison, not yet" says Mirror.

"Oh, Gabriel! I thought you would have trusted me by now," says Maddison.

Mirror steps back towards the exit, turns the handle and looks back towards Maddison. "If you're lying, Maddison, and this is just a trick to help you escape, or to delay us in any way, if any more of the jurors die, I'll make it my life's work to hunt you down. Whether it's Albert Diamonds in front of me or Maddison Bartel, I will make sure neither of you will be able to do anything ever again," he vows.

"Oh, Gabriel, I will miss you too. Say hello to Frances for me. I do hope to meet her one day."

Mirror looks towards Maddison, disturbed that he knows about Frances. He points the laser cuff controller towards Maddison, presses release and quickly leaves.

All eyes stare at the viewers, shifting between Maddison in the interview room and the five mini-screens containing the panicking jurors. They watch as Maddison pulls the viewer tablet towards him, looks up at the camera to give his watchers a smile and a salute then stands up to walk around the table.

"He's playing games, he'd better hurry up, it's three minutes to midnight," says Captain Mason.

Mirror looks at mini-screen two containing Jade Andrews, the robotics engineer from Highgate, a law-abiding woman, a good job, a husband and two children. All she did to deserve her place on the viewer gameshow was to be unlucky enough to have been called up for jury duty nine years earlier. He takes his mobile viewer from his pocket, opens the flip cover and removes the five-leaf clover he'd found that same morning at Harrison's campsite. DS Bailey looks at Mirror's hand and then up at his face. “We need all the luck we can get hold of right now, Jana.”

Even with the tense situation at hand, DS Bailey is slightly taken aback by Mirror calling her by her first name. “Yes, sir,” she replies, feeling, if not strangely timed, a bittersweet moment of acceptance into the TSM-PD.

“Forty-five seconds,” announces DS Chang.

Maddison takes a final look up at the camera and casually walks round to the laptop. He swipes to wake the screen and taps the password into box one, stopping the mini-screen timer at twelve seconds to go. Almost immediately, the five juror boxes show live-streamed footage of each room expanding back to normal, and reports flood in from the field teams at the relevant addresses, confirming they have regained access to each of the victims’ Time-Share bubbles.

Mirror places the clover back into his mobile viewer case and flips it closed. He walks over to the interview room, tries the handle, but the door is locked. He presses the control panel for Time-Share room four and it shows an error code: “*Time-Share Room 4 bubble has disappeared.*” Mirror’s thoughts confirm what Maddison had told them. “Looks like he was telling the truth. DS Chang, switch the dampening field on.”

Captain Mason turns to leave. “I’ll go and sort out the mess in the waiting area and think of something to tell the media. DS Bailey, DI Mirror, get some rest.”

“Yes, sir, thank you,” replies DS Bailey.

DS Bailey walks over to join Mirror as he stares at the live stream of interview room four, watching as Maddison, or Albert, taps away on the laptop viewer.

“Look at him, Bailey. Who have we got trapped in there? No food or water and no way out. Is it a killer or an innocent man?”

“Don’t do that to yourself, sir. We didn’t have a choice. Five people are still alive because of us. Even if Albert is innocent, a killer is in there too, with no access to the outside world. There’s nothing he can do with that laptop viewer without a connection to a Time-Share server, however distressing it is, he’s trapped where he can never hurt anyone else ever again,” says DS Bailey.

“I know, I know, you’re right, DS Bailey. But I can’t help thinking, am I any better than Maddison now that I’m allowing a man to starve, die and decompose while we watch the events live on our viewers.

“Come on, sir, it’s one in the morning, let’s go get some rest.”

Mirror looks at DS Bailey and nods, “You’re right, Bailey, let’s go.”

They turn to the viewer for a final time and see Maddison’s face near to the camera, giving them a big smile and a wave as if knowing they are watching. He points to the desk then to his eye, beckoning them to watch. He walks back round to the laptop viewer on the desk and presses the enter key. Maddison looks back up at the camera, clearly mouths, “see you later,” smiles then wave again as he walks over to open the door.

Mirror and DS Bailey’s adrenaline pump around their bodies, they turn to stare at their side of the door. It was still closed. The observation viewer linked to Time-Share four goes blank and the words “*No signal*” appear on the screen.

A shocked Mirror and Bailey look at each other, cold chill flowing through their bodies. The screen resets to show a now empty room. Mirror runs over to the interview room door, the control panel showing the room re-connected and active, he opens it to an empty room. Maddison Bartel is gone, and Albert’s laptop viewer is sat on the table, beeping. Mirror walks over to the viewer. On its screen was an incoming message from a ‘Brian Todd Smale’.

DS Bailey joins Mirror at the table, “Who’s Brian Todd Smale?”

“There was a Brian Smale in the files, Bailey, he was the prison transport driver the day Maddison was sentenced.”

“Shall I open the message, sir?” asks DS Bailey.

Mirror nods.

Chapter 18
Letter From A Killer

Monday 29th September 2059 – 12.58 a.m.

The long grey-haired Brian Smale sat on a bench by Westminster pier, staring at the New Scotland Yard building. He took his mobile viewer from his bag and swiped it on. *Tonight's the night!* he thought to himself. He opened his email app, clicked on drafts and brought up the pre-written letter. He entered Albert Diamonds' email address and pressed send.

*

Monday 29th September 2059 – 1.00 a.m.

"Shall I open the message sir?" asks DS Bailey.

Mirror nods.

DS Bailey cagily opens the message.

Dear Detective Inspector Mirror,

Nine years in the hide have been hard, but I can honestly say, I've been looking forward to this moment and to talking to you again. Firstly, I would like to thank you and DS Bailey for the opportunity you gave me to escape all those years ago. If you had called my bluff, well then, I guess I would never have had that chance. What and how? you ask. Well, like every good psychopath, I have been dying to tell someone and enlighten them as to how I did it. Remember when I told you I had a few theories of what would happen if a bubble collapsed while someone was still in one? Well, I may have exaggerated a tad and manipulated you to believe that it would be the end for our juror friends, when in truth, I hypothesized that if a Time-Share bubble broke down, it would be forced to merge with its original timeline, and all other Time-Shares that had been assigned to that room would switch permanently to the time the collapsed bubble was first installed.

Can you imagine how messy it could have been if any of your other Time-Share interview rooms had been occupied when they merged? I guess it was lucky that they were empty. I wasn't sure it would even work, but let's face it, the alternative would have meant me being trapped forever. So, I set a delay timer into the final trap and stalled the program that would fully collapse the bubble, then hoped you would fall for my ruse, a ruse that you all did fall for so brilliantly. I was willing to bet not one officer would morally argue a case for the man you would leave trapped in a room to die, especially if it meant the jurors could be saved. It wouldn't have mattered if you had set a dampening field or not, the program was already running, and hey presto, the Time-Shares merged back to the original timeline, and I ended up in the past. September 1st, 2041, to be precise. I didn't half give the engineer a fright when I came out of the interview room, it was the day the Time-Share units were installed, and that date, at different times, was chosen for the interview rooms' Time-Share bubbles. I walked straight past him and out of the observation room without a single person asking or caring who I was. I walked along the long corridor, through to the TSM-PD front desk, and that's where I saw you, DI Mirror. You weren't a DI yet, just a fresh-faced detective sergeant, running around impressing your captain by trying to help everyone you met. You even said hello, I must have been looking a bit disoriented because you asked me if I needed help, so, of course, I couldn't resist saying yes, it was so surreal. I gave you a sob story of how I'd lost my wallet and that I needed to get a taxi home. Being the kind-hearted person you are, you gave me some money. You even called the cab for me. I left the building and jumped into the taxi. The driver you got me was very talkative, telling me how he'd recently divorced, had fallen out with his family, and had recently moved into a new flat. How convenient, I thought. Although he wasn't on a list, that taxi-driver became my first ever kill that didn't involve Time-Share. It didn't feel very artistic, but it did serve a purpose. So, I guess I have you to thank for that as well, DI Mirror. His flat was the perfect place for me to lie low and invent a new life. Giving myself a new name and identity was easy, I had eighteen years' more advanced computer knowledge than anybody else in that timeline. I became Brian Todd Smale. In case you're wondering why I chose that name in particular, DI Mirror, it's another anagram of my name. It felt so cheeky, but I did it to leave you a clue and a link as to who I was. My first instinct was to find my younger self and stop him from making the same silly mistakes I had, mistakes that would eventually get me caught. An eagerness to meet my younger self was halted by common sense and the reality of the butterfly effect that would have occurred. If I had stopped myself from being caught, I would never have been sentenced, pronounced dead, become Albert, woken back up, got caught again and finally escaped into the past. So, instead, I came up with a plan that would guarantee I would be here today, and at the same time, let me have nine years from 2041 to 2050 to create art without being disturbed. I decided to blend into society, I got a job working at His Majesty's Prison Services and waited. I knew I couldn't interfere with my younger self's development or arrest, I had to let the timeline play out the same as it had, or as I said, I might not have been here today. Of course, that didn't mean I couldn't nudge it a little in my favour. It was fun to see my younger self starting out on our path. While he was honing his skills, I was mastering them. When he was caught, my younger self was convicted of eighteen murders. They then added another three hundred and twenty between 2041 and 2050 to his tally. You see, they were partially right, the Maddison Bartel they caught didn't kill the extra three hundred and twenty, it was me, the older, much wiser Maddison. During the trial, I would drop myself off at the court and pick myself up after each session, now that was fun. I couldn't help but share a joke or two with myself, but as tempting as it was, I never once let on who I was. It's quite surreal that I was actually talking to my older self, but of course, I would never have known, I looked like a long-haired and bearded version of Albert, and as you now know, my face was reborn after my little accident. I was there the day I had my run-in with the fire extinguisher. It was me that placed it against the fire door then set it up ready for that bailiff to trip on. Lucky me that he was so clumsy! And it was me that pushed my younger self into its path. I laced the base of the extinguisher with my special mix of Tetrodotoxin, Bufotoxin and Datura Stramonium to ensure that when it hit my younger self, the mixture would enter my bloodstream, and it would simulate a near death-like state that would lower my heart rate enough to sufficiently fool most people into thinking I was dead. I already knew I would get a life sentence.

A paradox, I hear you say! How could I have been there? Surely I've altered the timeline from the original? Both valid questions, and if I'm honest, I'm still working it out myself. But Isn't it fun knowing for this period of my life there will be an endless loop of me, even now another Maddison is emerging in 2041. My hunch is that at some point, being the perfectionist and control freak I am, I just made the loop better. What other way to make sure things are done right than to do them yourself.

The aim, as you now know, was to get them to pronounce me dead so I would be set free, then reawakened not knowing who I was. They would believe that my younger self was gone and eventually leave me alone. I added extra Datura Stramonium to the mix to keep the younger me asleep for longer, and, voila, nice-guy Albert Diamonds was born. With Albert now in the driving seat, I knew I had to stop my art for a while, so Albert could build his life. I wasn't ready yet, I hadn't fully re-emerged. I tried hard not to give in to my urges, although I did relapse a couple of times, the odd ski-boat accident in New Zealand, and the influencing of a heart attack on the judge. But mostly, I kept myself busy, manipulating Albert's life, pushing certain people in his direction just so they would be all lined up for me when I woke up, and boy did I hit the ground running when I did! As I said, DI Mirror, nine years in the hide is a long time as a double spectator to Albert's life, but then, getting to watch my younger self reappear and create art with those jurors felt euphoric. I was watching myself become who I used to be and who I am now, and it was exhilarating. I was there at each and every one. My favourite, to this day, is still the elephant. My escape took longer than I would have liked, but now, things have come full circle. I can tell you that I am back. I'm sixty-two, a little bit older, certainly wiser, a lot more careful, and there's still plenty of time to create my art. I look forward to the games we will play in the future. As promised, you and DS Bailey will never be on one of my lists, but I do have a certain list to finish, and I've waited a long time to complete it – there are still five names to tick. From your perspective, my younger self started it two Fridays ago, but that was nine years ago for me.

Goodbye for now, DI Mirror. It's Monday, and it is time to create art…

Albert Diamonds *Brian Todd Smale*

Maddison Bartel